ALSO BY LIZ EELES

Annie's Summer by the Sea

LIZ EELES

bookouture

Published by Bookouture in 2018

An imprint of StoryFire Ltd.

Carmelite House
50 Victoria Embankment
London EC4Y 0DZ

www.bookouture.com

ISBN: 978-1-78681-326-8
eBook ISBN: 978-1-78681-325-1

For my wonderful mum and dad, Margaret and Ivor

Chapter One

I'm seriously starting to think there's a poltergeist at Tregavara House. Not some random woo-woo spirit of the undead who likes chucking stuff about. But a seriously narked ancestor of mine who gets his rocks off trying to brain me with masonry.

'Crikey, Annie. That could have been nasty.' Josh kicks at the shattered tile that missed my head by centimetres and glances up at the storm-battered roof. It's the second tile that's fallen off this week. 'Maybe I should get the ladder out and have a go at fixing it.'

As he pulls me close for a huge thank-God-you're-not-hurt hug, I wonder how best to broach that this is very possibly the worst idea in the world.

Josh, my gorgeous Cornish boyfriend who gives Poldark a run for his money, is a New Man in many ways. He helps me look after my great-aunt Alice. He does the washing up without being asked. He even cleans the bathroom without bragging on Facebook as though it's heroic.

But in a strange throwback to pre-feminist times, Josh still believes he has an innate ability to 'fix' things on account of his manly genes. As though DIY skills are passed from father to son at conception or transmitted by osmosis from one male to another. And he gets dead shirty if I imply otherwise. It's weird. My father, Barry, rarely seen without a hammer in his hand, is exactly the same. It must be a Man Thing.

Before I can inform Josh gently that his DIY skills are diabolical, my half-sister Storm bowls out of the front door and stops dead in front of the tile fragments scattered across the garden path.

'What the actual hell is going on? This place is falling down and you need to do something about it 'cos, if a bit of house lands on me, I'll have to sue. It won't be personal,' she assures me, brushing back a strand of purple hair that's caught in the sea breeze. 'But it would be daft not to. Kayla's cousin in Adelaide got ten grand for saying a scaffolding pole fell on her head. She was lying but Kayla reckons insurance companies are fair game.'

Not for the first time, I wonder whether my friend Kayla is a good influence on my sister. A while back, they hated one another and were having scowl-offs across the bar of my local, the Whistling Wave. But now they huddle together in corners and giggle about my crush on Paul Hollywood. It's very disconcerting.

Storm saunters on along the path, wincing at the squeals of two children rushing headlong towards the harbour with their mum trudging behind. I don't recognise them but Salt Bay is always full of tourists on a beautiful May day.

'Don't worry, Storm,' Josh calls after her, resting his chin on the top of my head. 'I'll get up onto the roof later and sort it out.'

Storm hesitates with her hand on the gate and snorts. 'Yeah, you do that, Josh, 'cos then everything will be just fine.'

She treats me to one of her teenage eye-rolls before heading for the village newsagent's where she works on Saturdays. Her arms are bare and, though we've only had a few days of unbroken sunshine, her skin already has a golden glow. She looks far healthier than when she first arrived at Tregavara House from London – and purple hair suits her. Dyed hair is frowned upon at her school but, now the summer term is in full swing, she's banking on the teachers being too knackered to care.

'We'd better get a proper roofer in. I don't want you falling off a ladder and breaking something, and I think it's gone beyond DIY.' I snuggle against Josh's soft T-shirt and breathe in his musky smell. 'How much do you think it'll cost?'

'To fix the roof?' His deep voice vibrates through me with its soft Cornish burr. 'Lots, I expect, so you'd better talk to Alice before you get someone in to look at it.'

He's only being sensible getting my great-aunt involved. The house belongs to her, after all. But my mood dips as I gaze across the china-blue sea that's lapping gently against the harbour wall.

Everything is wonderful right now. In front of me, seagulls are skimming sun-kissed waves and soaring high over granite cliffs that drop into the ocean. Tregavara House, built where the land meets the sea, is my new home and, best of all, Josh has moved in with me and my 'family' – a ragbag of bona fide relatives and Emily, Alice's live-in carer.

And he really is gorgeous. Josh and I have been going out for thirteen months now, not counting a slight blip late last year and, having kissed my fair share of frogs, I'm sure he's the man of my dreams. He's tall and dark and kind and funny – and only a tiny bit grumpy. Much less grumpy than he used to be, now he's happily settled with me.

Which means that my life is fabulous, or would be if Alice wasn't fading in front of my eyes. My great-aunt, a fiercely proud and independent woman, frightened the life out of me when we met for the first time sixteen months ago. But, these days, the scariest thing about Alice is her deteriorating health – and the last thing she needs are money worries.

So far, she's been pretty chilled about the fact that our ancestral home is in desperate need of repair. But it can't be ignored for much longer. Centuries of fierce storms are starting to take their toll and, to be fair, if I'd been standing in a Cornish wind for two hundred years, I'd be crumbling too.

'Talk to her,' urges Josh, dipping his head to plant a warm kiss on my lips. 'You can't shield her from everything, even though I know you want to. But she can take it.'

While Josh goes in search of a dustpan to brush up the shattered tile, I step outside the front garden to pick up an ice-cream wrapper that's dancing in the breeze. Flaming tourists! Why can't they take their rubbish home after their day trips instead of spoiling the village with litter?

I crumple the slimy Magnum wrapper and shove it into my pocket. Like a woman on a mission, I've become evangelical about protecting the village that I once hated. Every dropped crisp packet or cigarette butt strikes fury into my heart. Basically, I've become Mrs Angry of Salt Bay who runs after tourists and thrusts litter back into their hands. Josh often pretends he doesn't know me.

'What's going on out here? I heard a bit of a commotion.'

Alice steps into the garden as I'm walking back up the path. She carefully negotiates the lip of the front door and hangs onto the safety rail we've had installed just outside. It's only been there for a couple of weeks but it's already encrusted with salt from a fierce storm that blew up last week.

'Nothing to worry about,' I say, casually kicking bits of tile off the path and onto the garden.

'Hhmm. I'm not senile, Annabella, and there's nothing wrong with my eyes. I can see exactly what you're doing. Another tile, was it?'

'Afraid so.'

'Can Josh fix it?'

I wrinkle my nose, aggrieved that Alice automatically assumes Josh is more practical than me. 'I don't think so. It's probably time to get someone in to have a proper look at the roof. This house is getting really old and weathered, Alice. It could do with some TLC.'

Alice places her blue-veined hand on the thick stone wall of Trega-vara House and spreads her fingers wide. She closes her eyes and tilts her head to one side, as though she's communicating telepathically with the building. Which is bonkers and I mentally kick myself for being far too imaginative. Though I love every inch of this house, it's only stone and mortar – even though the wind whistling through tiny cracks in the walls sometimes sounds like breathing.

Suddenly, Alice opens her brown eyes wide and gives a tight nod. 'You're right. And if the roof needs work, I know just the man. Follow me!'

Uh-oh. Alice is heading for her Bodgers Bible – the dog-eared notebook in her handbag containing contact details of people who've worked on the house during the last ten years. The trouble is Alice tends to get her mates in when something needs fixing and, though they're lovely, salt of the earth Cornish folk, many of them are clueless when it comes to power tools.

I follow Alice as she shuffles through the narrow hallway and into the sitting room where her navy blue handbag is sitting on the sofa. She pulls out her notebook and starts leafing through it.

'There you go.' I'm not sure if Alice is waving the book at me in triumph or if her hands are shaking again. 'Paul Trefarron from Perrigan Bay is good with a roof.'

'Would that be the same Paul Trefarron who celebrated his eightieth birthday in the Whistling Wave last week?'

'Hhmm. I suppose he is getting on a bit now,' admits Alice who, almost four years older than Paul Trefarron, is no spring chicken herself. 'But he's still very sprightly with his new hip and knee. I'm sure he could still nip up a ladder and patch the roof together.'

'It might need more than patching, Alice. We don't want the rain coming in.'

Alice sinks with a loud *oof* onto the sofa and adjusts the skirt of her spotted brown dress. 'We certainly don't. Damp is very bad for old houses – and old paintings. Toby will have my guts for garters if The Lady is damaged.'

She waves her arm at the gilt-framed oil painting that dominates the sitting room wall, opposite the stone fireplace. A pretty woman looks out from the canvas, her back to the sea and sunlight glinting on her dark hair. She's wearing a long dark skirt and white high-necked blouse with a cameo at her throat, and she's just about to laugh. The artist has perfectly captured a moment in time, an emotion, and the woman – an ancestor of mine – seems alive. As though she might step out of the canvas and share the joke.

To be honest, the painting gave me the total creeps at first. Eyes following you round the room and all that. It made the back of my neck prickle. But I gradually fell in love with the picture's rich colours and enigmatic subject – even before we discovered that it was painted by artist Ludo Van Teel in the mid-1800s and was worth a fortune. Though, I must admit, that made me love it just a teensy bit more.

Taking the notebook from Alice, I pop it back into the top of her open handbag. 'Why don't I find someone to mend the roof? So you don't have to worry about it.'

Alice gives me a sharp look before smoothing down her thick white hair. 'I'm perfectly capable of sorting out repairs and I'm not some old dear who needs to be mollycoddled, Annabella. I'm just a little tired at the moment.' She rests her head on the back of the gold velour sofa and closes her eyes.

'Which is why it makes sense for me to sort out a quote for the work and then I'll discuss it with you before anything's decided. Is that OK?'

Alice sighs with her eyes still closed and says quietly: 'I suppose that would be acceptable.' Her words seem to slur into one another and within a few moments she's asleep, although she only got up an hour or so ago.

Gently lowering myself down beside her, I study the wrinkled skin on her face. She looks pale in the light streaming through the stone-framed window. Alice was a force of nature when we first met. A woman who'd survived the loss of husband, child and brother with grit, determination and a sharp tongue. One of those people whose life force vibrates like an aura and seems inextinguishable.

But recently she just seems like a very tired old lady. And tired old ladies aren't immortal, are they.

Alice's mouth falls open as I softly place my hand on hers, swallowing hard to clear the lump in my throat. My beloved great-aunt's papery skin is cool but warms under my touch as I sit for ages, watching her chest gently rise and fall.

Chapter Two

The phone call I've been dreading arrives a week later – on an ordinary Friday afternoon while tourists in shorts are eating butter-yellow ice cream outside the office window. It seems everyone is gagging to get their legs out as the temperature rises, and there's no end to the heatwave in sight.

The weather, for want of a more meteorological term, has been freaking fabulous for days. And Cornwall is roasting in golden sunshine that makes the sea sparkle like it's sprinkled with glitter.

I love scorching hot weather – the iron smell of baked earth, sun reflecting on glass, not having to wear a coat. But it's sparked a massive moan-fest from work colleagues Gayle and Lesley, who reckon their bodies aren't sufficiently beach-ready to be bared. They both look fine to me, and does it really matter if there are a few wobbly bits? Just shove yourself into an M&S swimsuit and give a mental V-sign to anyone who gives a damn. But they've been scoffing chocolate eclairs to cheer themselves up so there's no end to the moaning in sight.

When they launch into yet another calorie-fuelled self-hate sesh, I resist the urge to yell 'Step away from the cakes' and retreat to the loo for a few minutes of peace. And that's where I am when the call comes in.

'Annie,' yells Lesley, rushing into the ladies' as I'm turning on the tap. 'You've got to come now. Emily's on the phone sounding upset and she says it's about Alice.'

So this it, then. Out of habit, I swoosh my hands under the water, barely registering that it's far too hot, and rush back to my desk without pausing to dry them.

The office phone is next to my keyboard but I hesitate before picking up the handset. Why can't things stay the same? I'm happy with my life here in Cornwall, happier than I've ever been and, if I don't pick up the phone, I can pretend nothing has changed.

But real life doesn't work that way. Lesley grabs the phone and passes it to me with a sympathetic smile before going back to her desk. She and Gayle start tapping at their keyboards to show they're not really listening in, but the air is thick with tension.

When I press the handset to my ear, water droplets fall from my hands and start dripping down my neck.

'Emily, is everything all right?'

'Annie, there you are. I tried your mobile but it went to voicemail and I don't like ringing you on your work phone but I needed to get hold of you and I didn't think you'd mind this once if—'

'Just tell me what's happened.'

Emily takes a deep breath. 'It's Alice. She's got a fever and seems confused and keeps talking about someone called Freddie and she looks ill. Really proper ill. And I'm not sure what to do so I—'

'Have you called the doctor?' Emily's been Alice's carer for a year now and isn't usually a panicker but she's gabbling.

'No, I spotted Roger walking past and he's gone to get his car so we can take Alice to A&E at Seawinds. I don't know if she needs to go but he says it's better to be safe than sorry.'

Emily begins to sob as I balance the receiver between my chin and shoulder, already pushing my arms into the sleeves of my cotton cardigan.

'Listen to me, Emily. Go with Roger, get Alice to A&E and I'll meet you there.'

'OK. But get there as quickly as you can.' Emily's breath is still coming in fast gulps but she sounds calmer. 'Thanks, Annie. I'll see you soon – and don't worry.'

Don't worry? Emily bangs down the phone while I start scrolling through the contacts list on my mobile for a taxi company. I'll get to the hospital a.s.a.p. and text Josh from the cab on the way there. He was going to visit his mum straight after teaching and might be at her house already.

Summer traffic has clogged Cornwall's roads and the taxi driver takes backstreets to avoid the snarl-ups. But it still seems an age until he pulls up outside the main entrance to Seawinds Hospital. The Victorian building has been added to over the years, with an ugly 1970s concrete extension and a more modern wing that's mainly glass and huge yellow panels that glow like giant bananas in the sunshine. But the A&E department is located in the old part of the building that has high ceilings and tall, thin windows looking out onto a blue sky.

The windows, I realise, rushing along endless corridors, remind me of the six months I spent in my teens at a Victorian school in Islington. Before Mum insisted that we move again. We were always on the move from Mum's demons, as though she could pack up and leave her mental health problems behind. If only it had been that easy.

Reaching A&E at last, I barrel in and spot Roger straight away. He's leaning against the reception desk and Emily is standing next to him, biting her lip.

'What's going on? Where's Alice?' I puff.

'There you are.' Emily pushes her long, mousey-brown hair behind her ears and pulls me into a tight hug. 'She's OK, I think. They've taken her straight through and told us to have a seat until they call us. I've given reception your name as next of kin.'

'Next of kin?'

'Yeah, just standard stuff,' Roger assures me, scratching at his belly which is bulging through his grey T-shirt. 'So there's nothing we can do except sit down and hope they won't be too long. Bags I don't sit next to the screaming kid.'

He leads us through the rows of blue metal chairs that are fixed to the floor, presumably to stop local drunks using them as weapons on Saturday nights. Roger, long-time landlord of the Whistling Wave, isn't the most agile of people and I follow behind murmuring 'sorry, sorry' to the people whose feet he stands on. A seventeen-stone man squashing your toes when you've already had a run-in with a chainsaw or fallen headlong down the stairs isn't ideal.

At last, he sinks onto a chair and gestures for me and Emily to take the seats next to him. Ugh, they're as uncomfortable as they look – and sticky. There's a puddle of what I can only hope is orange juice on the floor and I use a tissue to mop it up before someone slips – health and safety and all that.

On the wall in front of me, subtitles are scrolling across a sound-less TV screen but everyone's ignoring it and staring at their mobile phones instead. They're probably tweeting about their day taking an unexpected turn. Or putting cryptic, attention-seeking posts on Facebook: *Why is the wait in A&E always so long?* (Passive-aggressive subtext: Ask why I'm here or I'll de-friend you.)

'Thanks so much for driving, Roger.' I lean across Emily and pat his arm, which is covered in a film of dark hair. 'It must be at least ten miles from Salt Bay. I'm surprised you got here before me.'

'I'm not,' mutters Emily. 'Roger drove fast and often on the wrong side of the road.' She gulps and wipes a hand across her forehead, which is beaded with sweat.

Roger shrugs. 'No court in the land would convict me for straying over the centre line a few times. It was an emergency.'

'What about driving the wrong way up a one-way street, blaring your horn? Or yelling at that bloke to get out of the effing way or you'd run him over? He had a white stick.'

'He was dithering and it was a matter of life and death. I had to get here pronto for Alice's sake.' Roger folds his arms and pushes out his bottom lip as I get the feeling he quite enjoyed being Lewis Hamilton for half an hour.

'Well, I'm just grateful that you brought Alice in. How was she when you got here?'

Emily pushes her glasses up her nose and shakes her head. 'No worse, though she said she was feeling sick. Ooh, here's Kayla. She looks a bit frazzled.'

'Frazzled' isn't really the right word. 'Demented' is more like it. Kayla's rust-red hair, usually in soft curls down her back, has turned to frizz in the sun and is sticking up. Her cheeks are glowing pillar-box scarlet and there are damp patches on the back of her yellow T-shirt. For an Australian, Kayla is totally rubbish in the heat.

'There you are!' Spotting us, she rushes over, treading on the toes of the same people who were Roger-d just a few moments ago. 'How's old Alice doing? I was shopping in Penzance and got a call from Florence to say she was here.'

'How did Florence know?'

'She heard it from Jennifer who heard it from Gerald who heard it from Dan who's holding the fort in the pub, seeing as Roger's here.'

Not for the first time, it strikes me that things rarely stay secret in Salt Bay for long. Living in London, I didn't know my neighbours' names but here I know the ins and outs of Gerald's brother's prostate problems, and I've only ever met him twice.

'Alice is with the doctors now and we're waiting to hear, so you'd better take a seat.'

As Kayla drops onto the chair next to me, her Boots carrier bag clunks onto the floor and a jumbo box of tampons skids across the tiles. The screaming child, who's being placated with a Curly Wurly, kicks it back towards us.

'Cheers, mate.' Kayla rams it back into the bag before clasping my arm and giving it a squeeze. 'So tell me what's been going on then.'

'I haven't seen Alice yet, but Emily rang and said she had a temperature and was confused. She didn't look well when I left for work this morning. I really should have stayed home.'

Kayla's frizzy hair shudders when she shakes her head. 'There's no point in beating yourself up. Alice is in the best place and all we can do is wait. At least there's a telly.'

She stares at the screen, which is showing people bidding at auction on what looks like a chamber pot. It's double-handled and huge with raised green vines picked out beneath the rim. 'Unbelievable!' she breathes when the winners hug one another, beaming with delight. 'Why anyone would pay good money for something that's been sat on by bare arses, is beyond me.'

In spite of feeling sick with worry, I grin. Kayla might not be the best person to count on in a crisis. She has a horrible habit of collapsing into giggles at inopportune moments. But you can always count on her to cheer you up.

As the minutes tick by, I check my phone, but there's nothing from Josh. The phone signal at his mum's house in Trecaldwith is pretty hit and miss, and both his mobile and her landline go straight to voicemail when I try calling again. So there's nothing to do but wait for word of Alice – and one thing I'm really not good at is waiting. I don't even realise my foot is tapping against my chair until the woman opposite gives me a glare. She's nursing a bloodied hand and looks the sort of person who'd punch a wall on purpose, so I tone down the tapping and try to concentrate on the TV instead.

At last, after forty-five long minutes, a nurse calls my name and beckons for me to follow her. She gives me a beaming smile as she holds a door open for me, and asks in a broad Irish accent: 'Are you with Alice Gowan? My name's Siobhan.' She wouldn't look so jolly if it was bad news, would she? She wouldn't be smiling if Alice was dead?

One of my favourite TV programmes ever is *24 Hours in A&E* – I'm a sucker for medical reality shows that make me cry. So the scene in front of me when the door swings open looks familiar. A woman with a stethoscope slung round her neck is poring over a computer screen as nurses bustle past her. There's a low hum of background noise and a shrill phone ringing nearby. It's organised chaos and, in spite of why I'm here, a thrill of excitement tingles through me. Many jobs are nine to five, boring, repetitive, occasionally satisfying if you're lucky. But here, it's life and death every day.

I follow Siobhan past a row of bays, deliberately not looking at the patients lying on narrow beds, until we reach the final bay, which is shielded by a green curtain. The curtain catches as it's pulled back and Siobhan curses under her breath before giving it a violent tug.

'Someone to see you, Mrs Gowan,' she says in a sing-song voice, cheeriness restored. 'Give me a call if you need anything.'

'Alice!' I rush forward and grasp my great-aunt's hand. She's lying on her back, looking disgruntled and small. On the back of her other hand, a thin needle threads into a vein that's blue and raised under her almost translucent skin. 'I was so worried about you. Are you OK?'

'Obviously not or I wouldn't be in here. Though Emily and Roger overreacted.' She gives my hand a tiny squeeze and clears her throat.

'Do you need a bowl? Emily said you were feeling sick.' I glance around the cubicle for anything that looks robust enough to hold vomit.

'I wasn't feeling sick until Roger started driving like an absolute lunatic. He mounted the pavement at one point and people had to jump for their lives. Or maybe I'm imagining it. I think I've been a bit confused.' When Alice shakes her head, her snow-white hair spreads across the sheet she's lying on. 'But this is ridiculous. I'm perfectly fine now and want to go home. Everyone's making a terrible fuss.'

She starts raising herself up on her elbows until I gently push her back down onto the bed. Her face still looks flushed and her eyes are bright. 'You have to stay here, Alice. Until we know what's wrong with you.'

'I know exactly what's wrong with me. I had a funny turn and now it's gone. But they still insisted on poking me with needles and putting me in this awful gown thing. But they can't make me stay here.'

'I don't suppose they can, but I'd like you to stay until we're sure you're well enough to come back to Tregavara House.'

'If I ever come back,' she mutters, squeezing my hand. 'I know what happens when you get old and ill and go into hospital. They ship you off to some godawful care home or keep you in hospital until you die. Enid went in after breaking her hip and never saw Salt Bay again. Promise me, Annabella, that you won't let me die in hospital.'

'Of course, I promise,' I say brightly, though inside I'm panicking. Should I make a promise I'm not sure I can keep? 'You're going to be fine and you're coming back to Tregavara House. There's no dying allowed today.'

'Definitely not,' says a deep voice behind me. A doctor has stepped into the cubicle and, even though my stomach is churning with anxiety, I register that he's handsome. Film star, just-stepped-off-the-cover-of-a-magazine handsome with a chiselled jaw and perfect caramel skin. No wonder some of the younger nurses are so glammed up.

After giving me a cursory nod, he stands next to Alice's bed and peers down at her. 'Our tests indicate that you have a urinary tract infection, Mrs Gowan, which is why you've been feeling so unwell. But a course of antibiotics should do the trick. I'll get that organised right away and it might be best if you stay in hospital for a day or two.' Dr Delectable spots Alice's scowl. 'Or I suppose you can go home earlier if you have constant care.'

'She does. Alice lives with us and we can look after her when she's well enough to come home.'

'We'll administer some antibiotics and if there's a rapid improvement, you might be able to go home quite soon. Is that all right, Mrs Gowan?' he asks loudly, patting her hand like she's a sandwich short of a picnic. Alice's eyes narrow but she nods without saying a word. Blimey, she really is under the weather.

When the doctor sweeps out of the cubicle, I scurry after him. He sits down at the desk, starts studying an X-ray on screen and doesn't look up until I speak.

'Thank you for treating Alice. So she'll definitely be OK, will she? She reckons she's indestructible and I must admit I sometimes think she'll live forever.'

Dr Delectable glances back at the screen, which shows thick white bones surrounded by a grey fuzz. 'I'm afraid I can't guarantee immortality. Antibiotics will clear her infection but your mother—'

'Great-aunt,' I correct him, wondering exactly how old I look right now. Jeez, stress must add decades to your face.

'Your great-aunt is elderly and rather frail with some underlying chronic health conditions. People don't last forever,' he says with a frown.

'Which I know all too well. My mum died of cancer almost five years ago and she was only in her early forties.'

Nope. Not a flicker of sympathy. He just stares at me as though I'm a particularly annoying patient.

'Just so long as Alice will make it to Wednesday at least.' I grin to show that I'm joking. 'It's her eighty-fourth birthday and she'll be heartily peed off if she misses it.'

'She should be on the mend by then.'

Dr Delectable goes straight back to studying his X-ray without even the hint of a smile. What a shame. Looks aren't everything and his missing sense of humour will drive most women mad once they get past the tearing-his-clothes-off stage. Josh has a grumpy vibe going on sometimes, especially when his team loses at football, but he also makes me laugh more than anyone I know.

Talk of the devil. Josh suddenly pokes his head around the door and starts beckoning furiously at me. Thick, dark hair flicks into his chocolate-brown eyes with every beckon and there's a hint of stubble on his strong jaw. Wowzers! Eat your heart out, Dr Delectable, because my boyfriend is seriously stiff competition. And he tells jokes.

A young nurse, with golden-blonde hair pulled into a swinging ponytail, starts making a beeline for Josh but steps back when I get there first.

'Is he with you?' She laughs, revealing perfect pearly-white teeth, and I'm tempted to ask why she thinks that's so amusing. *Because she can't believe you've managed to nab such a gorgeous boyfriend,* whispers my inner bitch voice but I ignore it. My inner bitch is proving a bugger to shift, even though Josh and I have never been happier, but now isn't the time to take it on.

'I came as soon as I got your message, Annie. Is Alice all right? You sounded so worried on the phone,' says Josh in a rush, his forehead creased with concern.

'The doctor says she's going to be fine. She's got a urine infection and they're treating her with antibiotics.'

'Phew, that's a relief! I thought… well, it doesn't matter what I thought.'

The door swings shut behind Josh, who pulls me into his arms and hugs me tight. I breathe in his familiar sandalwood smell as I wrap my arms around his waist and realise that my legs are feeling wobbly. It must be all the adrenaline that's been whooshing through me for the last hour.

'Why don't I go and sit with her while you tell everyone outside that she's going to be all right,' murmurs Josh, stroking my hair. 'It's like a Salt Bay convention out there and the receptionist is getting antsy.'

Josh wasn't joking. Seven people jump to their feet and look at me expectantly when I walk into the waiting area.

'She's not dead is she?' blurts out Storm, whose hair, now faded to a soft mauve, gives her complexion an unearthly tinge.

'No, she's going to be fine. But how come you're here?'

'I was at Serena's when Josh found out.' She nods at Josh's seventeen-year-old sister, standing next to her.

'So we all came,' butts in Josh's mum, Marion, stepping forward and kissing me on the cheek. Her grey-streaked hair is pulled into a bun and she smells of freshly baked bread, like all mums should. 'We were all worried about Alice and that's great news she's going to be all right. What's wrong with her?'

'It's an infection and they can treat it,' I say vaguely, not sure that Alice would approve of me discussing her urinary tract in public.

'Well, I'm relieved my expert driving got her here in time, and it's just as well she's not dropping off the perch.' Roger nudges Kayla, who's looking even hotter than the last time I saw her. 'Annie doesn't want to lose Alice when she might be losing you too.'

'Losing you too, you what?'

When I turn to Kayla, she frowns. 'Roger is talking out of his backside, as usual. Ollie's being interviewed for a promotion today.' She puts 'interview' and 'promotion' in air quotes, though I'm not sure why. 'And if he gets it, he reckons he'll be moving to some awful place up North. Only he won't 'cos Ollie will never leave his beloved Cornwall. I'm the adventurer in our relationship and he's the stayer.'

Which is true enough. Intrepid traveller Kayla is nine thousand miles from home and has backpacked across much of Europe, while Ollie, her local boyfriend, thinks a day trip to Bodmin Moor is pushing it. But she's been settled in Salt Bay for a while now and that's largely due to Ollie, though she'd never admit it.

The thought of being tied down gives footloose Kayla nightmares and she totally freaked when Ollie proposed last year. They only got back together because he promised he'd never marry her in a month of Sundays. Ah, true love.

'So there's absolutely nothing to worry about,' says Kayla, pushing damp strands of hair off her shiny forehead. 'And, as a feminist, Roger, I resent the implication that if Ollie did move, I'd automatically go with him. Nothing is going to change.'

And she says it with such conviction, I want to believe her. But Kayla's wrong. Everything changes, from the weather and people's minds to Alice's health. And however much I want my life in Salt Bay to stay the same forever, I know in my heart that it won't.

Chapter Three

Dr Delectable is right; Alice does get better. But her recovery's slower than anticipated and she ends up spending two days in hospital before she can come home. As expected, this is not well received by Alice, who complains she's been kidnapped, and Emily, Josh and I take it in turns to sit by her bed so she won't do a runner. She wouldn't get very far but there's always the risk of her falling during a shuffling getaway.

All things considered, both we and the hospital staff are delighted when Alice is finally discharged back to Tregavara House, which has seemed horribly empty without her. Emily goes full *Great British Bake Off* and makes a fabulous iced Victoria sponge in celebration. And I'm touched to find Storm sitting next to Alice on the sofa while she's catching up on the *Doc Martin* she missed.

'Well, someone has to keep an eye on her. Though she seriously needs to upgrade her viewing preferences,' mutters Storm when I thank her. 'The place wasn't the same without the old lady.' And I have to agree, it really wasn't.

Alice wakes feeling more full of beans on her birthday, especially when she spots all the cards she has to open. Amongst the pile, there's one from my dad, Barry, who's in Sutton Coldfield on tour with his latest band, and even my distant cousin Toby has remembered to send one, thanks to a nudge from me via text. I can't take the day off work because Gayle and Lesley are away on some tedious training course, but people have already started calling in to pass on their best birthday wishes by the time I leave for the office.

'She's loved it,' reports Emily when I get home hours later, feeling hot and sweaty. All the windows are flung open but it's not doing much good. Usually Tregavara House is buffeted by strong Atlantic winds but today there's only the faintest hint of a breeze, tinged with salt.

'She's been like the Queen Mother of Salt Bay, holding court from the sofa,' laughs Emily, lifting up her thick brown plait and fanning the back of her neck with a *Radio Times*. 'There's been a steady stream of visitors and most have brought presents. She's got enough chocolate to keep Jennifer's shop stocked until Christmas. She's had a good day.'

Later that evening, I pour a glass of ice-cold water from the fridge and take it up to Alice, who's sitting in her four-poster bed, looking at the cliffs through her window. The house is quiet because everyone's at choir rehearsal except me – I'm giving it a miss to keep an eye on my great-aunt and spend time with her on her special day.

'Here you go.' I place the glass on Alice's bedside table and adjust the rose-coloured counterpane that's pulled up to her thin shoulders. 'You really did do well for presents.' Tubs of Roses, boxes of Milk Tray and fancy toiletries are piled up on the plush, button-back chair in the corner.

'People have been very generous, though they're trying to finish me off. I'll overdose on sugar if I eat all that chocolate. Is *Coronation Street* taping?'

'Yes, don't worry. Maybe we can get a TV organised in here, actually.' I glance around the room to see where an aerial socket could be installed but Alice shakes her head.

'No need. I'll be properly up and about in no time with none of this going to bed at seven o'clock nonsense.' Her legs shift as though she wants to prove it right now, but I put my hand on her knee through the cover.

'In a day or two, maybe. I don't want you rushing things and ending up back in hospital. It's so lovely to have you here on your birthday. Tregavara House wouldn't be the same without you.'

'I should think not,' harrumphs Alice, reaching for the glass. I perch on the edge of the bed and put my arm round her shoulders for support as she sips. The wind has picked up and is pushing against the thick brocade curtains which brush the floorboards.

'Thank you, Annabella. You are good to me.'

She wipes the back of her hand across her mouth and settles back against the pillows plumped up behind her head. She's looking much better these days but so old and worn out it breaks my heart.

'Don't look so worried, child.' When Alice smiles and touches her throat, I notice that she's wearing her pearls in honour of her birthday. 'My father used to say, "if the wind changes, your face will stick like that."'

'My mum used to say that too.'

'Did she? I expect she heard it from her father because these silly sayings are passed down through families. No doubt, you'll say it to your children one day.'

'Hang on a minute,' I laugh, moving the glass so Alice will be able to reach it in the night. 'Who says I'm going to have any kids?'

'I'm sure you will.'

'I don't know,' I say, suddenly serious. 'I don't feel grown-up enough and I'm not sure I'd be very good at it anyway. Being a mum, I mean. I didn't really have a great—' I was going to say 'role model' but stop and chew at my lip. Mum did her best. It wasn't her fault that she was often unwell and life was difficult.

'You are not your mother, Annabella.' Alice shuffles in the bed to get more comfortable. 'Joanna was a one-off, and it would be a shame if the difficulties of your past affected your future because I know you'd be a wonderful mother. Look at how well you've coped with Storm and stepped into her mother's shoes. You've given her stability that was seriously lacking.'

'It's you and Tregavara House and Salt Bay who've given her stability.'

Alice shakes her head. 'Don't underestimate your impact on that girl, and I know it hasn't been easy.'

Which is lovely of Alice to say – and one hell of an understatement. Storm's mum ran off a few years ago, leaving her in the care of our dad, Barry, who's not such a great role model himself. He loves Storm but the life of a wannabe rock star is chaotic and she arrived in Salt Bay angry, undisciplined and, quite frankly, a right royal pain in the backside.

At first it was awful. I'm surprised we have any doors left with all the hormonal slamming that went on. But over the months Storm and I have grown closer to the point where sometimes I do feel more like her mum than her half-sister – and I quite like it so maybe I am mother material. Surely coping with a baby would be easy-peasy compared to a teenager in a tantrum?

Alice gives me a none-too-gentle nudge with her shoulder. 'Anyway, if you are going to have children you'd better crack on because you're getting on a bit.'

Cheers, Alice. Just what every thirty-year-old childless woman needs – a great-aunt-shaped biological alarm clock.

'Times are different now.' I grin. 'No one has babies until, ooh, at least thirty-five. Some women wait to have their first babies until they're in their forties.'

'Huh, that's far too old and their eggs will be good for nothing. The trouble with you young girls is you think you can have it all, but you can't. Are you sure that you haven't thought of having children at all?'

'Not really, though I've got some favourite names on stand-by just in case I happen to have a child at some far-off stage in the future. Not that I'm planning to,' I add quickly when Alice's dark brown eyes flash with excitement. 'Do you want to hear them?'

'Of course. Just so long as they're not ridiculous modern names, like Firefly.'

'I'm not sure anyone anywhere has ever been called Firefly but, don't worry, the names I like are very traditional. If I had a girl, I'd quite like to call her Phoebe Alice Joanna.'

Alice pulls herself higher in the bed and her broad smile sharpens the cheekbones in her wrinkled face.

'Both your mother and I would be honoured and Phoebe is such a pretty name. I knew a Phoebe once who had a very sad life and ended up in jail for soliciting in Penzance.'

O-K. Maybe not Phoebe then.

'And what about if you have a boy?' asks Alice before starting to cough. I pass her a tissue and wait for the coughing to ease before answering.

'If I have a boy, I'd like to call him Freddie.'

Alice stiffens and, to my horror, tears start spilling from her eyes. They dribble down her cheeks and plop onto the counterpane, leaving dark patches on the silk.

'I'm so sorry, Alice. I didn't mean to be insensitive or upset you but I've always loved the name and thought it would be in memory of your little boy.'

'My dear girl.' Alice sucks her wobbly lower lip between her teeth. 'Forgive me but I'm annoyingly over-emotional at the moment with everything that's been going on. It would be wonderful for Freddie's memory to live on when I'm gone. But would Josh be all right with the name?'

'I expect he would be,' I tell her, feeling warm and fuzzy at her assumption that Josh will be the father of my children. If I have any. Which I might not. But my life has changed so much in the past year, who knows what will happen in the years to come? Maybe I'll end up with twins. Or triplets. Eek, I'm now picturing myself pregnant, the size of a beached whale.

Alice brushes away her tears and gives a little sniff. 'You've become very special to me, Annie, and I'm so glad you turned up on my doorstep last year. You're a wonderful young woman and my life would have been the poorer for never knowing you.'

'Stop it, Alice, or you'll make me cry too,' I wail, clasping her hand and softly rubbing my thumb across her knuckles. 'One of the best things I ever did was make that journey from London to Cornwall, even though I hated it here at first.'

'Didn't I know it!'

'Really? And I thought I hid it so well.' I wink at the old lady who has wormed her way into my heart. 'Better than Storm did at least.'

'That's true enough.' Alice stifles a yawn and settles back against her pillow. 'Though Salt Bay has worked its magic on that girl, too.'

She's right. Storm now has a part-time job in Jennifer's shop, she sings with the choir and she's settled pretty well into school. She's even taken a few exams and hasn't mentioned going back to live in London for ages. I've got used to having her around so haven't mentioned it either. She'd only end up getting in with the wrong crowd while Barry's away on tour.

'What's that noise?' asks Alice, glancing at her bedside clock. Outside her open window, a low hum of conversation is mingling with the dull boom of waves hitting the harbour wall. 'There seem to be a lot of people heading for the harbour at this time of night. I hope no one's organised one of those seaside rave things.'

She frowns as the hum gets louder and the garden gate squeaks open. 'Take a look, Annabella, and see who's calling at this late hour. It's most inconvenient.'

The bed creaks when I stand up and look out of the window. In the shadow of the cliffs that drop into the sea, a little huddle of people is trudging along the garden path – and I know every single one of them.

Josh spots me and puts his finger to his lips while he shepherds Salt Bay Choral Society under Alice's bedroom window. It's a bit like herding cats but he eventually gets them into a group and stands facing them. Storm, who's loitering at the back, gives me a shrug, Josh raises his hand and tenor Gerald plays a single note on his harmonica.

'What on earth is going on?' calls Alice from her bed, craning her neck.

'You'll see.' I smile at her as the first notes of 'Lamorna' waft in through the open window. It's a traditional Cornish song we performed last year when the choir competed for the Kernow Choral Crown and it helped us to win first prize in the New Choirs category. Josh knows it's one of Alice's favourites.

'Oh, that's lovely,' says Alice, recognition flooding her face. 'Are the choir here to sing just for me? That's so kind of them.' Her smile suddenly freezes. 'They don't think I'm dying, do they? Is there something you haven't told me?'

'Absolutely not, Alice. They merely want to do something special for your birthday.'

'Did you know about it?'

'I didn't. It must be an impromptu performance.'

Alice beams when the choir launch into 'Happy Birthday' and throws back the covers. She's looking very chic in the pink satin pyjamas that Emily bought her. 'Get my dressing gown immediately, Annabella. I want to see this.'

Dressing gown on, she walks slowly to the window listening to the choir sing 'Kumbaya', which is another of Alice's favourites. Josh must have noticed which songs Alice likes the most, the tunes she hums when she's shuffling around the house, which makes me love him all the more.

A loud cheer reverberates from below when Alice reaches the window and looks out. The setting sun is hanging deep red in the sky and its light casts an aura around her as she waves at the choir and blows them a kiss.

And that's how I'll always remember my feisty, funny great-aunt: giving a regal wave in shocking-pink pyjamas to her adoring public from the Salt Bay bedroom where she was born.

Chapter Four

Alice Jean Gowan – cherished sister, adored wife, firm friend and beloved great-aunt – dies ten days later.

It's nothing to do with the urine infection. She recovers from that and I start believing she'll be with us for a while to come. I let my guard down and feel happy again.

But her heart is old and tired and simply stops while she's dozing in her favourite chair that overlooks the harbour. Alice always did hate making a fuss and she slips away without any drama.

So in the end, there's no dreaded phone call at work or urgent dash home. I simply take her a cup of tea on a Sunday afternoon and stand frozen in the sitting room doorway, tea dripping onto the carpet when the cup slips in its saucer. Alice has gone. It's obvious from the way her arm is hanging loose over the side of the chair and the tilt of her head, chin to chest. And when I touch her lovely face, her skin is white and cool.

Josh rings Dr Rivers and I sit by Alice, holding her hand, and wait for him to arrive. Outside, tourists are walking from the harbour into the village and their snatched conversations drift through the window and hammer home that I'll never chat with Alice again.

We'll never sit in the garden at the end of the day and watch a golden sun sink slowly into the sea. Or roll our eyes in mutual solidarity when Storm flies into a mega-strop and stomps out of the house.

Emily and Storm are sitting pinch-faced with shock on the bottom stair when Dr Rivers arrives and takes over. He assures us that Alice's death was peaceful and painless, and that's some comfort over the next few days as we go about making funeral arrangements. But we're devastated to lose her and, though the sun is blazing outside, the house is cold with black shadows lurking in gloomy corners.

We all react to Alice's death differently. Josh switches into practical mode, which his mum says is how he behaved sixteen years ago when his step-dad died in the Great Storm that killed seven local fishermen. Emily is permanently in tears and Storm won't admit it, but she's knocked for six. The usual back-chat stops and she retreats to her bedroom, only venturing out for meals that we all pick at in silence.

For me, losing Alice has stirred the same ragged, suffocating feelings of grief I experienced when Mum died. *I must tell Alice*, I think several times a day, when I spot an oystercatcher in the bird bath or Jennifer tells me some juicy gossip or *Death In Paradise* is on the telly. And there's always an icy rush of sorrow when it hits home that she's gone forever.

But it's comforting that I was able to keep my promise and she died in Salt Bay among people who love her, rather than in hospital among medical staff who didn't know her at all. The cycle of Alice Jean Gowan's life began and ended at Tregavara House – and she wouldn't have had it any other way.

Josh is brilliant from the moment the undertaker takes Alice's body away and I collapse in floods of tears. He holds me while I cry great snotting sobs into his jumper and snivel in the dark hours of early mornings. And he comes with me to discuss plans with the funeral director who also organised the burial of my grandmother Sheila a year ago. She and my grandfather Samuel lie in Salt Bay's tiny clifftop cemetery which will one day fall into the sea.

Alice, ever pragmatic and practical, has left detailed instructions with the funeral director and paid upfront. So there's nothing for me to do except circulate the funeral arrangements around the village and steel myself for our final goodbye.

A strong wind is blowing over a raging sea when we all gather on the clifftop two weeks later. Almost the whole village has turned out and we're spread like a black carpet along the cliff edge with the cemetery behind us.

The memorial service in Salt Bay Church, where Alice and her husband, David, were married five decades ago, was a beautiful celebration of a life well lived and a woman well loved. And though Alice would have grumbled at us for making a fuss – I could imagine her standing at the back of the church, arms folded – I think she would have been pleased.

Jennifer and old boy Cyril, who sings with the choir, were among the locals who stood up and shared their happy memories of Alice. And I did too. Voice shaking, I only managed to get halfway through how Alice welcomed me to my new life in Salt Bay before the lump in my throat threatened to strangle me. But Josh, tall and handsome in his coal-black suit, leapt up and held my hand while he read out the rest of my words.

Any self-composure I had left finally splintered when Salt Bay Choral Society, conducted by Josh, sang Alice's favourite hymn, 'Amazing Grace'. I don't think there was a dry eye in the house and even Jennifer's solo was wobbly.

The church service marked Alice's life anchored in Salt Bay and now, high above the village, we're about to let her go. I hug the heavy plastic urn to my chest and deliberately turn into the squall of rain that's stinging my face. I'm glad the heatwave has finally broken and the sun has disappeared. This is perfect Cornish weather for what we're here to do.

Alice left us one last surprise. Everyone expected her to be buried in the clifftop cemetery next to David but she left strict instructions that she should be cremated and her name inscribed next to her beloved husband's. So a small ceremony was held for close friends and family at the crematorium a few days ago and I collected her ashes this morning, before the memorial service began.

People were surprised by her choice of send-off but I get it. Alice loved the ever-changing ocean and Cornish countryside and, this way, she'll be a part of the sea and the wind forever.

There's a hush from the crowd as Josh helps me unscrew the lid of the urn and I take a few steps towards the crashing waves far below us. Toby, in a sharp black suit with a tidy goatee, steps forward too and ignores a loud tutting from Florence.

My distant cousin Toby Trebarwith has been persona non grata in the village since they discovered he fathered a child with Josh's sister Lucy and then scarpered off to London for years. They don't mind the sex and illegitimacy – there's been a lot of it round here over the years apparently – but they disapprove of him not taking responsibility for his own child.

'Christ, it's a long way down,' mutters Toby, swallowing hard and inching back towards Josh, who's helping Alice's elderly friend, Penelope, stay upright. 'I'm not great with heights so you might need to do this on your own. The old girl wouldn't mind.'

For a moment, I hug the urn to my chest. 'Goodbye, darling Alice, and thank you for everything,' I whisper, concentrating hard on not dropping the slippery damp plastic as I turn it upside down.

A stream of gritty white ash pours from the pot, is caught by the wind and dances in front of us before being whipped across the grey water. For a few moments the ashes rise and dip above the white-flecked waves before melding into the churning sea and the huge Cornish sky. Alice is gone.

We're a bedraggled bunch, trudging down the cliffs towards the huddled houses of Salt Bay. I wouldn't mind if the rain stopped now and sun peeped through the thick banks of grey cloud. But a good old Cornish mizzle – a soaking blend of mist and drizzle – has set in for the day. My navy-blue coat is heavy with damp and my feet are soggy.

'This weather has totally knackered my new shoes,' moans Storm, pushing past me and almost sliding on the wet grass. She grabs my arm to steady herself. 'Are you feeling all right? I'm going to miss the old lady, though it was pretty sweet letting her ashes go like that so she flew across the sea. Oh. My. God!' She stops abruptly and starts brushing the top of her head with both hands. 'I think that's some of her falling out of my hair.'

As she careers off, Josh links his arm through mine and pulls me in close so we match strides. 'Just when I think she's starting to be less annoying…' He gives a short laugh. 'It's nice that your dad managed to be here.'

Barry is ahead of us, chatting with Josh's mum and I feel a rush of affection for the ageing rocker. He's put his best black jeans on specially and his long hair is tied back in a tidy ponytail that's curling on his shoulder. Isn't it funny how things change. When we met for the first time last October, I couldn't wait to be shot of him and now I look forward to his visits.

'It's a good job his band has a gig in Falmouth this evening. If they were still in the Isle of Sheppey, or wherever it was they were touring last week, he'd never have made it. Apparently, this new band is his big break at last.' I give Josh a rueful smile. 'Anyway, Alice wouldn't have minded if he couldn't get here.'

'Not ever-practical Alice,' agrees Josh, pushing his dripping fringe out of his eyes. 'She wouldn't have wanted him to waste his money on the travel.'

'True but it's lovely to see him and I'm glad Storm and Emily are around too. The house would be too quiet without them, now Alice has gone.'

We've reached the gate to Tregavara House and Josh pulls me closer and kisses my damp hair. 'You're not on your own any more, Annie. Don't forget that. You'll always have me whatever happens.'

Chapter Five

Emily and I have been buttering bread and shoving sausage rolls in the oven all morning so people can come back for a cup of tea and a snack, though we're screwed if more than twenty-five people take up the invitation – especially if one of them is Roger. He's the only man I know who can eat two Shredded Wheat plus a full English and still have room for Hula Hoops an hour later. No wonder he's the same shape as the barrels of ale stored in his cellar.

Fortunately, Roger declines because he's due back behind the bar and only a dozen people follow me into Tregavara House, most of them choir members. Oops, we'll be eating ham sandwiches for days.

I've been mingling for a while, feeling slightly guilty as though I'm taking Alice's place as hostess, when Kayla's arm snakes around my waist and she rests her pointy chin on my shoulder.

'How are you doing then, Sunshine?'

Kayla thinks it's a great laugh to call me by my middle name. The full name bestowed on me by my mother is Annabella Sunshine Trebarwith. Which is awful, isn't it, and why Kayla sniggers whenever she reminds me of it.

'I'm not so bad, considering. You look nice in that dress.'

Kayla has ditched her usual jeans and brightly coloured sweatshirts for black boots and a grey dress with a nipped-in waist and neon-pink buttons scattered across the bodice.

'I thought Alice would appreciate me making an effort so I picked this up in the Cancer Research shop in Penzance. Though I can't believe she's carked it. It's so sad... Alice was a real one-off.' When Kayla shakes her head, red curls tumble around her face. 'But it's good to see how everyone's been pitching in today – they're good people in Salt Bay. And Jennifer is really getting in on the act. Have you seen her over there?'

I hadn't, but Jennifer has put on a Birds of Cornwall apron and is pushing a platter of sandwiches under people's noses. It's Alice's apron, the one she wore for making pastry, and a shiver runs through me at the sight of Jennifer in it. But I take a deep breath and get a grip on myself. Alice wouldn't mind – she'd say there's no sense in ruining a perfectly good dress with mustard stains – and it's kind of Jennifer to help. Though I'm sure the sandwiches still had their crusts on when we left for the clifftop.

'She insisted on cutting off the crusts so I let her get on with it. I wasn't going to start arguing about bread,' says Emily, wandering over. Her eyes are red-rimmed and she sniffs loudly in my ear when I give her a hug.

'Where's Jay?'

Emily shrugs. 'He had a lot on so couldn't come today. To be honest' – she sighs and her bottom lip wobbles – 'we've split up. It's for the best, really. He's been rubbish since Alice died and he's not really what I expected. He's not terribly...' she searches for the right word '... kind. He's quite self-centred actually.'

'Self-centred? He's a total tw— Ouch!' Kayla squeals when I tread on her toes but clamps her mouth shut after catching my eye. Harry Styles lookalike Jay, eighteen years old and full of himself, is shallowness personified and it's great Emily has finally seen through him. But first love hurts like hell so I wrinkle my nose in sympathy and make soothing noises.

Tom, a lovely tenor from the choir, is loitering nearby and moves a little closer. All gangly arms and legs, he's been earwigging shamelessly. He tugs at the waistband of his trousers which are falling down as usual, revealing black boxers.

'That Jay's not worthy of you, Emily,' he says gruffly and then flushes bright pink. There's a dusting of hair across his chin – 'bum fluff' my mum used to call it – and the faintest hint of a moustache on his upper lip.

'Aw, you're such a lovely person, Tom,' says Emily, hardly giving him a glance. 'I'm off all men at the moment but you don't count 'cos you're like my gay friend.'

'Um, I'm not gay,' mumbles Tom, going even pinker.

'I know but it's like you are 'cos we can talk about all kinds of things without that boyfriend-girlfriend stuff getting in the way.'

Poor Tom's face falls but he gamely carries on. 'Maybe we can make a nice afternoon of it, Ems, and head for the pub in a bit. Would you like to come, Annie? It'll be fun.' Alarm suddenly sparks in Tom's grey eyes and he draws his face into a serious expression. 'Though, of course, I'm terribly sorry for your loss, Annie.'

For your loss? He's been watching far too many schmaltzy American TV shows.

'Thanks, Tom. You two should go and maybe I'll see you there later. Do either of you know where Storm is?'

Around me, people are chatting in subdued little groups, but my sister is nowhere to be seen.

'She ran upstairs as soon as she got back, yelling that she had to wash her hair,' sniffs Emily. 'I read that grief can make people behave erratically so there's no hope for her. She was terminally weird to begin with.'

I don't deny it as Tom links his arm through Emily's and pulls her towards the platter of curling ham sandwiches that Jennifer's currently forcing on Josh.

'Phew! It's a relief she's ditched gel-head,' whispers Kayla, who reckons Jay's obsessed with hair products and regularly buys out Boots. 'I was only going to agree with her decision so you didn't need to break my toes.'

'Sorry but you're not always the most sensitive of people. No offence.'

'None taken,' says Kayla, who revels in being an outspoken Aussie. 'Do you think she'll ever get it on with Tom? He's so sweet.'

'I doubt it. She seems adamant they're just friends. Poor Tom.'

'Yeah, poor old thing. He'd make a brilliant boyfriend.'

Kayla and I both sigh as Tom feeds Emily a sausage roll with a goofy smile on his face.

'Talking of brilliant boyfriends, what's happening with Ollie's promotion prospects? Is he going to be moving up North?'

'Of course not. They still haven't made a final decision, or so he says.' Kayla grins and taps the side of her nose. 'But mark my words, there won't be any promotion or moving out of Cornwall. Ollie's just trying to seem more adventurous in my eyes because I keep calling him provincial.'

'I dunno, Kayla. Josh says this promotion stuff is all legit.'

'Nope. They're in it together. Ollie will never leave Cornwall for good unless it's in a box and he's crazy about me so there's no way he'd risk losing this.' Kayla waves her hand up and down her body and winks. 'Oops, knobhead alert!' she murmurs, scuttling off.

The knobhead in question is Toby, who's been standing alone at the sitting room window for ages but is now wandering over. There are pale flakes of pastry scattered across his black cashmere jumper.

'That's it then,' he announces, brushing the flakes onto the carpet. 'Alice is no more. I'll quite miss the old girl though she had a good innings.'

Wow, a good innings? Toby is so blunt he makes Kayla seem uber sensitive.

'How long will you be in Cornwall?' I ask, keen to move the conversation on. 'You could have stayed here, you know.'

'Obviously, but I thought it best to stay in a hotel this time, especially if your father's around.' He raises his eyebrows at Barry, who appears to be shoving two sandwiches into his mouth at the same time. 'Anyway, personally I don't enjoy death,' he adds with a shudder as though the rest of us find the Grim Reaper a great laugh. 'I suppose I'd better stay in Cornwall until tomorrow so I can see Freya. I'd have brought her today, but Lucy didn't think she was old enough to come to Alice's send-off.'

'How's it going with Freya?'

Toby shrugs. 'OK, I think. She loved the new dolls' house I got her and I'm paying for Lucy to take her to Disneyland Paris.'

'Crikey. It sounds like you're spending lots of money on your daughter. I'm sure she'd be just as happy with your time and company.'

'But what would we do? I don't know how to talk to six-year-olds. You can't discuss the stock market or latest thinking on Renaissance art with someone who finds splashing in puddles exciting.'

If there's one man who'd benefit from joyful puddle splashing, it's Toby. But he'd never even countenance it.

'Why don't you try doing something simple with her?'

'Like what?'

'Maybe you could take her out for a burger.'

Toby frowns and shakes his head, not convinced that spending quality time with his daughter would be better than shelling out a shedload of dosh. Though to be fair, I don't know many six-year-olds who'd choose an afternoon at McDonald's over a holiday with Mickey Mouse. But at least Toby's now in touch with his daughter after ignoring her for years.

'Anyway.' Toby pushes up onto the balls of his feet and clasps his hands behind his back like he's Prince Charles. 'I suppose I'd better start making plans for this place. You do know, of course, that Alice left me Tregavara House in her will?'

'I assumed as much,' I say, heart sinking. 'Um, but what exactly do you mean by plans?'

'Don't worry, Annie. You did me right by Freya. You put me in touch with her even though your boyfriend threw a wobbly about it and I won't forget that. I'm not about to make you all homeless.' Toby's humourless laugh sounds more like a bark. 'So I'll give you time to find somewhere else though it shouldn't take long to secure a rental property in the area. I expect you're looking already.'

I shake my head, open-mouthed. 'We assumed we could stay on at Tregavara House if we paid you the market rent. I didn't think you'd want to live here yourself.'

'Heavens, no. I can't think of anything worse. I'm a Londoner through and through but it's good to have a family pile and somewhere to stay when I'm visiting Freya.'

I try not to stare at a yellow flake of pastry stuck to the corner of Toby's mouth that's wobbling with every word.

'Also, some of my colleagues have hinted they might like to spend a few days here occasionally. Apparently, Cornwall is a desired holiday location though I can't for the life of me understand why. Given the choice I head for New York or a capital city on the continent. It's far more chic and the weather's not so appalling. Still, each to their own.'

'Wouldn't it make more sense for the house to be occupied when you're not around? You could still come and stay with your friends and we'd love for Freya to stay over. Josh is her uncle, after all.'

Toby groans. 'If it was just you, Annie, maybe. But I don't think it would work with your family around all the time and especially not if he's here.'

He tilts his head at Josh, who's munching his way through yet another sandwich that's been thrust upon him by Jennifer.

'Are you sure this is what Alice would want?' My voice is getting louder and people turn round and stare.

'It doesn't really matter because Alice isn't here any more.' Toby sees my face fall and his expression softens. 'Look, I don't want to fall out with you, Annie, but I've made up my mind. I'll give you a few weeks to find somewhere else. Perhaps you and Pasco could rent a cosy cottage together, if you could bear it.'

'What's that about a cottage?' Josh has wandered over and is standing extra close to me like a sexy guardian angel.

When Toby bristles, the lip-flake of pastry flutters to the floor. 'I was just telling Annie that although the house belongs to me now she can take a few weeks to find somewhere else for you all to live. She is family, after all.'

'Good grief, man! Are you really throwing Annie out after she gave up her life in London to look after Alice?' splutters Josh, an angry red flush creeping above the collar of his white shirt.

'Oh, don't be so dramatic, Pasco. Of course I'm not throwing her out – you'll all have time to find somewhere else. But what you have to remember is that Tregavara House is now mine.'

Toby's hooded grey eyes narrow and the faintest hint of a smile plays around his mouth. Beside me, Josh tenses and I place a steadying hand on his arm.

'Please leave it, Josh. We may not like it, but the house will soon belong to Toby and he can do what he wants.'

'But throwing you out is not what Alice would want,' says Josh, dark hair flopping into his eyes. He rakes long fingers through his fringe and sucks in a steadying breath of air.

'I know but Alice made her will a long time before she met me and there's nothing we can do about it.'

'Well, at least one of you is talking sense,' huffs Toby, who seems determined to wring the very worst out of a rubbish situation.

I'm worried Alice's wake is about to turn into a punch-up, but Josh takes another deep breath and says pretty calmly, considering: 'Are you throwing Annie out because of me, Toby? She shouldn't have to suffer because of our history.'

'Don't flatter yourself, Pasco. This house – the Trebarwith family home – belongs to me and I want it to myself.'

'So you're not punishing her for falling in love with me?'

'Absolutely not, though I have to say there's no accounting for taste.'

At that comment, Josh takes a step towards Toby, but I pull him away before more's said that we might regret. Toby's regularly seeing his daughter now and paying maintenance which has eased the financial pressure on Josh's family. The last thing I want is for that to be wrecked – even though losing Tregavara House so soon after losing Alice is almost too much to bear.

This marvellous old house is my anchor and the antidote to my lonely chaotic life in London. Of course, I knew it would go to Toby but I hoped our relationship had improved to the point where he'd let us stay. It seems I was wrong.

The atmosphere in the room has changed and Gerald, who was standing close enough to overhear the whole conversation, starts moving around the room, murmuring to other choir members.

One by one, they glare at Toby, who fetches his coat without another word and heads for the door. He's itching to leave Salt Bay and I'm relieved to see him go. My cousin reveals an occasional flash of humanity. Sometimes I even feel sorry for him in his carefully constructed, sterile world. But, when it comes to the crunch, he's a bit of a bastard.

'About time that poncey idiot left.' Barry is still clutching a handful of sandwiches and leaves a trail of breadcrumbs when he marches over. 'Can I have a word with you in private, Annie? In the kitchen.'

Oh, what now?

'We can talk about all this later,' says Josh, giving my shoulder a sympathetic squeeze before I follow my father into the kitchen.

Wow, it looks like a bomb has hit this room. Used teacups are piled up in the sink, stray crusts are scattered across the worktop and there are piles of tea plates on the table. In the background, Radio 2 is playing quietly on the old-fashioned Roberts radio that lives on the windowsill near the back door.

'Take a seat,' says Barry, pushing the plates to one side. 'Look, I just wanted to say how sorry I am that old Alice is pushing up the daisies. She was a real lady. A bit scary sometimes but she took me and Storm in – both of you did – and I'll always be grateful for that.'

'Alice was a very special woman.'

When Barry nods and pulls off the black band around his ponytail, his hair falls to his shoulders and reveals the spreading bald patch on his crown. He looks less Bono and more dishevelled monk these days.

'So will Storm have to leave now?' he asks abruptly, twanging the hairband onto his wrist. 'That probably sounds like I'm selfish and only worried about her and me but, to be honest, she's much better here. She got away with murder in London.' He colours. 'Well, that was partly down to me. But here, she's going to school and she looks on you as a mother figure now Amanda's got her brand new lah-di-dah family.'

Oh, give me a break, Barry! The responsibility of being Storm's stand-in mum is suddenly too much on a day like today; a day of final farewells to Alice and finding out we'll soon be homeless. I put my elbows on the table – Alice would *not* approve – and my head in my hands.

'What are you up to, Barry?'

Storm is standing in the doorway, her freshly washed hair wrapped in a towel.

'I was just talking to Annie about what happens next, now Alice has gone.'

'We can stay here, can't we? It'll be weird without the old lady and she'd better not start haunting us 'cos I don't do ghosts, but nothing else will change, will it, Annie? Why are you looking so stressy?'

'I'm afraid lots is going to change,' I say gently, 'because the house doesn't belong to me.'

'Who the hell does it belong to then? I thought—' The penny drops and Storm's jaw drops with it. 'You are totally kidding me. Not Tosser Toby!'

'Afraid so,' I sigh, having given up the fight months ago to stop Storm from dissing my cousin. 'And he wants us out.'

'Oh. My. God. I can't believe… he wouldn't… what a total…'
Storm claws at the towel on her head and throws it dramatically onto
the kitchen tiles. She's almost beside herself and looks scary with her
damp hair sticking up on end and muddy-brown eyes blazing. Barry
hauls himself to his feet and drapes his arm around his daughter's
shoulders.

'Don't worry about it, love. We'll work something out if you have
to come back to London. Mugger Mike's getting a new place soon
which'll have a spare room and a proper bathroom and everything.
And he's off the drugs now. He hasn't been arrested for ages. Hey,
what's that they're playing?'

Dropping his arm, he strides over to the radio and turns it up
full blast. The final chords of a song echo across the kitchen as Storm
pushes her lips into a full-on pout and shakes her head at me. This is
odd behaviour, even for a man who once walked from Tower Bridge
to St Paul's dressed as a chicken drumstick for a bet.

'For goodness' sake, Barry. I'm having a mega meltdown and you're
only interested in listening to some crappy song on Radio 2. And I
can't believe you lot listen to Radio 2, anyway, 'cos it's for, like, ancient
people,' whines Storm.

'That crappy song was my crappy song. But how can it be on the
radio? I wrote it years ago when I was with Va-Voom and the Vikings.'

'Oh, not that stupid band you belonged to about a hundred years
ago. You're obsessed.' Storm kicks at the towel lying in a sodden heap
on the floor. 'My life is imploding here, Barry, and you're going on
about some stupid song on the stupid radio that you didn't even hear
properly. That was not your song, you're never going to be a rock star,
you are totally off your head and you don't care about me. No one
cares about me.'

With a dramatic sob, she rushes out of the room and slams the door so hard, the teacups hanging on the dresser chink together.

'I could have sworn I recognised that song but I must have been mistaken.' Barry drops into a chair, still looking puzzled. 'And I'm sorry about Storm throwing a hissy fit. She's just like her mother – very highly strung.'

'It doesn't matter, Barry,' I sigh, picking up the soggy towel and hanging it over the handle of the Aga.

'Yeah, we're all upset about Alice at the moment and not behaving normally.'

I nod, though Storm throwing a wobbly and flouncing out isn't that unusual. Whereas me picking up her wet towels is totally normal and even more thoughtful Emily often leaves hers in a sodden heap. Today's world-weary teenagers have longed consigned Santa and the tooth fairy to the realms of make believe but still believe in the Spirit of Terry Towelling who magically clears up the bathroom after them.

'So what happens now Toby's throwing you out?' asks Barry, puffing out his cheeks. 'I always knew he was a bit of a tit but that's well out of order. Would it help if I had a word with him?'

'No! What I mean is, he's made up his mind so there's no point in you getting involved. I'd hate for you to be distracted from your music when you've still got so much to give.'

Fortunately, Barry takes the bait and all thought of confronting Toby is forgotten while he agrees that the world needs his undistracted musical prowess. He witters on for a while about the joys of performing live and the discomforts of on-the-road budget hotels before pushing his hand across the oak table and laying it on top of mine.

'But that's enough about me. What will you do now you've lost Alice and your home, Annie? Have you thought about going back to London with Storm and persuading that man of yours to go with you?'

'Huh, fat chance! Josh thinks London's awful. He's wrong, obviously, and I miss it loads but I'd miss Salt Bay more. It's daft, isn't it, when I spent almost thirty years in London and I've only been in Cornwall for one and a bit. But what I've found here is more than just this house and Alice. It's the village and the people and the peace.'

'I'll give you it's quiet around here. Or it would be if it wasn't for those damn birds squawking and pooing all over the place. I thought London pigeons were bad until I came face to beak with a Cornish seagull.'

'I don't mean the actual quiet. I mean the peace of mind. In London I was always a bit jittery inside – it's a jittery kind of place, I suppose. But here, it's different. It took a while but I feel calmer in Salt Bay. I feel better here.'

I stop, embarrassed at baring my soul to Barry, who doesn't really do deep. But he surprises me.

'Peace of mind is underrated and you must do all you can to hang onto it,' he says, stroking his calloused guitar-playing fingers across the back of my wrist. 'So if you're planning on staying in Cornwall, what happens now?'

'I don't know but I'll do what I can to sort things out for everyone including Storm.'

'I know you will, Annie, because you're a lot like Alice.'

Which is the very best thing to say and the very worst because it makes me cry. Fat, salty tears plop onto the table as my dad scrapes his chair round next to mine and puts his arm across my shoulders.

And even though my father can be a bit of a tit himself, his presence is comforting on a day like today when everything's been turned upside down and the cold hard reality of being a grown-up starts hitting home. Change is coming. Big change – and it's scary.

Chapter Six

'Are you all right?'

Josh sits next to me on the damp wooden bench and looks across Alice's garden at the harbour. The mizzle has lifted but the sky and sea are still steel-grey and the grass on the cliffs is a washed-out green. Vibrant colours have leached away with Alice and the world seems drab.

'I'm glad people came back to the house after the ashes scattering, but I began to think they'd never leave.'

'Me too. Jennifer was determined no one would escape until all the sandwiches were gone. I saw her shoving a couple into Florence's handbag when she wasn't looking.'

When I laugh, the sound carries and startles a seagull that's strutting along the path like he's king of the garden. Is it OK to laugh when someone you love has just died? I'm pricked by a sharp shard of guilt.

'I think Alice would have enjoyed her wake,' I say, shuffling along the cagoule I'm sitting on so Josh can benefit from the plastic too. He pulls it under his backside and shifts across until our thighs are touching.

'She would have had a lovely time. Though she wouldn't have been happy that Gerald was smoking in the kitchen.'

'She'd have been furious.' I give Josh a sideways smile 'cos smiling's probably OK, and he laces his fingers through mine. His skin is smooth and warm. 'I'm not sure I could have got through today without you. Thanks for being here.'

'Where else would I be?' he says, simply, nudging his shoulder against mine, and my heart brims over with love. Yep, I've become one of those loved-up saddos who floats around with a daft smile on her face, but I've never felt like this before – completely at ease with another person and desperate to snog them senseless. But today there's an added frisson of fear because loving someone means there's a lot to lose and losing people hurts.

'I miss her.' Turning my head, I stare at the village that Alice loved with all her heart for eight decades. It looks the same. Of course it does – honeysuckle will still frame the front doors of granite cottages and the crystal-clear river that cuts across the village green will continue to flow into the sea. Life in Salt Bay will go on even though Alice has gone.

'I know. Me too.' Josh swallows hard. 'People dying reminds you of other deaths, doesn't it? Other people who've left us.'

'Yeah, it's reminded me of Mum. I thought I'd come to terms with her dying and had put it behind me but it's like Alice's death has ripped off the sticking plaster covering up the wound.'

I bite my lip, feeling foolish. My outrageous, annoying, fabulous mum died of breast cancer almost half a decade ago. So I should be over it by now, shouldn't I? Stiff upper lip and all that.

But Josh nods. 'It never fully goes away however long ago it happened. I thought of Dad while we were up on the cliffs.'

'Your step-dad?'

'My step-dad and my real dad. I was only a kid when he died but I still remember the shock of it. I still remember him.' Josh rarely mentions Mark Pasco, who died of a heart attack more than twenty years ago and I hold my breath, waiting for him to go on. 'I sometimes wonder what he'd think of me now. Whether he'd be proud of me and happy with the way my life's turned out.'

A single tear trickles down Josh's cheek and he brushes it away with a frown. My boyfriend is much less repressed these days after being bathed in my emotional intelligence – though he will insist on referring to it as emotional incontinence. But being touchy-feely sometimes takes him by surprise.

'Of course your dad would be proud.' My fingers catch slightly on the dark bristles across his chin when I stroke his lovely face. 'Just look at you – a successful teacher who's doing a brilliant job of looking after his family, and with an absolutely gorgeous girlfriend to boot.'

Josh snorts and pulls me close against him as a broad brushstroke of lemon sunshine breaks through cloud and falls across the garden. 'I suppose you're not bad in spite of having an utter git for a cousin.'

Often I stick up for Toby when he's getting a bad rap. Blood is thicker than water and all that caboodle. But not today. I get that the house should be his even though he doesn't love it like I do. But telling us on the day of Alice's funeral that he's chucking us out is utterly git-like.

'You know what.' Josh swivels around on the bench to face me. 'I know leaving Tregavara House will be hard for you but maybe it's for the best in the long run. It'll be a fresh start. We can find a little place for the two of us – somewhere cosy with an open fire and a sea view. Just you and me. What do you reckon?'

I reckon being holed up with the man of my dreams in a tiny seaside cottage sounds wonderful. I can see us now, a modern day Ross and Demelza, facing the world together from our cosy Cornish home. We can make love in front of a roaring fire with no worries about Storm bursting in at a climactic moment – at Tregavara House, we've taken to wedging a chair under the door handle.

But it's just a dream. Having spent most of my twenties successfully avoiding responsibilities in London, I've acquired a shedload since coming to Cornwall.

'I'm sorry, Josh. That sounds amazing, but I can't leave Storm and Emily, and what about Barry? He'll need somewhere to sleep when he comes to visit. Storm hardly ever sees her mum so I don't want her to stop seeing her dad too.'

Josh sucks in his bottom lip and thinks for a moment, his thick hair caught in the breeze. 'We'll just have to get a bigger place for all of us then.'

'Are you sure?'

'One thousand per cent sure, which is why I teach English and music, rather than maths. My family's important to me and yours is to you. I get it.'

He grins and gazes out to sea, his face in profile, as I thank my lucky stars for having such a lovely boyfriend who'll help keep my dysfunctional ragbag family together. I don't want to lose them as well as my home.

A dark shadow cast by the thick stone walls of Tregavara House settles across my feet. It'll break my heart to leave this place but what choice do I have now Toby's gone all Lord of the Manor on me?

No choice at all, so buck up and get on with it, girl, says my inner voice, which is sounding more and more like Alice these days.

Chapter Seven

The offices of Jasper and Heel solicitors' practice are perched at the top of an old building squeezed between two bow-fronted houses in a Penzance backstreet. The carpeted staircase smells of fusty old books and there's a brass doorplate with the firm's name inscribed on it in curly copperplate. Surely I've strayed into a Dickens novel.

The Victorian vibe goes into overdrive when the door is flung open by an elderly, pinch-faced man in a tired black suit who introduces himself as Emmanuel Thistleton. Really? Some parents are just cruel.

'Do take a seat and we can proceed with reading the will,' sniffs Emmanuel after shaking my hand. 'And please do accept my condolences on the death of Mrs Gowan. I've looked after her affairs for many years and had become fond of her. She was a formidable woman.'

Toby's already here and gives a curt nod when I take the chair next to him, which is near a desk piled high with papers. He's perching on the very edge of the seat and jiggling his leg up and down, a bag of nervous energy. Or maybe it's excitement at the thought of all he's about to gain.

'No Pasco?' he grunts.

'He's at work.'

'That's a blessing. Shouldn't you be at work too?'

'My office is only around the corner and I've taken an early lunchbreak.'

Toby nods again but doesn't ask about my job. He probably doesn't have a clue where I work or what I do. If it's not happening in London, it's not happening at all, as far as Toby's concerned.

A younger man with short, greying hair and a straight Roman nose strides in from the book-lined room next door, places a manila folder on the desk and adjusts it until it's in perfect alignment with the inlaid blotter.

'This is my colleague, Elliott,' announces Emmanuel, settling into the tan leather chair behind the desk and leafing through the papers in the folder.

Ah, so this is Elliott, who contacted me last year to pass on Alice's invitation to visit her in Salt Bay. That was the first I'd ever heard of Alice and his letter changed my life.

'Miss Trebarwith, I presume. It's marvellous to meet you at last,' coos Elliott, caressing my palm with his thumb when we shake hands. A fleck of foamy spittle settles on his upper lip. 'You're quite as lovely as you sound on the phone. And what amazing blue eyes you have.'

Is this what a solicitor should be saying to a recently bereaved person? Elliott was annoying when he flirted with me over the phone but in the creepy flesh he's even worse. I pull my hand away and resist the urge to wipe it down my skirt.

'Let's get on, Elliott,' says his boss with a disapproving glance. 'I'm sure Mr and Miss Trebarwith have places to be.'

'Actually, I'm not sure why I need to be here at all,' I pipe up, taking off my cardi and placing it across my lap. It's really hot and stuffy in here.

'Exactly,' whines Toby.

'Really?' Emmanuel squints at me over the top of his half-moon glasses and frowns. 'You are Mrs Gowan's great-niece, aren't you? Did you bring your passport with you for identification purposes as requested?'

'Yes, but I don't see why…'

Oh, never mind. My question peters out as I realise it's best to just get this over with and focus on finding somewhere else to live. A lack of rental properties in the village means we'll have to move out of Salt Bay so being here to witness Toby take over Tregavara House seems extra cruel. He'll probably rip out all the old features and replace them with expensive modern tat to impress his friends. All the plaster coving will go. And the ancient fireplaces and thick oak doors. Within a few months, Tregavara House will be full of glass and stainless steel and concrete.

If only Alice was still here. I blink rapidly, determined not to cry – not here in front of Toby and creepy Elliott who's sitting in the corner, undressing me with his eyes.

'Right then,' Emmanuel picks up a sheet of paper and clears his throat. 'This is the last will and testament of—'

Suddenly, the door flies open and Kayla hurtles through it. Her face is glowing scarlet and she's wearing hardly any clothes – just a strappy T-shirt and a teeny tiny skirt that barely covers her thighs. Elliott's eyes open wide and he pulls his shirt collar away from his neck.

'Sorry, so sorry. The bus was late and packed with tourists who didn't know where to get off and then I couldn't find you and you've got *so* many stairs! I'm surprised you get any clients up here,' she puffs.

'What the hell is going on?' demands Toby, leaning across the desk towards Emmanuel and raising his hands palm-up to the ceiling. 'I didn't know she was coming. She's nothing to do with me or Alice.'

'What *are* you doing here, Kayla?' I hiss when she drags a chair to the desk and drops into it with a loud *oof.*

'Covering your arse, Sunshine,' she whispers loudly out of the corner of her mouth. 'I want to make sure you're not screwed by him over there, seeing as Josh can't make it. You're far too nice for your own good. Whereas I'm not.'

She folds her arms and glares at Toby, who taps his finger on the manila folder. Tap-tap-tap.

'Do you see what I have to put up with in Salt Bay? It's utterly ridiculous.'

Emmanuel ignores him, gives a tiny cough and pushes his glasses up his long, thin nose. 'Shall we get on if everyone is here? I do have another appointment at 12.30.' He glances again at the paper in front of him. 'This is the last will and testament of Alice Jean Gowan, made before witnesses on October the seventeenth of last year.'

'October the seventeenth of when?' A deep furrow has appeared between Toby's eyebrows. 'That can't be right. Alice made her will a few years ago.'

'Mrs Gowan made a new will five years ago, Mr Trebarwith. I remember you coming into the office with her. But she had her carer bring her in a few months ago in order to supersede her previous will with this updated one.'

'Did you know about this?' Toby turns towards me and sniffs in disbelief when I shake my head. 'Did that Emily girl know about it? Did she tell you Alice had—?'

'Mrs Gowan sent her carer away and had her come back and collect her later,' interrupts Emmanuel, who's starting to look thoroughly peeved. 'She wasn't the kind of woman who wanted others to know her business.'

'OK, mate.' When Kayla crosses her long, bare legs, Elliott almost faints. 'So cut to the chase then. What does the new will say?'

Kayla's never backward in coming forward. She claims it's a traditional Aussie trait though Roger reckons it's simply rudeness. Which is rich from possibly the rudest man in the Western Hemisphere.

Emmanuel glances through the papers in front of him and sighs. 'I can give you a full copy of the will to read at your leisure but the main points are as follows: "I, Mrs Alice Jean Gowan—"'

'Yes, yes, you've already done that bit,' says Toby, breathing rapidly. Tiny beads of sweat are scattered across his forehead and glistening in the sunlight coming through the wonky window panes.

Emmanuel gives the faintest of smiles. 'I, Mrs Alice Jean Gowan, leave Tregavara House and its contents to my great-niece Annabella Sunshine Trebarwith, on the proviso that Emily Trengrouse shall live there for as long as she wishes.'

'Get in!' yells Kayla, punching the air. 'Alice Jean Gowan, what a total beaut!'

Toby has jumped to his feet, but I'm frozen to my chair, unable to move, unable to breathe. Tregavara House belongs to me?

'What on earth is happening?' blusters Toby, his face puce and damp patches spreading under the arms of his expensive shirt. 'She can't leave the house to a woman she only met for the first time last year! My cousin has been manipulated and I'm going to fight this every step of the way.' He places both palms on the desk and thinks for a second. 'Alice had dementia, you know.'

'Ooh, that's low,' yells Kayla. 'Alice had all her marbles and was as sharp as any of us. She certainly knew what you were like.'

'Will everyone please be quiet!' barks Emmanuel. 'Take your seats because I haven't finished reading the will yet and this is most irregular.'

'Oh dear Lord, is there more? What a wicked old bat. Rest assured I'm going to fight this every inch of the way.' Toby sinks into his seat and puts his head in his hands.

'There is indeed more.' Emmanuel clears his throat again and starts reading. 'To my dear cousin, Toby Trebarwith, I leave a family heirloom, the painting of The Lady.'

Toby's head snaps up. 'She's left me the painting? The one by Van Teel? Oh Alice, how generous of you.'

'Oh, puhleez.' Kayla glares at Toby. 'You'd better hope Annie doesn't claim the painting back if Alice had dementia and didn't know what she was doing.'

'I misspoke because I was upset that Alice had forgotten me,' says Toby, smiling broadly, 'but now I'll always have the painting to remind me of her.'

No, he won't. The painting will be sold as fast as Toby's pudgy fingers can enter it into the next art auction where he works. And he'll soon have a big wodge of cash instead. Estimates put the painting at around three-quarters of a million pounds which is more than the house must be worth. But I couldn't give a monkey's. All that matters is we don't have to move out and leave Salt Bay.

'Are you all right, Miss Trebarwith?' asks Emmanuel. 'Would you like Elliott to get you a glass of water?'

I shake my head, unable to speak.

It's a shame the family painting will be sold but Alice, lovely Alice, must have seen that as a price worth paying to keep Toby off my back. She didn't know he was Freya's father when she made her new will, but she obviously pretty much had the measure of Toby. And I'm beyond touched that she judged me to be the better custodian of her beloved house.

'So now you've got your hands on the painting, Toby, you're not going to kick off about the house. Is that right?' Kayla nudges me to get involved in the conversation as Toby's lip curls into a sneer.

'Tregavara House is old and battered and will prove to be a financial millstone around Annie's neck. Have you seen the state of the roof? And when it does prove too much, and you come begging for help, Annie, don't expect me to pay top dollar for what should rightfully be mine.'

I swallow, finding my voice at last. 'I honestly didn't plan for this to happen, Toby, and I didn't know about the new will. Tregavara House has been in the Trebarwith family for generations and it's true I've not been around for long. But I'll take care of it, I promise. And you can come and stay whenever you're visiting Freya and bring her round. Things can stay like they are at the moment.'

'When can I have the painting?' Toby asks Emmanuel, totally blanking me. But I hardly notice his surly behaviour. Toby can huff and puff as much as he likes and Tregavara House will still belong to me. Me, the girl who's never owned as much as a car before.

I can hardly believe it. Two years ago I was living in a rented London flat with no relatives, no significant other and no responsibilities. And now I have a family, a steady boyfriend and a house. A big, falling-down house.

Toby's words about millstones and battered roofs start nudging at my brain but I close my eyes and send up a promise to my beloved great-aunt. *Alice, I won't let you down.*

Chapter Eight

I'm totally rubbish at work all afternoon. In my defence, it's hard to show interest in what the chief exec's doing next Wednesday when I've just become a property owner, when the girl who grew up moving from one grotty inner London flat to another has inherited a forever house in a place that feels like home.

I'm still in shock and don't say anything to Josh when he texts from school to say he hopes the will reading wasn't too upsetting. Some news is so momentous, it needs to be shared face to face.

And though Lesley and Gayle ask how it went and can tell something's up from my general uselessness, I keep my answers vague. They're both broke and the funding situation at work is uncertain so it seems insensitive to announce I've just been given a kick-arse house.

A kick-arse house in need of serious dosh – the bloke who patched up the roof warned me a new one would be needed before long, and Emmanuel said something about inheritance tax as I was leaving. But a house nonetheless and I can sort out any problems later. That's what I tell myself when I buy a huge bar of Dairy Milk from the vending machine in reception and scoff it until I feel sick.

Nothing has physically changed when I get home from work. Tregavara House is still a handsome granite building standing where land meets sea. But it feels different when I turn my key in the lock and step into the hallway. These worn flagstones are mine, and the twisted-wood banisters and the intricate plaster coving too. This is my home and no one can throw me out. Wow, this owning property thing is really blowing my mind.

The first thing I do after kicking off my sandals is run upstairs to Alice's bedroom. It is exactly as she left it. A faint scent of lily of the valley lingers in the air – an echo of Alice – and I often go into her room and sit on the bed. It's been almost three weeks since my great-aunt died and her floral smell is gradually fading. But for now it envelops me like a hug whenever I perch on the edge of her four-poster.

Sitting on the soft bed, I can picture Alice standing at the window in her pink pyjamas and waving to her adoring public. Was that only last month? Now the candlewick dressing gown she wore is hanging limply on the back of her bedroom door and I'll have to do something with it eventually. Maybe take it to a charity shop? A wave of grief overwhelms me and I press the balls of my fists into my eyes. All of Alice's possessions will need to be sorted through and some disposed of, but not yet.

'Thank you, Alice, for entrusting your most precious possession into my care,' I whisper into empty space. 'But are you sure? Toby's right that I only knew you for a little while so maybe the house should be his. Am I up to looking after this place?'

But there's no answer. There never will be an answer from Alice.

The fists-in-eyes thing isn't working and tears start streaming down my face. Here we go. Some women are genteel criers with trembling lips and pink cheeks – think Anne Hathaway all dewy-eyed in a romcom – whereas I am the Gorgon of Sobbing. There's gulping and puffy cheeks and snot. So much snot… and Storm is just the same. Being crap at crying must be genetic. But sometimes you just have to give in and let it all go.

And it's while I'm ugly-sobbing that the answer drops into my brain. Alice wanted me to have this house because Toby doesn't need it or love it like I do. This house is full of Trebarwith history and I belong here. That's what she knew and now I just have to believe it too.

Five minutes later, when my rasping sobs have turned into tiny hiccups, the front door slams so hard the polished floorboards in Alice's room judder. Which can mean only one thing – Storm is home and I can share my momentous news at last.

I scrub my cheeks with a tissue and head for the hall to find that Storm and Emily have come in together. Emily's been for an interview for an office job in Trecaldwith and hit the shops on the way home, judging by the bulging supermarket bags she's carrying.

'I don't mean to be harsh, but you look gross. What's happened to your face?' demands Storm. 'Is Toby evicting us? There's no way I'm going back to London and moving in with Mugger Mike 'cos he's a grade one crack head.'

'There'll be no moving in with Mugger Mike. In fact, no moving at all.'

'You what?' pouts Storm. 'Has your awful cousin decided that we can stay in his house after all?'

'It's nothing to do with my awful cousin any more because it's not his house. Alice made a new will last year and the house now belongs to me.'

Emily screams – properly screams – and drops her bags, which thunk onto the hall floor. There's a sharp crack as something glass inside shatters. Then she throws herself into my arms, swiftly followed by Storm, who's not a huggy person at all.

We're group-hugging, half laughing and half crying, when the front door swings open and Josh steps in. He's looking gorgeous in smart chinos and a white linen shirt that's extra bright against his black hair.

'What the hell's going on? Your phone's been off for hours and I wanted to tell you about a house I've found for us in Trecaldwith. It's perfect.' He waves the property pages from the local newspaper at us.

'We don't need a perfect house in stupid Trecaldwith 'cos the old lady left this house to Annie,' yells Storm in my ear, jumping up and down on my toes.

Josh freezes for a moment before dropping his heavy satchel onto Alice's poor tiles. *My* poor tiles! Then he strides forward and throws his arms around the huddle. My sometimes-buttoned-up boyfriend is joining in a group hug! This day keeps on getting more surreal.

'Sorry to be all mysterious and incommunicado but I wanted to tell you in person,' I tell him over Emily's head, which is buried in my shoulder. 'It's good news, isn't it? Don't you think it's great?'

There's the slightest of hesitations before Josh grins broadly and grasps my hand. 'I think your great-aunt was a class act.'

'She left me the house and left Toby the painting of The Lady.'

'Huh. Seems fitting seeing as the painting is what he's always wanted the most.'

'Mind you, he says the house will be a millstone around my neck and too expensive to keep going.'

My excitement is pierced by cold, hard reality and the fizzy feeling that's been rushing around my body starts to evaporate. How can I afford to keep Tregavara House going when I don't earn much, Emily's hardly earning at all and Josh is strapped for cash? He's still paying back the loan he took out last year to keep his family's head above water when his mum was ill and Toby wasn't contributing towards Freya's keep.

But Josh grasps hold of my hand and holds it tight. 'We'll manage, Annie. Whatever happens, we'll manage it together. All of us.'

'Yeah, all of us,' mumbles Storm, her cheek pressed up tight against my hair. 'We'll prove your lame cousin wrong and do the old lady proud. You'll see.'

And as we all stand there hugging, the back of my neck starts to prickle and I get the strangest feeling that Alice is watching us from the stairs. And she's smiling.

Chapter Nine

It's only a few days since Mr Thistleton dropped his bombshell but everyone in the village knows – of course, because blabbermouth Kayla was there. And everyone seems delighted. No one other than Toby seems to think I started living with Alice to get my avaricious hands on her house and the sitting room mantelpiece is covered in *Welcome to Your New Home* cards.

Technically, my home is not 'new' but Jennifer – never one to miss a retail opportunity – has persuaded people to buy the job lot of cards she got in specially. But she's pleased for me too. The last time I went into her shop, she gave me a rather stiff hug and declared me 'a true daughter of Salt Bay'. Which is totally over the top but lovely, nonetheless.

The only person who doesn't seem delighted is Josh. I'm used to my gorgeous boyfriend being quiet and his brooding, introverted vibe can be knee-tremblingly sexy. But this is something else. Josh, still loving and supportive to all of us, has clammed up as though he's frightened of what he might say. And though at first I kid myself he's simply tired from working or missing Alice, inside I know it's more than that. His hesitation on hearing of my inheritance might have been brief but it was long enough to set alarm bells ringing.

So a week after the will-reading, I grab Josh's hand when he passes me in the hallway, push open the door to the cellar and pull him down the dusty wooden stairs. A bare bulb swinging back and forth above our heads casts moving pools of light and shade across the bare brick walls.

'Whoah, what's going on?' Josh moves closer and puts his arms around my waist. 'I'm all for making out in new places but the damp down here has been terrible since the flood and it's absolutely freezing. We'll get hypothermia.'

When he kisses the tip of my nose, his lips warm my cold skin.

'That's not why I brought you down here. I just needed some peace away from Storm and Emily so we can have a conversation.'

'What sort of conversation?' asks Josh, letting me go. He runs a hand across the ancient bricks and frowns at the moisture on his fingers.

'A conversation about the house and why you've gone all weird about it.'

'I don't know what you're talking about. I'm fine.'

'No, you're not. You're distracted, which is why I need to know how you feel about me taking it on.'

Josh, who's rifling through a wooden crate filled with rusty gardening tools, stops and looks up. 'You didn't exactly take it on. Tregavara House was thrust upon you.'

'Which is exactly what I mean. You're obviously not happy about it and that bothers me.'

Josh shrugs and pulls out a lethal-looking pair of secateurs. 'Of course I'm happy that Tregavara House is yours, Annie. I know how much it means to you to have a home here, but I can't help being concerned.'

'Why, because of the millstone thing that Toby said?'

'Kind of. Toby is crass and insensitive and eaten up with envy that Alice left the house to you. But I can't help wondering if he's got a point and you're taking on too much. The roof's still dodgy and then there's the inheritance tax.'

Ah, yes. That bill's so big it made me cry and I'm still working out how best to pay it. Inheriting and staying in my ancestral home is going to cost me serious money. I lean against the wall and shiver when cold seeps through my T-shirt.

'So why didn't you say something to me, Josh? We're supposed to talk about things.'

'I know but I didn't want to pour cold water on everything so soon after you'd lost Alice. It didn't seem fair.'

'But you're glad that we can carry on living here?'

'Of course I am.' Josh's face is in shadow but he sounds like he's smiling. 'Who wouldn't want to live in a lovely old house by the sea? Just so long as you're being realistic and know what you're taking on.'

'I do. Don't forget I was the one almost brained by a roof tile. But the repairs have been done and the house is solid and we can relax once the tax bill's been taken care of.'

'And there's always the option of selling up and using the money to buy somewhere more modern that doesn't need as much upkeep.' He raises his hand when I go to speak. 'I'm not saying that's what you *should* do but that's what you *can* do if it all gets too much. You wouldn't be letting anyone down.'

'I know,' I lie, because even selling to Toby would feel like betraying Alice's trust in me. 'But I'm happy here with you and Emily, and Storm too when she's not deafening us with her music.'

Josh laughs and steps into the light. 'Yeah, if she doesn't turn down Kendrick Lamar I might have to chuck her speakers into the harbour. But if you're happy, I'm happy.' And then he pulls me into his arms and warms me up with a hot kiss.

In the end, we take out a mortgage on the house to pay off the inheritance tax in one go rather than pay in instalments plus interest. That seems best, especially since I can't shake off Mum's dread about owing money to the government. My poor mum became convinced Her Majesty's government was out to get her when her mental illness took hold. And though I know it was Mum's paranoia talking, the anxiety she drummed into my head is hard to shake off. Echoes of her illness sometimes ripple down the years.

But there's no respite from my anxiety about Toby's next move. So far he's been silent, other than a brief text to say he's arranged a courier to transport *The Lady* to London, and it's unnerving. My cousin's loaded with access to all sorts of fancy solicitors in the capital, and could still challenge the will. And though everyone seems confident I'd win, I'm not sure I could cope with a legal battle right now.

Dragging grief over Alice, money worries and uncertainty about Toby's next move start taking their toll and I turn into an early-morning waker. Usually I'm one of those annoying people whose head hits the pillow and – *bam!* – that's it for the next eight hours. But I find myself regularly stirring at 3 a.m. and staring at the ceiling for hours until pale light creeps under the curtains and across the floorboards.

Oh boy, am I sorry for insomniacs because everything seems *so* much worse when Salt Bay is unconscious – and so much more annoying. It's not Josh's fault that he sleeps soundly and his gentle snoring is usually soothing when I'm lying beside him, my arm flung across his chest. But in the early hours, every snuffle only serves to hammer home that I'm wide awake in a frighteningly uncertain world. My imagination goes into overdrive and, before I know it, I'm living in the roofless ruins of Tregavara House with nothing but seagulls for company – until the sun rises and burns away my fears like sea mist.

Josh gets fed up with me kicking him to shut up in the early hours and announces one Saturday that he's taking me out for a de-stressing treat. Which kind of counts as a mini-break, doesn't it? My gorgeous boyfriend is taking me on a one-day mini-break and I'm determined, à la Bridget Jones, to have a damn good time. Away from Salt Bay, the sadness and the anxiety.

So here we are on a Saturday in mid-July standing on Marazion Beach as the sun climbs higher in a blue sky scattered with trails of wispy cloud. It's only ten o'clock but warm already so I'm wearing a blue cotton sundress and Josh is in shorts. We've already spotted one of his pupils on the beach, who pointed at his legs, grinned and gave him a thumbs up.

Ahead of us St Michael's Mount rises steeply, just a few hundred metres off land. Lapped by deep blue water, its steep slopes are covered in trees and I can make out houses near the harbour walls. Plus, to make the mount even more perfect, there's a castle on the top. Yep, a real-life, flipping castle. It's *Game of Thrones* comes to Cornwall.

Josh hooks my arm through his and leads me onto the cobbled causeway that links the island and the land when the tide's out. Pools of water left by the retreating tide shimmer beside the causeway and I shiver at the thought of the path disappearing beneath the waves in just a few hours' time.

'Have you really never been here before?' asks Josh, squeezing my arm tight against his waist.

'I've seen the mount from a distance but whenever I thought about visiting, the weather was pants.'

'Then it's good you waited to see it with me while the sun's shining. It really is a magical place.'

He adjusts the straps of his backpack that's full of our picnic and says 'good morning' to an elderly couple strolling by. They're hand-in-hand and I wonder if that'll be Josh and me one day. Still in Cornwall, still together, still in love.

Five minutes later we've reached the island, and it's fabulous. Brown stone and whitewashed houses face the tiny harbour where boats are beached on wet sand – and the mount rises ahead of us. Wow, it's busy! Tourists are everywhere, clicking with their smartphone cameras and licking Cornish ice cream. It's hard to believe that I used to be one of them – and a reluctant tourist at that, keen to leave the back of beyond and return to London. And now I love Cornwall and I'm a property owner here. How quickly life can change in little more than a year.

'Let's go up to the castle first,' says Josh, grabbing my arm and pulling me past the gift shop.

'OK. There's no rush,' I laugh and then feel guilty. I didn't laugh for ages after I lost Mum but then I didn't have Josh. Or Cornwall. I was rootless and unloved and lost.

'Are you all right?' Josh senses my drop in mood and pulls me close. 'Come and see the view from the castle. It's awesome.'

Josh pays the National Trust fee and we start climbing the path, along with every tourist within twenty miles. We're swept along by a sweaty tide of people with sunburned shoulders but it's worth the climb when we reach the top because Josh is right. It is awesome. Perched above us, the grey-white castle seems to grow out of the rock, like a living, breathing part of the island. There are turrets and tall chimneys and tiny windows looking toward the land and out to sea. Give me Jon Snow and a circling dragon and we could be in Westeros.

'Look at this!' Josh pulls me towards the edge of the land, which drops across huge slabs of grey granite and bright splashes of brilliant pink flowers into an indigo sea.

The waves are sparkling in the sunshine as they lap against rock and I picture the people who've lived on this island over the centuries. People with joys and griefs and loves who stood in this spot and admired the same view. People just like us. They were living here while my ancestors were just a few miles away at Tregavara House.

'What do you think then?' Josh comes up behind me and snakes his arms around my waist.

'It's beautiful. I was thinking of all the people who lived here and raised families and died here.'

The 'D' word triggers a pang of sorrow, but I force a smile because I want to smile every time I remember my feisty great-aunt whose love and generosity have given me the roots I've always needed. And looking across the sea towards the land, I realise that I'll never go back to London now. Whatever happens with Josh or Tregavara House, Cornwall is my home.

'And this is definitely the best place to bring up a family,' I say, almost thinking out loud. Eek! Josh is 'a keeper', according to my London friend Maura, but we've never properly discussed having children. And there's nothing like impending parenthood to frighten off a boyfriend.

Josh tenses behind me and my heart sinks when he drops his arms and steps back. Way to go, Annie! I swing round to face him, oblivious to the tourists bustling about taking endless photos they'll never look at.

'I don't mean have a family right now,' I gabble. 'I'm not even a hundred per cent sure I want kids and I'd be a terrible mother. Maybe I'll have some one day but that doesn't mean it has to be with you.'

Jeez, I certainly don't mean that and I'm just making everything worse. I wince at Josh, who stares at me for a moment and then grins. He knows what I'm like.

'Come with me.' Grabbing my hand, Josh pulls me away from the chattering tourists towards a stone wall.

'Shall we do it?' he asks, his face so close to mine I can see streaks of gold in his chocolate-brown eyes.

'Do what? Have kids? I'm not sure I'm ready for that yet. I was just thinking aloud really and—'

'No, not have kids. Not yet, at least. What I mean is, shall we start our own dynasty one day at Tregavara House?'

Crikey, I need to give this conversation all my attention. But suddenly all I can think of are Linda Evans' ginormous shoulder pads in *Dynasty*. And her fabulously flicky hair style. I blink rapidly, trying to divert my brain from the deflection thing it's been doing for years whenever a conversation gets heavy. *You don't need to do it, brain – I can get heavy with this man,* screams my inner voice.

'Are you sure you're OK, Annie? You've gone a bit vacant. Look, what I want to say – though I can't believe I'm saying it in this soppy way – is that you've opened the floodgates to my heart.'

'Is that a good thing?' I ask, tentatively. I've had a thing about floods ever since Tregavara House was inundated last year when the river burst its banks.

'I didn't think so at first. It was a bit overwhelming, to be honest, when I thought you were a bossy, annoying control freak and now you've inherited an old house which is a huge responsibility and—'

'Um,' I interrupt, 'you were saying something about your heart.'

Josh takes a deep breath. 'I was. Before you came to Salt Bay, and even afterwards, I wasn't always very happy because I kept everything locked up inside me.'

'You did, and it made you a right miserable old grump at times.'

'What, me?' He shrugs and gives a rueful grin. 'Yeah, I suppose I was, especially when Mum was ill last year. Sorry. But you've changed everything, Annie. You've changed how I look at life and you've changed my heart. Not physically, obviously but… oh God, I'm making a right dog's dinner of this.'

When Josh drops onto one knee, tiny particles of dirt scuff up into a cloud and waft around us. 'What I'm asking you, Annabella Sunshine Trebarwith – extremely badly, I'm afraid – is will you marry me?' He shrugs again and gives the half-smile that makes my legs go wobbly. 'What do you reckon?'

I'm sure people being proposed to are supposed to act cool. Maybe give a tinkly laugh and a little speech about how they'd be honoured and then kiss their new fiancé passionately as time stands still. A moment to look back on and treasure.

I don't do any of that. I'm so taken aback, I lean too far over the edge of the stone wall and my bag falls off my shoulder and onto the rocks below. 'Bugger it,' I yell, as my keys, bank cards and mobile phone scatter across the rock shelf.

Josh pulls himself to his feet and peers over the edge. 'Oops. Does "bugger it" mean yes?'

'Of course it does, you plonker. There's nothing I'd rather do than become your wife.'

Thoughts of my possessions perched precariously above the ocean fly out of my head when Josh pulls me into his arms and kisses me.

A year ago, he'd rather have set his own arse on fire than kiss me in front of hordes of tourists at a popular beauty spot. He was that repressed. But love has flooded his heart. And mine. And now we're getting married!

'Get a room,' murmurs a young girl passing by but we giggle with our lips still pressed together and carry on kissing, his hands in my hair.

'Are you only marrying me now I've become a property owner?' I tease Josh when we come up for air.

'Obviously.' With the castle behind him, black hair caught in the wind and white shirt billowing, he looks more like a Cornish pirate than ever. 'Actually, I was going to propose a while ago but then Alice was ill and it didn't seem the right time. I'm not sure now's the right time either, with Alice passing away and the kerfuffle about the house, but I couldn't wait any longer. I don't think Alice would mind.'

'I'm sure she wouldn't because she'd be happy for both of us. It's such a shame she won't ever know.'

'But she did know,' says Josh, gently brushing a strand of hair from my forehead. 'I told her while she was recuperating from her infection. I sat on her bed and kind of asked her permission, seeing as Barry wasn't around and he could never have kept it quiet anyway.'

Which is very true because Barry adheres to the Kayla code of keeping secrets. And I'm so glad that Alice knew about the proposal.

'Tell me exactly word for word what she said.'

'She got very excited and said she had the ideal present for you, though she didn't say what. Presumably she meant the house. Then she promised to wear a big hat to the wedding.' Josh's smile fades and he cups my face in his hands. 'She'll be with us in spirit, Annie. Look, let's get married soon. There's no point in waiting and it doesn't have to be a big do unless that's what you want.'

'No, I don't need a posh dress and flowers and presents and neither of us have big families. But can we get married in Salt Bay Church for tradition's sake and have the reception at Tregavara House? Well, not so much a reception as a get-together for the people we care about. Then it'll be like Alice is with us.'

Josh grins. 'Of course we can. That sounds perfect and we can make plans. But first, what are we going to do about your bag?'

He pulls himself up onto the wall and dangles his long legs over the other side.

'No, please don't!'

But it's too late because Josh is already scrambling down the steep slope. Typical! I'm proposed to by the man of my dreams and now he's about to fall off a cliff and be dashed on the rocks beneath. I can picture the newspaper billboard outside Jennifer's shop: 'Salt Bay woman set to remain spinster forever after fiancé of five minutes falls to his death.'

But as with most of my anticipated disasters, nothing actually happens. Josh scoops up my bag and its contents and clambers back over the wall. A passing guide spots him and he gets a ticking off but that's as bad as it gets. It looks like the wedding's still on then.

Seeing as we're at the castle, we wander round it hand-in-hand, finding out about the St Aubyn family who've lived there for ages and the siege of fourteen-something-or-other but I don't take anything in. It's really hard to concentrate on stuff from the past when your future has suddenly become so much more exciting.

Josh is equally distracted and we soon ditch the castle and head for its mediaeval church. Inside, away from the buzz of tourists and screeching seagulls, it's cool and peaceful.

'Maybe this is where we should get married,' jokes Josh, striding towards the altar which sits below three beautiful stained-glass windows. 'You could body-swerve all the tourists when you walk up the aisle.'

'We'd never get Alice all the way up here,' I reply without thinking and a sudden whoosh of sorrow engulfs me. My mum should be at my wedding, flirting with the ushers and refusing to sing hymns because she's a pagan. And Alice should be next to her in the front pew with her best silk tea dress on and the hugest hat you've ever seen.

Josh says nothing but hurries over and puts his arms around me, which is far more comforting than words could ever be. He totally gets it because his dad and step-dad will be missing on our big day too.

A thought suddenly strikes me and I mumble into his shoulder: 'I don't want to be Mrs Pasco.'

'But you just said yes.' Josh pulls away and holds me at arm's length. 'You haven't changed your mind, have you? I know you can be indecisive sometimes but—'

'Of course I haven't but I want to stay a Trebarwith because that's who I am. Maybe I could compromise and call myself Mrs Pasco-Trebarwith though I'm not sure I can carry off a double-barrel. Or just Mrs Trebarwith, or Ms Trebarwith – though that sounds like I can't make up my mind. Or you could change your name to Trebarwith and—'

Josh grins and gently places his finger across my lips. 'You can call yourself Donald Duck if you like, just so long as you marry me. Why don't we go and get you a temporary ring in the gift shop to make it official? I didn't get you anything ahead of time so you can choose a proper ring when money's not so tight, plus you are a bit' – he chooses his next word carefully – 'particular about what you like. I'd only have got the wrong thing.'

'Hey, I'm not fussy,' I say, punching him playfully on the arm.

'Ow, I didn't say you were.'

'But that's what you meant. And I don't need a ring anyway.'

'I know you don't *need* a ring but I'd like you to have one. Come on. I think we've done the castle.'

The shop near the harbour is crammed with tasteful leather handbags, silk scarves, tea towels and biscuits. There's a small selection of jewellery and I choose a simple silver band twisted into a Cornish Celtic knot that costs less than forty pounds. And then Josh and I sit on the harbour wall, waiting for the boat that ferries tourists back to the mainland at high tide.

While we've been busy getting engaged and changing the course of our lives forever, the sea crept in as it's been doing for millennia and there's an expanse of deep blue water between us and Marazion Beach.

Josh takes the ring out of its bag and slips it onto my fourth finger. 'I'll buy you a proper one soon,' he promises.

I nod and smile as I twist the ring around my finger and it catches the sun but I know I'll never have another engagement ring. This one is just perfect.

Chapter Ten

'Woohoo, it's Annie Sunshine Trebarwith, mistress of Tregavara House.'

Kayla gives a mock bow while I'm weaving through the crowd and heading for the bar. Cornwall's summer season is in full swing, the sun is out, and the Whistling Wave is heaving with tourists, or emmets – the Cornish word for 'ants' – as they're known around here.

Kayla's wearing a strappy pink vest top and all the windows in the pub are flung open but it's hot and humid in here and Kayla's face is flushed.

'Too. Many. People,' she pants, pulling a pint with one hand and handing over change with the other. 'Roger needs to get more bar staff in here only he won't 'cos he's so tight.'

'Oy, I heard that,' shouts Roger, who's pulling a pint for Gerald. 'I'm not made of money, you know.'

'See, tight!' says Kayla, slopping the beer down in front of a man whose ice cream is dripping over the flagstones. She turns her back on a customer who's waving a ten pound note in her direction. 'Did you have a nice time at the Mount then? You look less stressed so going out for the day must have done you some good. What's that?' She stares at my ring after spotting it at last. I've been waving my fingers in her face since I reached the bar, like Marcel Marceau doing an intricate mime.

'Oh, this?' I wiggle my fingers some more and grin. 'I've got something to tell you so cadge a break from Roger and I'll meet you out the back in five minutes.'

'Five minutes, my tight Australian arse!' Kayla throws down the cloth she's carrying and yells: 'Urgent business. Back in a few minutes.' Then she rams her sunglasses onto her shiny face, grabs my arm and pulls me through the kitchen into the back yard.

There's a smelly dustbin out here and a skinny feral cat is grubbing in the dirt for fallen fish bones. But it's peaceful away from the tourists and inquisitive members of the choir.

Kayla parks her backside on a low wall, takes hold of my hand and starts pushing my ring up to the knuckle and back down. 'Is that what I think it is?'

'If you think it's an engagement ring, then yes, it is. Josh and I are getting married.'

'No way!' yells Kayla, throwing her arms around me so ferociously she almost knocks both of us off the wall. 'That's brilliant news! Let's go and announce it in the pub. You won't have to buy yourself a drink all afternoon and you'll be rat-arsed by teatime.'

'No, you can't tell anyone. I wanted to tell you first but Josh's family don't know yet, so you can't tell a soul.'

'Nooo. Don't do this to me,' wails Kayla, pushing her sunglasses up off her face and into her thick red hair. 'This news is mega and it'll cheer everyone up after losing Alice. You can't make me keep it quiet. It's cruel and inhumane and against my human rights.'

'What, against your human right to spill the beans? It's only for a day or two, Kayla, and I'm taking a risk here 'cos I know what you're like. So you have to promise me you'll keep it a secret.'

'Ugh, OK,' she says with a grimace. 'Honestly, the things you ask of me!'

'What are you two doing out here?' Ollie steps through the kitchen door and shields his eyes against the glare of the sun. 'Roger told me you were back here. He said, and I quote: "If that work-shy girlfriend of yours isn't back behind the bar in two minutes, tell her she can collect her P45".'

'Well, Roger can go whistle because Annie and I are out here on very important business.'

Ollie bounds over to Kayla and kisses her on the lips. Straw-blonde hair is flopping into his eyes and his short-sleeved T-shirt shows off his muscled rugby player arms.

'We were just having a quick chat, Ollie, about girl things.' I scoot along the wall so he's got room to sit between us.

'Annie and Josh are getting married,' blurts out Kayla.

'What the—? Really?' I stare open-mouthed at Kayla who at least has the good grace to look embarrassed.

'Sorry but you're asking too much of me. I said I wouldn't tell anybody but Ollie isn't anybody. He's the man I lo—' she hesitates, 'like spending time with.'

'Wow! That's amazing news, Annie. That Josh is a very lucky man.' Ollie envelops me in a quick hug and squeezes so tight I can hardly breathe. 'Marriage isn't for me and Kayla because we're both free spirits but it'll be great for you two. When's the big day then? 'Cos I'll have to make sure I get back for it.'

I breathe in slowly in case Ollie's cracked a rib or two. 'Back from where? You only live a few miles down the road.'

'Kayla hasn't told you then?' Ollie frowns. 'I've finally been offered that promotion at work. It's a really big jump up, to regional sales manager for the North-West covering the whole of Cumbria, Lancashire and part of Yorkshire.'

'Crikey, that's fantastic, though we'll miss you. Why didn't you tell me, Kayla?'

Ollie rests his hand on Kayla's knee. 'I only found out late yesterday and we haven't told anyone else yet. They need me in post by mid-October so I'll be upping sticks and heading off for good in three months' time.'

Beside him, Kayla is smiling although her boyfriend is about to abandon her and head up North.

'What about Kayla?'

A shadow flits across Ollie's invariably cheerful face. 'I've asked her to come with me and I'm hoping she will. In fact, I'm taking her to the Lake District for a few days to show her the area.'

Kayla gives a slight shake of the head but carries on smiling. It's very odd.

'Anyway, I've got to go or I'll miss the late kick-off. I only nipped in to check that we're on for meeting up later, Kayla.' Ollie leaps to his feet, shakes out his legs and grins when Kayla gives a mute nod. 'Brilliant. I'll pick you up at eight then. And that really is wonderful news, Annie. I'll ring Josh when I've got a signal to say congratulations.'

When he's bounded off, I fold my arms and wrinkle my nose at Kayla. 'Ollie, the man you're crazy about, is moving hundreds of miles away but you don't seem upset.'

'Oh, he's not going anywhere,' says Kayla, adjusting the straps of her vest top. 'He says I've filled his head with stories about experiencing new places and new opportunities and that's why he's giving it a go. But it's all for show. There's no way he'll leave his beloved Cornwall, especially 'cos he knows I'm not keen on moving.'

'But I thought you were a free spirit, a nomad, an Aussie backpacker who's only in Salt Bay for a while and can't bear to be tied down.'

'Which is true, and I've got nothing against moving, per se. But my next move will be south and Ollie knows that. The last couple of winters here have been dire and there's no way I'm going somewhere with worse weather. If that's even possible.' Kayla shudders at the memory of torrential rain and curling Cornish fog that lasted for days. 'Nope. Ollie's just trying to make me panic at the thought of him leaving and then he can make a huge gesture and stay.'

'Um, maybe.'

It doesn't sound like uncomplicated Ollie's style at all. Marriage has been off-limits with these two since he proposed in the pub last year and was turned down by a freaked-out Kayla. But the two of them have been pretty much joined at the hip in unmarried bliss since they got back together.

'Are you quite sure, Kayla? You reckoned the whole going for promotion thing was a ruse, but it's turned out to be real.'

'Absolutely sure. Ollie Simpson would rather walk through Salt Bay in a dress than move away from Cornwall and me.' She flicks her hair from her shoulders and smiles, convinced that her boyfriend can't possibly live without her. 'Anyway, onto real and more important things. Are you going to have a big society wedding with lots of guests and a huge do at a posh hotel? Ooh, you can have champagne cocktails and a cake with real gold flakes in it. I saw an amazing one in a magazine once and it wasn't even poisonous which surprised me.'

Firmly anti-marriage herself, Kayla obviously has no qualms about spending a shedload on someone else's nuptials.

'It's not going to be a big, expensive wedding,' I tell her, firmly. 'The ceremony will be at the village church and we're thinking of having a small reception afterwards at Tregavara House.'

'Hhmm.' Kayla looks doubtful. 'That might work, but you'll definitely need champagne.'

'Cava, maybe. But we need to keep a contingency fund for any house repairs so we can't spend much on a fancy wedding.'

'This owning property thing is a right drag,' huffs Kayla. 'No wonder Josh told Ollie he was worried about it. I think it's a shame Alice left that valuable painting to Toerag Toby or you could have sold it and had a mahoosive wedding with enough left over for a gold-plated roof. You could have had fireworks and a master of ceremonies to announce all the guests when they arrive. And doves! I saw a programme where the bride and groom released a basket of twenty white doves to signify their enduring love. It was so romantic.' She gazes dreamily into the distance.

'We don't need doves or fireworks or a master of anything, Kayla. All I want is to marry Josh and a small village wedding is fine, so Alice did the right thing about the painting.'

She definitely did because it would break my heart if I had to sell a family heirloom. Toby doesn't have any such qualms, so the guilt will sit more lightly on his shoulders when he pockets the proceeds.

'Kayla,' yells Roger from the kitchen door. 'You need to get your backside back in here sharpish. I've got emmets five-deep at the bar and it's getting ugly.'

Kayla gets to her feet with a sigh and brushes tiny stones from her backside.

'I'll catch up with you later, Annie, but I'm so happy about your news and I promise I'll keep it a secret. But don't wait too long before you tell everyone else 'cos there's only so much keeping quiet I can do.'

When she's scurried back into the pub, I sit for a while twirling my new ring round and round my finger. Josh has seemed more relaxed about taking on the house since we talked openly about it, but I wonder whether he told Ollie he was worried before or after our cellar heart-to-heart.

Which reminds me… pulling my phone from my bag, I use the Whistling Wave's Wi-Fi to log into my emails. I got a company in to quote for a brand new roof a few days ago – just out of interest because the roof repair seems solid – and I'm still waiting to hear back.

My inbox is clogged up with spam – delete, delete, delete – and there's a long list of ailments from Maura in London, who's pregnant with her second child. She'll end up giving birth soon after Pippa, a lovely soprano in our choir who's blooming at the moment.

I scan through Maura's long email and wince. Eew, who knew that being pregnant could cause itchy nipples and piles? Maura's never been coy about her body or her feelings and the brakes are off now she's awash with pregnancy hormones. She'll probably have an emotional meltdown when she hears I'm getting married.

Two emails below Maura's I spot the one I'm looking for and click on it. Good grief! I do a double-take when £30,000 leaps out from my phone screen – the estimator has helpfully underlined the figure in red just to make sure it's even more likely to give me a heart attack. That's crazy money!

The bubble of wedding euphoria that's surrounded me since Josh got down on one knee deflates like a pricked balloon. How can we build up a contingency fund like that and get married too? Fireworks and doves, indeed! This is going to be the most cut-price wedding Salt Bay has ever seen.

Chapter Eleven

Emily is overcome with excitement when we tell her about the wedding and totally beside herself when I ask her to be a bridesmaid. She went over the top at Christmas with gaudy Santa jumpers and flashing reindeer antlers on her head. But this is on another level. There's hyperventilating and screaming and a dash into Penzance to pick up a copy of *Brides* magazine. In contrast, Storm plays it cool and blanches with horror when the subject of being a bridesmaid is broached.

'There's no way I'm wearing some sad dress that looks like an explosion in a meringue factory,' she informs me. But she does give me a quick hug and whispers in my ear: 'He's quite fit for a teacher' which is high praise indeed.

When I text Barry with the news, he texts back from Hartlepool where his band's playing a pub gig: *Nice one and about time he made a decent woman of you. Don't worry, I'll be back to give you away x*

There'll be no 'giving away' at my wedding seeing as I coped perfectly well without Barry for twenty-nine years until he turned up on my doorstep. But he can walk me up the aisle if he wants to. I'd like that.

Josh's mum and his sisters are delighted with the news and Freya goes hyperactive at the prospect of being a flower girl. I'm happy too and can hardly wait to tie the knot but feelings of disloyalty niggle around the edges of my bright new life.

How can I be happy and looking forward to my wedding when I've just lost Alice? There seem to be two people in my head these days – sad Annie who aches inside at the sight of Alice's empty chair by the fireplace and giddy Annie who's dreaming of wedding dresses.

We manage to keep the news quiet over the weekend but it's a good job the choir has an extra rehearsal on Monday night to practise for Perrigan Bay's summer fete. There's only so long anything stays quiet in a close-knit community and these days I'm fine with that.

Catching the eye of someone on the Tube marks you out as a weirdo in London so Salt Bay, where everyone knows your inside leg measurement within a week of arrival, was too much at first. But I've slowly learned to appreciate being surrounded by people who give a damn about me. And then there's the choir.

Salt Bay Choral Society has and always will have a special place in my heart. The village was sad and subdued when I first got here and had never fully recovered from the Great Storm of 2002 which drowned seven singers in one night. That's why the original choral society was disbanded. But I helped to resurrect it and am so glad I did because it brought me and Josh together and helped me feel at home. I saved the choir and in return the choir saved me. So it's the perfect place to share our good news.

'We've got something to tell you,' announces Josh when all the choir have trooped into their seats and settled down.

'Thank goodness because keeping it quiet is killing me,' shouts Kayla. 'It's like knowing the *Strictly* result before everyone else and not being able to tweet it 'cos you'll get hammered by trolls.'

'Trolls? What on earth is the girl talking about and what exactly is going on?' Jennifer is fanning herself with the sheet music for 'Sunny Afternoon' that Arthur reckons is far too modern for us.

He gets in a right strop about singing anything composed after the Reformation.

'Annie and I are taking the plunge and getting married,' says Josh, giving me a sexy wink. I'm standing at the piano behind Michaela, who's flexing her fingers and ready to go.

'Woohoo, about time! I love a wedding,' yells Maureen, jumping up and squashing the bag of leftover cupcakes from her tea shop that will feed us at breaktime.

The church is suddenly filled with sound and everyone rushes forward to shake Josh's hand and give me a hug. Everyone except elderly Cyril, who hangs back but mouths 'Congratulations' at me. There are tiny scraps of bloodied tissue paper across his chin where his razor has nicked the skin.

'Did you know about this, Kayla?' demands Jennifer when the fuss dies down. 'Is that why you ran off when I tried to speak to you in the shop this morning?'

'Yep. You have no idea how difficult it's been keeping this quiet, but I knew if I told you it would be all around the… oops.'

'All around what? Are you implying I can't keep a secret?' snorts Jennifer, Salt Bay's biggest gossip whose encyclopaedic knowledge of every local affair, peccadillo and nose job is unmatched in the area.

'We're getting married in mid-September and we'd love the choir to sing at our wedding, which will be in this church.'

Kayla gives me a wink for coming to her rescue.

'We'd be honoured,' says Florence, ruddy cheeks glowing bright against her steel-grey hair. And the rest of the choir murmur in agreement.

'And you're all invited to a reception afterwards at Tregavara House,' adds Josh. 'Nothing fancy but it should be lots of fun.'

'Hey, Annie, you'd better sit down,' shouts Roger. 'Apparently it's not good to be on your feet too much in the early days.'

'You what?'

When I look at him in confusion, Kayla starts sniggering: 'He thinks you're up the duff 'cos you're getting hitched so quickly.'

'I'm definitely not pregnant, Roger.' I grin at Pippa, who's due in a few weeks' time and looks like she has a beach ball stuffed up her T-shirt. 'There's just no point in waiting and we'd like to have the reception in the garden so I'm hoping to catch an Indian summer before the bad weather sets in.'

Everyone nods, having experienced unforgiving Cornish winters when the wind is stiff with salt spray and wellies are the footwear of choice. Cornwall in the summer can be glorious. However in the winter, as Kayla's already discovered, not so much. And I'd rather not be married in a freezing gale with disorientated seagulls smacking me in the face.

I'm also keen to have the reception at Tregavara House as soon as possible – before something else falls off or falls in and it gets harder to justify spending money on anything other than the house. Josh went pale when I showed him the email from the roofing company and sometimes in the early hours, when sleep is impossible and courage deserts me, selling my ancestral home feels like the only long-term solution.

'Well, I think your great-aunt would be delighted at your news,' says Mary from the soprano section. 'This church hasn't seen a Trebarwith wedding since Alice and David walked down the aisle so it's lovely that you're getting married here. A Salt Bay wedding will be wonderful!'

'It'll be Emily and Tom next,' says Kayla, who can be a right old stirrer. She gives Emily a thumbs up.

'Ooh, are you young things courting? That's lovely. Here, have a cupcake to celebrate.' Maureen delves into her carrier bag and thrusts a squashed butterfly cake into Tom's hands.

'I think we're just friends, aren't we, Em?' says Tom, glumly, taking a huge bite of chocolate sponge. Buttercream squishes across his upper lip and sticks to his fledgling moustache.

'Yeah, best friends,' mumbles Emily, her face red-hot with embarrassment.

'Excuse me!' Arthur is waving his hand in the air like he's back at school. 'We're happy to sing at your wedding but you won't expect us to perform that dreadful *Robin Hood* song, will you? That one about everything you do being for you? If so, I'm afraid I'll have to abstain on principle.'

'Don't worry, Arthur. It'll be old-fashioned songs and hymns all the way,' Josh reassures him with a glance at me and I nod in agreement. After being rootless for so long, I'd like our special day to be steeped in family tradition and echoes from the past. Maybe we can include music that Alice and Josh's mum had on their wedding days.

It takes a while for the choir to settle down after the wedding announcement. But all in all, the rehearsal goes pretty well and Maureen's cupcakes go down even better during the break. We decamp to the Whistling Wave when we're all sung out and Kayla was right – Josh and I are plied with drinks and don't need to get our money out once. Everyone's delighted for us and, since the death of Alice has rocked the community hard, seems happy to have something to celebrate at last.

Kayla's kept busy behind the bar because she's off to the Lake District with Ollie tomorrow and Roger's getting his wages' worth out of her while he can.

'When will you be back?' I ask her as she pushes a gleaming glass under the gin optic with one hand and pushes the till drawer closed with the other.

'Friday.' She rolls her eyes and swooshes the gin with tonic before banging it down in front of Maureen. 'He's still going through with this ridiculous charade but at least I get a few days away out of it. Though it's up North which everyone keeps warning me is grim, and the weather forecast is awful. I was quite keen to get out of baking-hot Australia for a while with this colouring' – she waggles a strand of auburn hair in front of her green eyes – 'but there is a limit and I think the Water District might be it.'

'The Lake District. And what if it's not a charade, Kayla – which Josh says it definitely isn't? What if Ollie really is going to move up there, whether you go with him or not?'

'He wouldn't. He'd never leave me and his family behind,' scoffs Kayla. But uncertainty flickers across her face before Gerald bangs a tenner on the bar and insists on buying me and Josh a short to celebrate. We are going to be totally bladdered but what the hell! You only get married once, fingers crossed, and it's lovely that everyone's so happy for us.

The only person not likely to relish the Trebarwiths and Pascos being legally joined is Toby – but he's just going to have to lump it.

Chapter Twelve

Toby has disappeared off the radar since the reading of the will. But he turns up in person a couple of days later and my stomach lurches when I open the door to find him leaning against Alice's safety rail. Duty visits to his great-aunt are no longer required so is he here to lay claim to the house? Surely he's satisfied with the painting, which is worth far more.

'I was in the area on business,' he says, tapping his foot impatiently on the step. It's cloudier today and there's a cooler breeze but, behind him, tourists are still heading for the harbour in shorts and skimpy tops. I open the door wide but Toby hesitates.

'Are you coming in then?'

'If you're sure that's all right, seeing as it's your house now.'

'It's absolutely fine. Alice would want us to get along,' I mutter through gritted teeth, wondering why Toby has to make everything difficult.

'If that was the case, maybe she should have been less cavalier with her possessions.'

Toby steps past me into the hallway and hangs up the jacket that's hanging over his arm. It's soft grey suede and must have cost a fortune. Then he stands by the coatstand like he's waiting for something. Well, this is awkward.

'Would you like a cup of tea?' I venture at last.

'Lovely. No sugar.' Toby stalks past me into the sitting room and I head for the kitchen to make a brew, grateful that no one is home except me. My cousin in a foul mood plus Storm in a strop is like matter and antimatter colliding – explosive and unpleasant for anyone in the vicinity. And when Josh gets involved too… I give the leaves in the teapot a vigorous stir and tip biscuits onto a plate, keen to get Toby out of the house a.s.a.p.

When I carry the tray into the sitting room, Toby is sitting in Alice's chair, sprawled back against the gold velour with his legs outstretched on the footstool where Alice would rest her stockinged feet in the evening. And he's still got his dusty brogues on.

'Here you go.' I place his tea on a side table and make a space for my mug on the bureau, which is covered in documents and information about the house. Lying on top is the email from the roofer that I've printed out for filing and the red-underlined £30,000 catches my eye. Has Toby seen it? He sips his tea without expression while I shuffle the papers together and stuff them into a drawer.

'So what brings you to Salt Bay, Toby?'

D'oh! He's here to slap an expensive law suit on you, you idiot, and you'll all be ruined, says my inner voice unhelpfully.

Toby uses his snow-white handkerchief to mop a splash of tea that's dribbled into his tidy goatee. 'I wanted to see you because we didn't part on the best of terms at the will reading. And that's a shame because now my parents and Alice are gone you're the only family I have left.'

'Apart from your daughter.'

'Apart from Freya, of course.' He smiles but there's a flash of annoy-ance in his hooded grey eyes. 'Anyway, I'd prefer that we're on good terms seeing as we're the only Trebarwiths left. Or at least the only ones bearing the Trebarwith name.'

My tension-tight shoulders start to ease down from my ears. 'I'd prefer that too. Are you planning on seeing Freya during this visit?'

'I saw her briefly yesterday and took her to a soft play area so we could spend some quality time together.'

'That sounds great. How was it?'

'Awful. I didn't realise such places existed – there were ridiculously loud, feral children screeching and crying everywhere. Needless to say, we didn't stay long and I don't know why you suggested it in the first place.'

I'm pretty sure my suggestion was a more general one about spending one-on-one time with his daughter, but I let his complaint wash over me. Now isn't the time to be picky.

'Did the painting arrive in London OK?'

We both glance at the wall where the oil painting used to hang. I haven't got around to putting anything in its place and the empty space catches my eye whenever I'm in the room – a constant reminder that Alice has gone and things are changing.

Toby sniffs and pushes his fingers through his short brown fringe. 'The courier company charged a fortune but they did a good job and it arrived undamaged, thank goodness. It's currently in the vault at my office for safe keeping.'

'Are you planning on putting it up for auction?'

Toby shrugs. 'I'm not sure. I must admit I was planning on selling it but now it's in my possession I might hang onto it for a while. Parting with such a glorious painting that's part of Trebarwith heritage would be a wrench.'

'So you'll keep it?'

'Yes, I do believe that I will for the moment.'

Crikey. That's a turn-up for the books. I was sure the wrench of parting with the painting would be softened by its new owner handing over three-quarters of a million pounds. But maybe fatherhood is bringing out the best in Toby after all.

'Do you want a biscuit?' I hand him the plate of chocolate digestives like a peace offering but Toby shakes his head and balances the plate on the footstool.

'I'm watching my waistline,' he says, staring at mine. 'So what else is happening around here now Alice has gone?'

'Um…' I swallow, annoyed that the thought of telling Toby my good news is making me nervous. It's ridiculous, just as ridiculous as sweeping the engagement cards on the mantelpiece into a tidy pile when I saw his car pull up outside. So I'll just say it… 'Josh and I are getting married.'

Toby carefully places his cup back in its saucer. 'Are you, indeed. So tell me, Mr Pasco, what was it that first attracted you to property owner Annabella Trebarwith?'

'That's not fair, Toby. Josh and I have been going out for a while and he was going to propose before Alice fell ill.'

'If you say so, and there has been a slight improvement recently from the humourless paragon of virtue he used to be. But a Pasco owning Tregavara House, who'd have thought it?' Toby gives a yelping laugh that doesn't reach his eyes.

'It will belong to both of us.'

I hold my breath, waiting for Toby to make his own claim on Tregavara House but he grabs hold of my left hand instead. 'Let's have a look at the ring then.'

He peers at the plain band while I bite back the urge to explain that it's only temporary and I don't want a platinum-set blingtastic diamond anyway. Simple silver will do me just fine.

'It's very you,' says Toby at last, shaking his head like he's trying to dislodge the thought of me and Josh getting hitched. 'Look, I can't stay but the main reason I'm here is to talk about the house.'

Here it comes. He takes another sip of his tea and waits while I take a seat opposite him. I get the feeling I'll need to be sitting down for this.

'I was shocked by Alice's will because I was sure she'd leave the house to me seeing as I've known her for years and you only turned up eighteen months ago.' He sucks in air and breathes out slowly. 'Of course it was entirely up to Alice how she disposed of her property but I'm here with a proposal.'

'Which is?'

'All in good time, but first I think I might have been a little hasty about asking you to leave when I thought the house was mine. My behaviour was inappropriate and for that I apologise. To be honest, Alice's death has hit me harder than I thought it would and I'm more attached to this house than I realised.'

Wow, this is weird. Thoroughly disliking Toby would be so much easier than the ambivalence I often feel when my cousin is around – he's unkind and irresponsible and a terrible snob but he shows just enough flashes of loneliness, hurt and humanity to keep me on his side.

'Why don't we forget it? We were all upset at the time.'

'That's true. It was a difficult day.'

'So what exactly is your proposal?'

'I've thought of a way we can all benefit,' says Toby, leaning forward with his elbows on his knees. 'You can't afford to live here and keep this place going.'

'Did you read my email?'

'I couldn't help noticing it with all that underlining but I'd guessed as much anyway. Anyone with half a brain can tell this place is crying

out for some TLC or it might not last another hideous Cornish winter.'
He shudders. 'Anyway, I might be willing to buy Tregavara House
from you at a very reasonable price and let you stay on indefinitely
as a tenant.'

'I thought you wanted the house empty for yourself and your
friends.'

'I've had time to think about that and it would be better if the
house was occupied rather than being prey to local burglars. So in
effect the house would still be your home but I'd be paying the repair
bills including funding a new roof, though thirty grand sounds a bit
steep. That roofer saw you coming.'

'We won't need a new roof for ages because the repair will hold,'
I assure him, crossing my fingers behind my back. 'But what's in all
this for you, Toby?'

'Sometimes you do remind me very much of Alice.' He leans back
in her chair. 'OK, cards on the table. I could pursue this legally but that
would cost both of us money and time and would mostly benefit the
lawyers involved. But I don't like not having a toehold here, especially
now I'm visiting Freya.'

'You could rent or buy somewhere else nearby.'

'I could, but I've been visiting Tregavara House since I was a child
and it feels like home. I don't want to see it fall down because you can't
afford to repair it and my way is win-win.' He ticks off the win-wins
on his fingers. 'You get to live here, Pasco and your various hangers-
on still have a roof over their heads – a roof that won't blow off in a
storm – and I can stay whenever I'm in the area. Alice would approve.'

Would she, when she deliberately left the house to me?

'Of course you'd need to pay the appropriate rent,' adds Toby. 'I'm
not a charity.'

'Of course.' The thought of Toby being even a smidgen charitable is hard to fathom.

'So shall I get a price over to you that I'm willing to pay? I've already taken advice about what Tregavara House is worth but I'll obviously need to take into account the cost of a new roof and other repairs. But you'll still get a better price and a quicker sale from me than from anyone else. And the house will stay in the Trebarwith family – it would break Alice's heart for it to go to an outsider.'

My cousin steeples his fingers under his chin while I try to work out whether I'm dealing with Toby One or Toby Two.

Toby One is a heartless, avaricious snob who abandoned his responsibilities as a father and screws people over. While Toby Two is a sad, lonely soul who's trying to make amends with Freya and helped get me and Josh back together during a sticky patch last year. The second version is rarely glimpsed because it's buried deep, but it's there nonetheless.

'Why don't you get more information about your proposal to me and we can discuss it. Obviously, I need to talk to Josh about it first.'

'Obviously,' says Toby with the faintest hint of a sneer. 'Josh Pasco married to a Trebarwith and living at Tregavara House. Whatever next? Doctor Who getting it on with the Daleks?'

He smiles at his own joke, which has taken me by surprise. I'd have thought *Doctor Who* was far too plebeian for a man of Toby's calibre but there's a lot I don't know about him. He doesn't let anyone get close, which is so like me and my life before Salt Bay, Alice and Josh, when I was haring round London cultivating friendships and relationships, almost all of them superficial. It was safer that way.

Toby crosses his legs and finishes his cooling tea while I wonder what it is that keeps *him* awake at night.

'So what do you reckon he's up to?' asks Josh, peering over the edge of the cliff at the perfect curve of sand far below us. 'I know he's seeing Freya now and paying maintenance but I don't trust him. He's still the man who ran away from his own child and left us to pick up the pieces.'

He turns face-on into the breeze and pulls at his white T-shirt, which is sticking to his back. Thick grey clouds have smothered the sun and the air is heavy with the threat of a storm. Climbing the cliff path was absolutely knackering.

'I think – I like to think – that Toby has the best interests of the house and the Trebarwith family at heart.'

'Then you're definitely a better person than me, Annabella Sunshine.'

'Or more gullible?'

'Or that,' says Josh, wheeling his hands around his head to chase off a swarm of midges. The unusually hot weather we've been having is an aphrodisiac for insects and Salt Bay is teeming with the tiny flies.

'So what do you think we should do?'

'It's your house so it's up to you.'

'No, it's *our* house and I want you to be happy with what's decided.'

When I lace my fingers through Josh's, he swings our arms back and forth with a thoughtful look on his face. 'Well, look at the options. We either stay put, try to make it work and hope the roof doesn't fall in. Or we could sell to an outsider or to Toby, at what I'm sure will be an advantageous price to your cousin, and buy somewhere else.'

'He said we could stay on as tenants.'

Josh wrinkles his perfect nose. 'Like I said, I don't trust him and the rent would probably be extortionate. I'm sure we'd end up moving somewhere else.'

'Somewhere else not in Salt Bay.'

'Probably. Nothing much in the village comes on the market until people die and most local properties are too small for us all anyway. But there's nothing wrong with Trecaldwith.'

Hhmm. I shrug because there's nothing wrong with Trecaldwith at all. It's a small town with a harbour, shops, my future in-laws and the school where Josh teaches. It's got lots going for it but it's not Salt Bay. And I can't imagine leaving this close-knit, sometimes infuriating community.

Josh spots my frown, puts his arms around me and kisses the top of my head. 'Come here. Alice gave you a wonderful gift and she'd hate that it's causing you such stress.'

'I know, and I love living here and am so grateful to her for choosing me as guardian of the house.'

'Guardian? You make it sound like a child rather than a building,' chuckles Josh into my hair. 'What's your gut feeling about the right thing to do?'

'Honestly? Keeping Tregavara House and making it a wonderful home for all of us feels right. But there are bills coming in and a wedding to pay for and sometimes I think it would be better in Toby's safe keeping.'

'Or someone else's safe keeping.'

I pull away and raise my eyebrows at my tall, dark, handsome fiancé. 'Huh! You just can't stand the thought of Toby getting what he wants. But I couldn't let Tregavara House go to anyone other than a Trebarwith.'

'Even if that Trebarwith is an idiot? Honestly, your family and its blood is thicker than water shtick can be a bit trying at times.'

Biting my lip, I wonder if I am being over the top about my family ties. It's so hard to keep things in perspective when having roots is so new and wonderful for me.

'Look, Annie, we don't have to make any decisions straight away so why don't we let Toby stew for a while?'

'You'd like that, wouldn't you?'

Josh grins. 'I must admit, I would. And it'll give us a chance to concentrate on getting married instead seeing as that's less than two months away. Our wedding doesn't have to cost loads as long as you're sure you don't mind not having a *big* Big Day.'

'I don't need a big wedding, Josh. All I want are a few friends and family there – and you, of course, looking handsome in your suit.' When I playfully pinch his backside, he gives me a sexy wink. 'But even doing it on the cheap costs money. There's the food and drink for the reception and wedding dresses cost a lot. Even simple ones without a veil and all that malarkey. Kayla's been looking at some wedding dress websites and reckons I'll need to sell a kidney or go on the game.'

'Kayla is not a good influence on you. Honestly, you can get married in a black bin bag if you like. You'll still be the most beautiful woman in the church.'

And that's why I'm marrying him. Here I am, standing on a cliff in my old jeans with spaghetti bolognaise on my top and no make-up on, and he still reckons I'd look good in a bin bag. He's either the best boyfriend ever or he seriously needs a trip to Specsavers.

Fat seagulls screech and swoop over the waves as I thank my lucky stars I came to Salt Bay last year and stayed. And I send up a special thank you for Alice, whose name is now inscribed in gold on a stark granite tombstone in the cemetery behind me.

Would she rather Josh and I scraped our pennies together in a falling-down house or sold it to Toby and moved on? I'd give almost anything for her advice and for her to be guest of honour at my wedding. If only she'd put off dying for one more summer.

Blinking in the breeze, I link my arm through Josh's and run my thumb along the silver band on my fourth finger.

'Tregavara House means the world to you, doesn't it, Annie?'

'It's the first place that's ever really felt like home.'

'And Alice knew that. She knew you loved the place and she left it to you so we'll see what we can do to make it work.'

'Like what?' I ask, squinting as the sun peeks through a gap in the clouds and blinds me.

'I have no idea but Alice left Tregavara House to you for a reason and Toby has the painting so he's not exactly hard done by. For now, let's just enjoy getting married.'

The heat builds and thunder rumbles far out to sea in the early hours while I lie awake with Josh snoring gently beside me. *Please don't let a storm roll into Salt Bay.* I cross my fingers under the duvet and think about London Annie, who would never have lost sleep over the course of a thunderstorm and the efficacy of a roof repair. My mum wouldn't have either. She dealt with problems by running away from them, but it didn't do her any good in the end, nor me. Staying and sorting stuff out is what being grown up is all about. I drift back to sleep as lightning arcs above the sea and the thunder rumbles on.

Chapter Thirteen

Letting Toby stew is all very well but it's me who seems to be going crazy. I'm expecting Toby's written proposal to land in my inbox the next day, but nothing arrives then or the day after. And the postman only brings his usual haul of charity letters, bills and holiday brochures.

I'm not planning to accept Toby's offer. There's no way I want to let Tregavara House go but it's unfinished business and he's got under my skin.

'What's up with you?' asks Storm, watching me flick through the post in the sitting room and throw it into a pile on the floor. 'What are you expecting?'

'Nothing,' I lie because there's no point in worrying or unsettling her. She's still more subdued than usual following Alice's death.

Storm rips open an envelope adorned with an animal charity logo and hoicks out the pen inside. 'I'll have that, thank you very much. Have people replied to those lame wedding invite cards you and Josh posted round the village?'

'Some have sent acceptance cards, but most people just say yes when we see them in the pub. Actually, talking of wedding invitations, I've got some cards left and could—'

'Nope! I've already told you there's no way I'm inviting my mum to come and see me in some sad dress and spend time in the same church as Barry. The last time they got together she threw a pint of beer down his sweatshirt.'

'I'm sure they could behave like adults on my wedding day.'

'You have no idea,' mutters Storm. 'But she wouldn't come anyway.'

'She might if she was invited by you. What about when you next see her? It's not long until you're off to Richmond so could you raise it with her then?'

'Yeah, OK, I'll ask her.'

That was far too easy. I know Storm has no intention of mentioning it to her mother and she knows I know but it's an efficient way of bringing the discussion to a grinding halt. Accusing her of being economical with the truth would only herald the onset of World War III and my nerves are frazzled enough.

Storm wanders off to have a shower and douse every available bathroom surface with water while I fetch the remaining invitation cards and envelopes from the bureau.

Mr Joshua Pasco and Miss Annabella Trebarwith invite you to their wedding at St Piran's Church, Salt Bay at 11.30 a.m. on Saturday, September 22nd. A reception will be held at Tregavara House. RSVP to Tregavara House, Salt Bay. No gifts required.

The glossy cards with navy blue edging were ordered online and didn't cost much. But seeing the details of our wedding in black and white is a thrill every time. Would it be such a bad idea to send one to Storm's mum behind her back?

I pop an invitation into an envelope and pick up the charity pen that Storm left on the sofa. But I know deep down that I can't address it and put it in the post. Storm's trust has been hard won and would be easily lost. It looks like I won't be the only one missing her mum on my wedding day.

Toby's offer for Tregavara House arrives via email two days later.

'He's offering how much?' Josh squints at the laptop screen and sucks air in through his teeth. 'Oh, that's clever. Very clever. He's offering just over the market value, when you take into account the thirty grand he's deducted for a new roof, so that we'll sell to him rather than someone else.'

He takes another look at the email just in case the figure being offered has magically changed.

'Perhaps he really is missing Alice and has feelings for the old place. He's not all bad, you know, and he's trying very hard with Freya.'

'But he still always puts himself first so why do you want to defend him?'

'I dunno. He's the only member of the Trebarwith family I've got left and I'd rather he wasn't a sleazeball, I suppose.'

Pulling my sleeve over the heel of my hand, I rub a viewing circle in the steamed-up windscreen. We're crammed into Josh's battered old Mini because we needed somewhere private to talk. We told the girls we were going to Tesco in Penzance and have driven up onto the moors instead. But Storm presented me with a shopping list before we left so I guess we'll have to traipse round the supermarket once this is resolved.

'So what *are* we going to do about his offer?' asks Josh, cracking open his window. Rain is drumming hard on the roof and the sweet summer smell of hot, damp earth floods the car.

'Presumably you want to tell him where to stick it.'

'Oh, yeah and I'd be happy to help him do it.' He leans forward and peers through the windscreen at a blur of green moor and grey sea. 'But we need to be realistic, Annie, and accept that we might need to let Tregavara House go.'

'You said we could make it work.'

'I said we'd see if we could make it work but things aren't improving, are they?'

He's got a point. My boss Celia called a meeting at work yesterday and warned us that 'the funding situation going forward is rather challenging', which Gayle and Lesley later informed me is corporate code for 'we're screwed'. At the moment Josh and I are managing to pay off the mortgage and his loan and put a bit aside for the wedding and the roof fund but if I lose my job, our finances will be well and truly shafted.

'So are you saying we should sell Tregavara House to an outsider?' I can't help shuddering.

Josh laughs and closes the laptop lid. 'We wouldn't be handing over the house to an alien, Annie. It would go to someone who'd probably love it like we do but could give it the money and attention it needs. And don't forget you were an outsider in Salt Bay not so long ago.'

It's true that I felt like an outsider at first. But it didn't take me long to realise I was more of an outsider in London where I'd lived all my life than in Salt Bay. Alice took me in, filled in the gaps and gave me what I was missing. And now I miss her.

'I can't,' I say in a small voice. 'I know you think it's crazy and I'm letting my emotions win but if we sell to anyone it has to be Toby because he's—'

'A Trebarwith. I get it.'

'And I can't let Alice down. Are you fed up with me?'

'Not with you, just the situation. We should be looking forward to our wedding and celebrating having the house but it's all a bit of a mess at the moment.' Josh swivels his backside round towards me and curses when his knees hit the handbrake. 'Actually, I admire your family loyalty because I'd walk through hell and high water for mine. Mind you, they're not duplicitous toerags.'

'Perhaps Toby isn't either. Maybe he's changed.'

'And maybe I'll be invited to take part in the next series of *Strictly*.'

'Cor, you'd look gorgeous in sequins doing a samba with your chest out.'

We both laugh which helps to ease the tension that's started threading through our relationship. It's hard when your boyfriend is ruled by his head and insufferably sensible whereas you appear to have morphed into a quivering blob of heart-led irrationality.

But we both want the same thing – the best for all of us. I take a deep breath of damp air and curl my hands into fists. 'I'm so fortunate that Alice left me the house and I feel terrible selling it, but Toby's offer is the best compromise. We could stay in Salt Bay, pay Toby rent and invest the money from the sale. It makes sense.'

'Believe me, the thought of Toby as our landlord doesn't fill me with joy and we'd need to get things in writing. But this way would give us breathing space to sort out what to do next. I love living in Salt Bay too, Annie, and want you to be happy.' Josh nudges me with his shoulder and grins. 'We could spend more on the wedding and get some of those doves Kayla was going on about.'

'And fireworks. And a ginormous cake with gold flakes. But we wouldn't have to sell until after the wedding, would we? It feels important that the house is mine when we hold the reception there.'

Ugh, irrational feelings again. My eyes are filling with tears and Josh squeezes my leg.

'We don't have to do anything right now. Selling is a huge decision and the thought of Toby getting what he wants is killing me so let's sleep on it. No decisions today, OK?' He winds his window down further and pokes his head outside. 'The rain's stopped so we could have a quick walk and get some fresh air before we hit Tesco. What's Storm put on her list?'

I fish the crumpled paper out of my pocket and scan down it. 'Just the usual. Crisps, white bread for toast, chocolate milkshake and ice cream. Good grief, the girl's a nutritionist's nightmare and I'm supposed to be in loco parentis.'

'You've got a lot on your plate, Annie. Though not as much as Storm, obviously,' he sniggers.

It's a terrible joke but I love my strong, sensible boyfriend for trying to cheer me up. He deserves more than me moping about all over the place.

'Come on,' I say, giving my door a hefty kick because it's the only way to get out of this rust bucket. 'Let's walk to the old tin mine and make out.'

Chapter Fourteen

The next morning I take a walk into the village. The ground's damp from the overnight rain so the cliff path will be too slippery and treacherous. It's cooler today and still overcast, though the sky is light grey rather than the bruised-purple clouds that bunched over the sea last night.

'Morning, Annie. Not so many emmets about at the moment,' calls Cyril as I'm walking past the village green. The river that cuts across the open space is lower than usual in spite of yesterday's rain and the water is swirling and eddying around stones on the river bed.

'That's because the sun's disappeared for the last few days, Cyril.'

I sit beside him on the bench where he's resting his legs. The hem of his trousers is frayed and there are breakfast stains down his shirt but it's good to see him out and about. Before he joined the choir, Cyril was the village recluse and still grieving the loss of his wife. I understand that – shutting yourself away when the safe world you know crumbles around you. But it's not healthy to keep yourself apart, not in the long run.

'You look tired, girl. Are you off work because you're ill?' Cyril stares at me without blinking.

'No, I've taken a day's leave to catch up on stuff. I'm not sleeping too well at the moment but I'm fine.'

'Why aren't you sleeping? You're not having second thoughts about young Josh, are you? He'll do you right.'

'I know he will.' I pat Cyril's arm, which feels insubstantial beneath his cotton shirt. 'But I'm missing Alice, and Emily's still looking for a job and Storm can be challenging sometimes and the house is lovely but quite a responsibility and, to be honest, we're considering selling it to Toby.'

Eek, I didn't mean to say that. One question and it all came burbling out, which only goes to prove I'd be the worst spy in the world. *'Tell me all your secrets, Mr Bond.' 'Uh, OK.'*

'Toby Trebarwith? That's interesting.'

What sort of interesting? 'What a fantastically good idea' interesting or 'you've clearly lost your mind and Alice would be appalled' interesting?

'Only the house would have gone to Toby anyway presumably if I hadn't been around and the roof's dodgy and there are bills to pay and we could probably pay rent and stay on in the house anyway and... I'm burbling. Sorry. But what do you mean by interesting?'

'Just that Toby Trebarwith is local Cornish but he doesn't fit in round here.'

'So you think selling to Toby would be a bad idea.'

Cyril places his cool, veiny hand on top of mine. 'You don't want to take advice from an old codger like me, Annie, and I'd never make a fuss but I know some folk who would if Toby took over Tregavara House.'

Great. It seems I'm damned if I do and damned if I don't.

'Sorry, Cyril. I didn't mean to load all my worries onto you.'

Cyril gives a gappy grin because he's forgotten to put his false teeth in again. 'It's a long time since I've been useful so load away! And if you want my opinion, a young girl like you should be all excited about her wedding, not being dragged down by responsibilities. You need a break,

Annie. Somewhere you can get some peace and quiet, away from work and calls on your time and this social media stuff that's addling people's brains.'

'I'm fine, honestly, and where in the world is more peaceful and gorgeous than Salt Bay?'

Ahead of me, pretty cottages are clustered along the valley which rises steeply away from the sea. The air is fresh with salt and ozone and there's no need for Cyril to worry about frazzled brains because my social media consumption has plummeted since I arrived in Salt Bay. The Internet disappears into a black hole around here and now I don't much miss it. All that Facebooking and tweeting to convince everyone that my life was perfect turned out to be exhausting.

So Cyril's wrong. I don't need to go anywhere else. In fact, people would pay to change places with me.

Whack! That's the sound of a Brilliant Idea slapping me around the chops. What if I could give people the opportunity to enjoy what I have here – sea air, huge arcing skies, a community choir, real-deal Cornish pasties? Tregavara House would be a fabulous venue for a B&B.

My brain starts whirring while Cyril and I sit on the bench in companionable silence. A B&B would bring in money and help Tregavara House pay its way. And Emily could run it with some help from the rest of us – she told me once she was interested in the hospitality trade and this would give her brilliant experience.

'Are you all right, dear?' asks Cyril, patting my knee. 'Only you've gone a funny colour.'

'What about a B&B?'

'Eh?' He squints at me and rubs the white bristles on his chin.

'I was thinking that we could maybe turn Tregavara House into a B&B and that would help to pay for its upkeep so we could hang onto the place and not sell to Toby.'

'A bed and breakfast establishment in Salt Bay? I suppose it's about time we had one of those.'

'But please don't tell anyone about it.'

I'd better discuss what might be a madcap scheme with Josh before my idea is talked about in the pub and Jennifer's saying a five-star hotel's planned. Some of the locals are set in their ways and might not like outsiders 'invading' the village. Mind you, according to Cyril they'd also freak at the thought of Toby owning Tregavara House.

'Don't worry, I'm the soul of discretion and can keep a secret,' says Cyril, tapping the side of his nose. 'I've never told anyone what Arthur got up to in Rhyl.'

What on earth did upright, uptight Arthur get up to in Rhyl? All kinds of scenarios are running through my mind – Arthur rat-arsed in a gutter, Arthur off his head on E in a night club, Arthur having it away with a stranger behind Rhyl Bus Station.

I'm tempted to beg Cyril to spill the beans but can't really, seeing as I've just asked him to keep a secret for me.

So instead I ask him: 'What do you reckon Alice would think about me opening a B&B?'

'She always was a very practical woman and it's better than you selling the house to Toby. If she'd wanted him to have it, she'd have left it to him. You need to do what's best for you and that young man of yours and those girls you've taken in. And if that means turning the house into a bed and breakfast establishment, so be it.'

I can hardly wait to run my idea by Josh and pounce on him the minute he comes in from the summer school he's helping to run during the holidays.

'Slow down – slow down,' he laughs, pushing me onto a kitchen chair. 'Do you really think people would pay to stay here? It's not exactly The Ritz, is it.'

He's got a point. The walls in here could do with a freshen-up coat of paint and the back door is scuffed from Storm kicking it closed. But the Aga still cooks up a mean full English and our guests could eat at the solid oak table.

'I'm sure it would be all right if we tarted the place up a bit. We could convert the dining room into another bedroom and then have two couples staying at the same time to bring in regular income.'

'But what could we offer people?'

'Good Cornish home cooking, fabulous views of the cliffs and the harbour, bracing sea air, a local pub, Poldark.'

'Poldark?' splutters Josh.

I shrug. 'The house was built using the proceeds from tin mining so we can spin a Poldark connection. And you do look rather brooding and swashbuckly.'

Josh raises his eyebrows. 'Will I be required to stride around in boots and breeches with my shirt off?'

I give myself a delicious moment to fully picture this while Josh laughs and pours us both an orange juice from the fridge. The back door and windows are wide open and a cool breeze is snaking through the house.

'Plus, the village is pretty,' I continue, 'and the view from the cliffs is awesome and there's a beach.'

'Yeah, if people want to break their necks scrambling down the cliff path to get there.'

That's true. Guests hurtling off the Path of Doom wouldn't be great publicity.

'OK, maybe we don't mention the beach. But Salt Bay has lots of day-trippers and I'm sure some of them would like to stay in the village overnight.'

When Josh stays quiet, I wrinkle my nose at him. 'Do you think it's a daft idea?'

'No, not really. But it's not going to bring in loads of money so finances will still be tight if we don't sell the place. And there are rules and regulations about B&Bs. You can't just open them willy-nilly and the authorities won't be too happy if our roof's about to fall in.'

'But it's not. The roof's been patched up and will be fine for ages,' I say, crossing my fingers behind my back.

'Hhmm. You have more faith in this house than I do.'

Josh is being infuriatingly practical but how frustrating will it be if we need income from the house to keep it going and save up for a new roof but we can't get that income until a new roof is on? I slurp my orange juice and drum my fingernails on the table.

'Anyway, I thought you were coming round to the idea of selling to Toby,' says Josh gently. 'It grieves me letting him have what he wants but I can see it's probably the most sensible option.'

'So can I but I don't feel sensible. I feel guilty because Alice left her beloved house to me and selling it feels like going against her wishes. And I feel sad that she's not here so I can explain and ask her if she'd mind. And I feel awful that I'm messing you about and behaving so… Ugh, what's the word I'm looking for?'

'Emotionally?'

'Yep, you probably think I'm being all emotionally incontinent again. I bet you wish you'd chosen someone else now. Someone not so—'

I was going to say 'mental' but that's what the kids in the school playground used to call Mum when she turned up to collect me in poncho and slippers. As her bouts of illness progressed, her fashion style got even more eccentric until she didn't turn up to collect me at all.

'I don't want anyone but you, Annie. And I get why you're all over the place at the moment.'

Hhmm. I wouldn't have put it quite like that but whatever.

Josh sips his orange juice and looks at me across the kitchen table. 'You're still grieving for Alice and reeling from the shock of inheriting this house and the responsibilities that come with it so it's hard to know which decisions are the right ones. Look, why don't we leave Toby dangling for a bit longer and you can check out your B&B idea to see if it's a go-er?'

'Are you sure?'

'Why not? It's good to look at other options before Toby gets his hands on the place. And anyway, having to wait for an answer will drive him demented.'

'Then I'll check out the planning rules and see what we'd have to do. I bet we can get round things… and don't people round here say you should never underestimate the Trebarwiths?'

'I wouldn't dare,' murmurs Josh, scooting round to my side of the table, putting his hands on my cheeks and lifting my face for a kiss. 'If anyone can sort things out, you can, dodgy roof or no dodgy roof.'

Which is lovely and all that but, without a nifty thirty grand in my back pocket, I'm not one hundred per cent sure that I can.

Chapter Fifteen

Kernow Coast Council has a planning application advisory service which is tucked away at the rear of a soulless office block, a few streets from the sea.

'Here you go, dear.' A woman in a green trouser suit holds open the door for me and an acrid smell of sweat hits me when I duck to get under her arm. Her face is pink and shiny and the man behind the front desk is equally frazzled. He's called Warren, according to his lanyard, and looks about twelve years old. At first I take him for a work experience lad but his lanyard is dated six months earlier. Oh, great! I'll soon be commenting on how young the police look these days, like Jennifer does whenever the local community support officer calls in to discuss her shoplifting complaints.

'Air conditioning has packed up,' says Warren by way of greeting. 'All they've given me is that.' He points at the small fan next to him which is wafting humid air from one place to another. 'It's probably illegally hot in here. Anyway' – he snaps back to what he's supposed to be doing – 'how can I help you?'

'My name's Annie Trebarwith and I'm here about my property, Tregavara House in Salt Bay.'

'Ah, yes,' says Warren, reaching for a big brown box file on the shelves behind him. 'There's already some info about that. I think you spoke to my colleague about it a few days ago.'

Before I can disagree, he pulls out a piece of paper. 'Here we are. You wanted to know what permissions would be needed to demolish the property and build flats for holiday usage on the site. Or to retain the house and convert it into flats.'

'Ugh, no.' I stare at Warren and shake my head. 'That wasn't me.'

'It says Trebarwith on here which is an unusual name.' Warren stares at the paper and then starts gnawing his lip. 'Ah, but it wasn't you who saw my colleague. Sorry about that. You said it was your property?'

'Yes it is,' I say, trying to read upside down but Warren stuffs the paper swiftly back into the file. It doesn't matter. It could only be Toby contemplating knocking down Tregavara House to build holiday flats. How could he?

I thought Toby had some feeling for family tradition and wanted to maintain links with his past, but I failed to spot the pound signs in his eyes. I'm such an idiot! Just because my cousin is trying to forge a relationship with his daughter doesn't mean he's gone all family-friendly.

'So how can I help you?' asks Warren, folding his arms and then unfolding them when he realises it'll just make him hotter.

'I'm here to ask about changing Tregavara House into a B&B and what I would need to do.'

'It depends. You might need planning permission for change of use and then there are building regulations to consider as well. I've got some info here about it.'

He roots in his desk and hands me a leaflet that I flick through. 'Do you get a lot of people in here asking the same thing then?'

'Uh, yeah, 'cos tourism is one of Cornwall's main money-spinners. We're overrun with German tourists at the moment – they can't get enough of the place. Do you speak German?'

I shake my head, wishing I'd paid more attention in language lessons at school. Getting my head around 'le' and 'la' in French was fine but discovering German words could be neutral as well put the kybosh on it for me. That was far too complicated when I had more pressing things in my life, like whether Mum was mentally well enough to get up and dressed.

Warren pulls the fan closer to him. 'It doesn't matter much anyway. They all speak English better than we do.'

I push the leaflet into my bag to study it later. 'Hypothetically, Warren, if I did fancy knocking Tregavara House down and building flats there, would it be allowed?'

Even asking the question feels horribly disloyal to Alice and the many generations of Trebarwiths who preceded her.

'Probably not because it's listed and Salt Bay lies in a conservation area. But that wouldn't necessarily stop it from being converted into flats as long as the right permissions were sought first.'

That's good to know, but it doesn't really matter whether Toby would be able to go through with his grubby plans or not. It's obvious he has no intention of letting us stay at Tregavara House and he doesn't give a monkey's about the building.

He must never get his hands on it.

Chapter Sixteen

On the way home, I call into the Whistling Wave for some brash Aussie advice from Kayla. This is a bold move because the art of people-pleasing has passed my friend by. But her forthright opinions are often right, and I'm putting off telling Josh about Toby because he'll totally go off on one – and he has every right.

He and Toby have forged a fragile peace for the sake of Freya but their old enmity runs deep. It was Josh who picked up the pieces when Toby abandoned pregnant Lucy and left her family to bring up Freya. That's one reason why he's so strapped for cash now. And more proof that my cousin is a duplicitous toad will push the Toby Trust Swingometer straight to Total Git.

Kayla's dislike for my cousin is less entrenched – or so I thought until she launched into a two-minute rant. I switch off after thirty seconds as swear words rain down thick and fast but I get the gist. To paraphrase, Kayla believes Toby is behaving appallingly, Alice would be turning in her grave if she had one, and Toby's parentage is questionable.

Once she's spent, Kayla slumps next to me in a window seat, fanning herself furiously with the bar menu. The window's open and a strong breeze is moving the horse brasses on the bumpy white walls. But the low-ceilinged pub is gloomy even though it's so bright outside.

'What are you going to do then?' Kayla demands, waving at Tom, who's just come into the bar. 'You definitely can't sell Tregavara House to him now, even if the roof blows off and you're totally destitute. Though' – she adds, glancing at my ashen face – 'that is so not going to happen, like ever.'

'Let's hope not. But whatever happens, there's no way I can let him get his hands on Alice's house.'

'Your house,' Kayla reminds me, shaking her head as Tom wanders round the pub like a lost soul. 'He keeps coming in to check if Emily's here. That boy has got it bad, poor lovesick loon.' She turns to me. 'Anyway, what were you doing at the planning place?'

'I was checking out maybe bringing in some money by turning Tregavara House into a B&B.'

'Hhmm, that's not the worst idea you've ever had and you might make enough to keep the house, for longer at least.' Kayla beckons at Roger, who's currently propping the pub door open with a huge chunk of grey granite. 'What do you reckon about Annie's idea to run Tregavara House as a B&B then, Rog?'

Roger wipes his sweaty hands down his grease-spattered T-shirt before answering. 'I've never fancied taking in paying guests myself – they're far too much trouble. But it might work if you can be arsed to be on your best behaviour all the time.'

'What might work?' Oh, no. Arthur and Fiona have just come through the door with their labradoodle, Pickles, who's the closest thing I've ever seen to a living teddy bear. Roger sniggers at Pickles, who he reckons is 'not a dog for a real man', and grabs three empty glasses from the table next to us in one huge hand.

'Annie's setting up a B&B at Tregavara House. Bedrooms overlooking the sea, home-cooked food, excellent pub just up the road...'

'Um, it's just an idea at the moment. Nothing's settled,' I squeak, but Arthur's arms are already folded.

'Well, I don't know about that. A bed and breakfast establishment isn't really in keeping with the village.'

'What, a village that's full of emmets all summer?' snorts Kayla, rolling her eyes at me. 'The place is heaving with them every day and the Whistling Wave would go tits up without them buying loads of beer and chips. No offence, Roger.'

'None taken. Tourists are damn annoying, but we can't do without them.'

The young couple bowed down with backpacks, who are waiting to be served at the bar, give Roger a filthy look but he's too oblivious to notice.

'Exactly. Having tourists here during the day is fine,' snorts Arthur. Fiona gives me a sympathetic smile and I smile back. The poor woman has to put up with Arthur being bombastic every single day. 'But tourists leave Salt Bay when the sun goes down and that's just how we like it. We don't want the village overrun with them all evening as well.'

'It'll be even worse if Toby—' Kayla blurts out but stops mid-sentence when she spots my expression. Arthur's comments on my cousin's plans are so not needed right now.

'The village wouldn't be overrun because we'd only be able to accommodate two couples at most,' I explain to him, but he shakes his head.

'No, no, no. It's a slippery slope, Annie, and what's next? Muggings on the cliffs, black masses at the church, raves on the beach?'

'We're talking about a small B&B in Salt Bay, Arthur mate. Not the fall of the Roman bleedin' Empire,' says Roger, puffing out his cheeks and making me grin.

'It's not a laughing matter,' huffs Arthur, pulling himself up straight. 'What experience do you have in the hospitality trade, anyway? You can't just sling people in your spare room and get them to muck in with the rest of you. There are rules and regulations to be followed and you'd need to observe other businesses and see how they do it.'

'Absolutely, Arthur. I'm thinking of staying in a B&B somewhere to get a feeling for it. Somewhere different but still by the sea. Maybe Southwold or Morecambe. Or Rhyl.'

Oh, I know I shouldn't and Kayla is looking at me as though I've lost my mind. But Arthur is seriously getting on my nerves with his litany of complaints before my B&B idea even gets off the ground. If people round here don't like the thought of a B&B in Salt Bay, heaven help Toby's holiday flats.

Arthur's eyes narrow when they meet mine, then he grabs hold of his long-suffering wife's hand. 'Come along, Fiona. Let's get a drink and sit outside so Pickles can have a run around.'

'Silly old fool can't bear change,' mutters Roger loudly as Arthur drags Pickles towards the bar. 'If he had his way, we'd still be sending kids up chimneys and using leeches to treat infections.'

'I guess he's got a point. Not about the leeches or the village being the wrong place for a B&B. But about me having no experience of this sort of thing. Josh and I might jump through all the hoops but still be awful at it.'

'Or you might hate having strangers in your home,' Kayla butts in. 'You wouldn't be able to walk about with your bits out after a bath. Though some guests might appreciate that kind of service.'

'We have to cover up anyway with Emily and Storm about.'

'Ooh, ooh, I know!' says Roger, his belly bouncing up and down when he does a little jig. 'What you need is a dry run and I might know just the thing. Hold on.' He lumbers behind the bar while I sip my lemonade and Kayla aims a surreptitious V-sign at Arthur's back.

'Here it is!' Roger has arrived back at our table, clutching a scrap of paper. 'I had a call from some French bloke a couple of days ago asking if I did B&B. When I said no, he insisted I take down his details and get back to him if I could think of anywhere nearby. He seemed very keen on staying in the village if possible. So why don't you put him up for a few days?' He waves the scrap of paper in my face. 'His name is Jack Boo-something. He spelled it out for me. He was quite a forceful bloke.'

The till receipt has 'Jacques Bouton' written in Roger's scrawl across the back, along with a phone number.

'But we're not a registered B&B yet.'

'Whatever,' says Kayla, with a dismissive wave of the hand. She leans forward, her green eyes bright with excitement. 'That is a surprisingly good idea from Roger. You can tell that Jackie bloke he can stay with you as long as he contributes towards the food which is, like, £50 per day.'

'Blimey, I'm not planning on feeding him foie gras.'

'Nah, you can just serve up your usual slop – oops, sorry. I didn't mean to be rude about your cooking. But it'll get around the whole charging him to stay thing.'

'I don't know. Having a stranger to stay would be a bit weird.'

Running a B&B seemed like a good idea – a helping hand out of our financial problems – but the nitty-gritty is suddenly hitting home. I'll need to share my beloved Tregavara House. With some random French bloke called Jacques. But it's better than selling up to treacherous Toby.

'Sunshine.' Kayla grabs my hands and swings me round to face her. 'The very nature of a B&B is that loads of strangers come to stay. It's really no different from when you took in Barry and Storm last year. You'd never met them before and they were freaking awful back then.'

Eek! I can't cope with guests like my father and half-sister, who caused chaos when they turned up announced just before last Christmas. I'd never met Barry until he arrived on my doorstep and I was clueless about Storm's existence. Getting rid of them was my sole aim, but now… now, I love having them in my life.

'What was this Jack bloke like?' Kayla asks Roger.

'I dunno. French. Good English. Bit bossy. Said he ran a bakery business.'

'There you go then,' says Kayla. 'He sounds just right to be your first guest so, Rog, you can ring Frenchie Jack back and, Annie, you can launch into your new career as a B&B-er. Simples.'

'OK. Let's give it a go.' I give a thumbs up and smile to show that I'm up for this latest adventure which is my last hope.

Kayla starts getting to her feet when Roger heads for the bar but I pull her back onto the window seat.

'You're not going anywhere until you tell me what the Lake District was like. We haven't had a chance to chat since you and Ollie got back and I want all the gossip.'

Kayla sniffs. 'It was all right, I s'pose. Lots of lakes and tea shops and appalling weather. I didn't know rain could hit you horizontally and it's hard to appreciate a view when you can't see further than your nose. And that's in the summer! If people up there have got any sense, they hibernate through the winter.'

'It can't have rained all the time so what did you do when it stopped?'

'Ollie made me climb up what the locals call a "fell" which turned out to be a freaking mountain. Halfway up, I thought I was gonna die. But the view from the top was pretty awesome. Do you want to see my photos?'

She shoves her phone in front of my face and starts scrolling through pictures. There are jagged peaks fading to grey in the distance, huge lakes surrounded by trees, and selfies of Kayla looking sweaty, puce and close to death.

'And this is Keswick, pronounced "Kezzick", where Ollie was looking at flats to rent.' She scrolls through multiple pics at high speed. 'It was quite a nice town actually and it has an actual pencil museum. Like, a proper museum that's all about pencils!'

'Hang on, backtrack a bit. Ollie was looking at flats to rent?'

'Yeah,' says Kayla, wrinkling her nose. 'But it's all part of his ruse to make me think he's adventurous and about to leave his beloved Cornwall.'

'Or it's not a ruse, he really is moving to the Lake District in October and you're in denial.'

Kayla shakes her head but starts scratching her neck which is what she does when she's anxious.

'So let's say for the sake of argument that Ollie definitely *is* leaving' – I hold up my hand when Kayla goes to speak – 'and he's going to be five hundred miles away. Are you going with him or staying here?'

Kayla keeps on scratching at her reddening skin. 'I don't know, Annie. Tell me what to do. Would you miss me?'

And suddenly it hits me just how much I will miss Kayla if she leaves Salt Bay. She took me under her wing and made the village bearable when I first arrived from London, feeling angry and lost. And though we're different in lots of ways, she still helps make life bearable when people like Toby disappoint me – or I disappoint myself.

'Of course I'd miss you horribly.' I take a deep breath. 'But this isn't about me and you've been talking about moving on somewhere else ever since I've known you. So why are you holding back?'

'Because if I follow Ollie up North it'll send all the wrong signals, like I'm totally committed to him and then he'll start talking about getting married again and, before I know it, I'll be just like the Smug Marrieds – hitched, pregnant and terminally boring.'

'Is this what all the angst is about? You're worried you'll end up like your sisters?'

Kayla nods, red curls tumbling around her face. 'They say I'm missing out 'cos I'm not married to some tedious accountant with two-point-four children and a pointless career. But they're so scared of life they've never been outside Australia yet they still look down on me and think I'm weird 'cos I want to travel and be free. They're just narrow-minded and provincial and… and…'

'Smug?'

'Yeah, hideously smug. And I'm never going to be like them,' she declares, folding her arms and pulling her mouth into a pout.

Oh, where do I start? I rest my head in my hands for a few moments, not sure how best to unpick the tangle Kayla's got herself into. It seems we're not so different after all – I can't wait to marry Josh and she can't bear the thought of matrimony but we're both great at getting ourselves into a muddle.

'You're so different from your sisters, Kayla, that you'll never be like them whatever you do. So if you don't want to leave Cornwall with Ollie, that's fine – plenty of people have long-distance relationships and some of them even work. Look at Prince Harry and Meghan.'

'Who have loads of cash to spend on transatlantic travel and don't work for a slave driver like Roger.'

'True. But I'm sure you could both make it work if you wanted to. Just make sure if you stay in Salt Bay that it's for the right reasons and not because you're a wuss when it comes to commitment. Ollie's a lovely bloke and moving to the Lake District would be an adventure.'

'Not so much an adventure as a cold and rainy challenge,' mutters Kayla. 'And I don't appreciate Ollie putting me under pressure.'

'All he's doing is taking up the chance of promotion in the Lake District and he'd like you to go with him. The only person piling on the pressure and making it any more than that is you, you eejit.'

'Kayla!' bellows Roger across the packed pub. 'There's people here who need serving if you've finished your little chinwag.'

'Duty calls,' she sighs, getting to her feet. 'Thanks for the chat, Annie.'

Kayla wanders off towards the bar, deep in thought, as I realise I'm a prat. Kayla's the woman who keeps me sane when Storm's kicking off and Barry is being… Barry-like, and here I am persuading her to move away.

But friendship is wanting each other to be happy – and Ollie makes her happy, even if she's too pigheaded to recognise it. Salt Bay won't be the same without her but nothing stays the same forever. However much we might want it to.

Josh is surprised by the news that we're having a Frenchman to stay but remarkably unfazed by my bombshell about Toby.

'Lying to us and planning on carving the house up into flats is typical Toby. I knew his proposal was too good to be true,' he says, hitting his stapler extra hard with the heel of his hand. He's photocopied some musical scores for the choir and is fixing the sheets together.

'But I feel so stupid for believing him.'

'Did you really believe him, though, deep down? You must have had some niggles to come up with the idea of running a B&B.'

'Maybe I wasn't sure about him letting us stay on in the house but I never thought he'd start ripping out walls and changing the whole character of the place. You're right. I am horribly gullible.'

Josh stops stapling and pushes the music scores to one side. 'Don't be too hard on yourself, Annie. It's Toby who's at fault here, not you.'

I sigh, unwilling to let myself off the hook because disappointment is coursing through me. Disappointment in my cousin for turning out to be the weasel Josh said he was. And disappointment in myself for letting Alice down. How could I have ever considered letting the house fall into Toby's avaricious clutches?

'What upsets me the most is that he'd like to knock this place down.'

'You're kidding me.' Josh's composure is starting to slip. 'He wants to knock it down? Converting into flats is one thing but wanting to bulldoze this house when he knows what it meant to Alice and how much it means to you is downright cruel.'

'He wouldn't get permission to knock it down, but he made enquiries about it.'

'Unbelievable! Just when you think Toby Trebarwith has scraped the bottom of the barrel, he sinks even lower.'

The muscles in Josh's jaw have tightened and I see a flash of the man I first met early last year. Back when he was angry and resentful and stressed out by the demands of looking after his family. Before we fell in love and brought out the best in each other.

'I'm going to ring him,' he announces, standing up so quickly that pieces of photocopied paper flutter to the kitchen floor. He marches into the sitting room with me scurrying after him and starts flicking through Alice's address book, which gives me my chance.

I position myself between him and the landline because, though the situation is bad now, it could become catastrophic if Josh rings Toby in a temper. The two have made peace for the sake of Freya and she'll suffer if their whole hating-each-other thing kicks off again.

'Please don't ring him.'

Spreading my arms wide, I shuffle backwards towards the phone feeling faintly ridiculous. I'm not on a protest march or protecting royalty. I'm simply asking my fiancé not to call my awful cousin. So quite why I'm adopting this position is beyond me.

However, it does the trick. Josh frowns – or it might be a suppressed smile; I'm not sure. But he puts the book down on top of the bookcase and folds his arms.

'Why shouldn't I ring him?'

'Because it wouldn't make anything better.'

'It'd make me feel better,' says Josh, dark eyes flashing.

'Which is exactly why you shouldn't call him. But we won't ever sell the house to him.'

'Hang on. Are you saying that you'd sell to someone else instead?'

'No, I'm definitely not saying that.'

'So you won't sell to Toby and you won't sell to anyone else and the roof needs a thirty grand makeover that we haven't got.' Josh sighs and rubs his eyebrows with the heels of his hands. 'Can you see that's not going to work, Annie?'

I want to yell: *Of course I can because I'm not an idiot but selling this house wouldn't work for Alice and it doesn't work for me.* And then fall into Josh's arms and snivel into his polo shirt while he rocks me like a baby.

But I don't because that won't help in the long run and there's one last hope for the Trebarwith ancestral home – a Frenchman who sells croissants for a living.

'Will it be all right if Monsieur Bouton comes to stay and we see how that goes?'

Josh shrugs. 'And if it doesn't work, will you give serious consideration to selling to Toby? He's got the money to replace the roof and, if the house is split into flats, at least it'll still be standing – now he knows he can't knock it down. Honestly' – he scrunches up his nose as if he's just sniffed a dead rat – 'what a moron.'

When I nod, Josh says: 'We'll push ahead with the B&B option and hope it works, seeing as Toby's living up to my expectations.'

Then he picks up the scattered music on the kitchen floor and staples the sheets with such force, I'm worried he's going to punch a hole through the table.

Chapter Seventeen

Cooking lunch, shovelling clothes into the washing machine and scrubbing the bathroom until it's gleaming helps to work off my agitation. And by the time I've washed up our plates and the omelette pan, I'm feeling more confident that our B&B plan might work. Knackered too, but exhaustion is a price worth paying for calm and clarity.

Josh disappeared straight after lunch and I find him in the garden, digging the hell out of the vegetable patch. He's so busy he doesn't spot me and I sit for a while on the bench where I used to sit and chat with Alice.

It's lovely watching Josh work out his frustration. He's taken his shirt off and the muscles in his lightly tanned back ripple and glisten under the sun. I'm starting to feel rather hot myself when Storm and Emily wander into the garden and plonk themselves down either side of me. It's quite sweet that they're spending so much time together these days – especially as they hated each other at first. Back then, they were chalk and cheese: sweet, naïve Emily with her old-lady fashion sense and bolshie, streetwise Storm with her bellybutton ring. But they've forged a firm friendship.

'Isn't it a bit hot to be digging, even if you are half naked – which is totally inappropriate?' Storm shields her eyes against the glare of the sun. 'Mate,' she calls out, 'do us all a favour and put a top on!'

Josh ignores her but pauses briefly to wipe his damp fringe out of his eyes.

'Don't blame me if he gives himself a coronary at his age. Or if a photo of his chest mysteriously appears on the school Facebook page,' huffs Storm, pulling her phone from her jeans pocket. There's a huge expanse of skin above the waistband because her tiny black crop-top finishes just under her boobs. 'What's he in a mood about anyway?'

'Nothing. He's fine. Actually, it's good you're both here because I wanted to run something by you.' I take a deep breath. 'We're thinking of running this place as a B&B and we might have a bloke called Jacques Bouton staying with us for a few days as a try-out, to see if it might work.'

'That's a weird name,' says Storm, snapping photos of Josh.

'He's from Paris.'

'So let me get this straight. Some random bloke from Paris is going to be sleeping here. Some random bloke who'll probably go mad in the night and slaughter us in our beds.'

'Monsieur Bouton is actually the chief executive of a bakery business who's visiting Cornwall on holiday for a few days. So, unless he's going to batter us to death with croissants, I think we'll be all right.'

'That's outrageous! You go full-on mental about me eating too many burgers but you're happy to let some weirdo you've never met before sleep next to my bedroom.'

Storm's mouth sets into a thin line and my heart sinks. I know that look, and if Storm launches into full passive-aggressive mode while our guest is staying it'll be a disaster. He'll return to la belle France deafened by all the door slamming.

'Look, Storm, we have no choice. This is something we have to try.'

'Is that 'cos you're having trouble keeping this house going?'

I give Storm a sideways glance. She's usually teenage-oblivious to anything that doesn't directly affect her. Although I guess losing the roof over your head is pretty much the definition of 'directly affected'.

When I don't answer, she shrugs. 'I do hear what you and Josh are saying, even when you think you're being all secretive, and roof tiles trying to smash my head in is a bit of a giveaway that this house is falling down. You could have told me. How much will the roof cost anyway?'

'A lot.'

'How much is a lot?'

'A new roof will cost about thirty thousand pounds.'

'That roofer bloke's having a laugh,' splutters Storm while, beside her, Emily rapidly blinks her pale blue eyes. 'That's it then. We'll have to leave and I'll end up back in London where I'll probably die in a crack den and get eaten by rats.'

I can't help but laugh at the look of horror on Emily's face.

'No one's going back to London. If we move, we move together but hopefully it won't come to that. The roof's fine for the time being and the B&B idea might work and bring in some money to keep us afloat.'

'Do you want me to move out?' blurts Emily, long mousey-brown hair falling across her pale face. 'I'm a dead-weight now Alice's gone and I'm hardly bringing in any money from temping. I'll totally understand if you want me to go.'

'Of course we don't want you to go, Emily, and Alice didn't want that either which is why she specifically mentioned you in her will. You'll have a home with us for as long as you want it.'

'That was so sweet of Alice.' Emily wipes away the tear that's sliding down her cheek. 'But you don't have to stick by it now she's gone. After all, I'm not real family.'

'What's real family anyway? Growing up it was just me and Mum and now my family's grown to include Josh and the people he loves and Barry and Storm and you, and Toby too, for better or worse. Anyway, I was thinking you could head up the B&B business if it comes off.'

'What, me?' Emily checks behind her in case some stranger with a shedload of hospitality qualifications has wandered in off the street. 'You mean me, running things?'

'Yes, you, if you'd like to. You're caring and organised and a good cook, and I think you'd be great at it. Though it's just a plan at the moment and might never happen so don't get too excited.'

'Wow!' When Emily smiles, her eyes sparkle with unshed tears. 'That sounds brilliant and I'd try really hard to do a good job. You're so much nicer to me than my proper family and I really don't want to move out.'

'You won't need to move out and, Storm, you'll always have a home here too as long as we do all we can to keep things going. Which means…'

'Yeah, yeah… letting random men into the house.'

'And being polite to said random men.'

'Whatever. Come on, Ems. I'll give you a lesson on using eyeliner 'cos the last time you tried it you looked like a panda.'

'I don't need to use eyeliner now I'm off men.'

Storm sighs and shakes her head. 'You still have so much to learn, Emily. Using eyeliner isn't about attracting men. It goes deeper than that. It's about enhancing what nature gave you and feeding your soul. It's about your self-esteem and self-worth.'

Emily frowns, unconvinced by Storm's cod psychology when it comes to make-up, but she allows herself to be led towards the house.

'Hey, Storm,' I call after them. 'Those photos had better not appear anywhere online.'

'Whatever,' drifts across the garden as the girls disappear into the kitchen.

Josh winks at me, his bad mood eased by hard labour, but my own mood is dipping fast. Placing my hand on the sun-warmed bench where Alice used to sit, I look past the cliffs and towards the harbour wall, which is glistening with spray at high tide.

A young woman in a tight scarlet sundress, who's standing looking out to sea, grabs the hands of her young family so they won't slip. And even though she's a size eight with honey-blonde hair and two perfect children, I realise that we have a lot in common. We're both doing what we can to protect the people we love.

My life has come full circle. As a child, I was the grown-up because Mum needed looking after. Then I fended for myself as an adult in London which was fine – it was all I'd ever known. But all that changed when I came to Salt Bay and met Alice, who cared for me while I watched over her. I relaxed and stopped feeling responsible for everything all the damn time. But now the weight of responsibility is back, even with Josh here to support me.

Closing my eyes, I listen to water lapping against stone and reflect on the fact that this being grown-up thing is a bit pants.

Later that evening I behave in a way that isn't grown-up at all. In fact it's probably downright childish but I need to hear what Toby has to say for himself and tell him what I think of his plans for our home. So I walk to the phone box on the green with Toby's number in my pocket.

This makes me a hideous hypocrite, I know, because I stopped Josh from calling him. But the difference is I'm not going to lose my temper and inflame the situation. Oh no. I intend to be as cool as a cucumber.

My plan starts going awry from the moment Toby answers the phone.

'Ann-ee!' he coos down the line as though I've suddenly become his BFF. 'How lovely to hear from you. I presume you're ringing to accept my very generous offer?'

But he drops the charm like a hot brick when he hears that's not why I'm ringing at all.

'You want to talk about something else? What else is there to talk about?' he snaps. 'I've got a cab arriving any minute so you'd better be quick. I don't want to pay for someone to sit outside my flat.'

'I was hoping to have a word about your plans for the house.'

'I was under the impression you and Pasco wanted to stay on in the house after I've bought it and paid out a significant sum for a new roof.'

'We'd love to stay on, but I understand you're planning on carving up the house into holiday flats.' Silence. 'Toby, are you still there?'

There's more empty space down the phone line before Toby answers, speaking slowly as though carefully choosing each word.

'"Carving" is rather an emotive word, don't you think? I'd rather use "transforming" or "improving" or even "enhancing". And how the hell did you hear about my plans anyway?'

'That doesn't matter. What does matter is, one, you lied to us to encourage us to sell to you and, two, Alice would hate you damaging the house.'

Oops, my resolve to be a beacon of serenity in the face of Toby playing hard and fast with the truth is starting to slip.

'There you go again using emotive words like "lie" and "damage".' Toby laughs as though I'm a silly child wasting his time, which really doesn't help my self-control. 'Here I am, offering you a good price and the house will still belong to a Trebarwith which seems to be important to you.'

'But you'd knock the house down if you could.'

'But I can't so what's the problem? Are you being hysterical because you're trying to say you won't sell me the house?'

Ugh. Falsely accusing a woman of hysteria is the last refuge of a patronising prat. Clenching my teeth, I rest my forehead against the cool glass of the telephone box and force myself to focus on the clear, soothing water of the river. I wish I was floating down to the sea and onwards towards the horizon.

'Annie?' Toby's tinny voice sounds in my ear. 'I said are you saying you won't ever sell to me?'

That's what I want to say, more than anything, but Josh's face pops into my head. His tired, stressed, sensible face when he's trying to make ends meet and do the best for all of us.

'No,' I sigh. 'All I'm saying is that we haven't made up our minds yet.'

'Then you need to get on with it because my offer won't be on the table forever. And my car's here so I have to go. We'll speak again soon and I'm sure you'll make the right decision if you stop overreacting. At the end of the day' – Toby gives a short laugh just before ending the call – 'it's only a house.'

I place the phone back into its cradle, step outside the box and take several gulps of clean, fresh air – because talking to Toby always leaves me feeling slightly grubby. Toby's final words are still ringing in my head because they sum up the problem perfectly. To Toby, it's only a house whereas to me and Josh and Storm and Emily, it's a home.

Chapter Eighteen

Monsieur Jacques Bouton arrives at Tregavara House early on Monday morning in a flash rented Mercedes that he parks outside the garden gate. As I peek from behind the sitting room curtains, he takes a smart leather case from the boot, sucks in a deep breath of salty air and strides confidently up the path.

At the door, he pauses for a moment and gazes at the sea before rapping on the brass knocker. Eek! Operation B&B, or 'Operation Axeman' as Storm's taken to calling it, has begun.

'*Bonjour Monsieur Bouton. Je m'appelle Annie et vous êtes bienvenu ici,*' I say in my best remembered French accent on opening the front door. Greeting him in his own language seems polite but fingers crossed he won't reply in rapid-fire French or I'm screwed.

'Thank you, and please call me Jacques,' he says in almost accent-less English. Phew! I hesitate in the doorway, not sure if he's going to kiss me on both cheeks, but he steps past me into the hall and puts his suitcase down onto the flagstones. He's older than I expected – maybe early sixties – with a shock of steel-grey hair above a handsome, tanned face.

'It's very good of you to accommodate me at short notice in your charming seaside home.' He waves his arm around the hallway. 'You are planning to open a small hotel, yes?'

'Well, more a bed and breakfast than a hotel.'

'Ah yes, Rupert at the public house explained it to me.'

I assume he means Roger but I don't correct him. 'Rupert' brings to mind a huge cuddly bear, which is actually quite a lot like Roger if you ignore the cuddly bit.

'We haven't actually opened as a B&B yet so it's very good of you to be our guinea pig.' I smile and nod but Jacques frowns.

'A pig?'

'No, I'm not saying you're a pig. Not at all. It's an English saying…' I trail off. 'Would you like me to show you to your room?'

'I think that might be for the best.' Jacques picks up his luggage, still looking puzzled, as I make a mental note to keep colloquialisms to a minimum.

Tregavara House has been cleaned to within an inch of its life. The weekend has been a bonanza of dusting, vacuuming and scraping mouldy bits off bathroom grouting. But when Jacques pads behind me up the stairs, I spot scuffs in the paintwork and a dark stain on the carpet – things I never normally notice but today they stand out. And from the look of Monsieur Bouton, he's used to the very best.

I'm a bit nervous about showing him upstairs but he gives a brief nod of approval at the stained-glass window on the landing that's throwing streaks of vibrant red and blue across the carpet. And there's a grunt of satisfaction when I show him the bathroom. It is looking pretty good – Storm's towels have been picked up, Barry's manky spare toothbrush swept into a drawer, and the pretty basin – with blue forget-me-nots picked out across the enamel – is gleaming. Jacques seems particularly taken with the Victorian claw-footed bath that was my great-grandmother's pride and joy.

But I hesitate when we come to Alice's room because it doesn't seem right bringing a stranger in here. Reminding myself that we're doing this to save the house, I take a deep breath and push open the heavy oak door.

'Jacques, this is your room.'

'But this is charming,' exclaims Jacques, dropping his case on Alice's bed before wandering over to the stone-framed window and peering out. 'And you are spoiling me with such a magnificent view of the cliffs and the sea.'

'The view is wonderful. Alice loved this room.'

'Alice?'

'My great-aunt who lived here most of her life until she died recently. She didn't die in this room,' I add quickly in case Monsieur Bouton has a thing about ghosts.

A furrow appears between Jacques' eyebrows. 'My condolences. Losing a loved one is difficult.'

'Have you lost someone?'

Way to go, Annie! Cross-examining a guest before he's even unpacked. 'I'm… I'm so sorry,' I stutter, 'I don't mean to pry.'

Jacques turns his back to the window and regards me coolly. The light behind him catches his hair and silver streaks shine amongst the grey.

'I lost my wife a while ago.'

He brushes off my condolences with a very Gallic shrug, moves back to the bed and runs his hand across the pillows while I force myself to smile. A strange man will be sleeping under Alice's covers but this is the best room in the house and my practical great-aunt would want it to be used. So it's for the best even though clearing out her possessions was the worst thing ever. Her dresses, books and ornaments are now piled up in my bedroom while we decide what to do with them.

'What made you choose Salt Bay, Monsieur… Jacques?'

'This and that. I have heard a lot about it and thought it was time to visit. Would you give me a tour of the village?'

I nod, taken by surprise. I hadn't reckoned on being a tour guide too. 'Of course, though it won't take long. Salt Bay is slightly smaller than Paris.'

Jacques ignores my pathetic attempt at humour and clicks open the shiny clasps on his suitcase. Inside there are piles of carefully folded clothes and a brown leather washbag with JB monogrammed in gold lettering. He pulls out a pale blue shirt and starts smoothing it across the rose-pink counterpane.

'If it's not too much trouble, do you think I could have a cup of coffee?'

'Of course, straight away,' I bluster, feeling caught out that I haven't already offered him a drink. Some B&B host I am!

By the time I bring up a cafetière on a tray – with a jug of milk, a bowl of sugar lumps plus ancient silver sugar tongs I found in a drawer – Jacques' clothes are hanging neatly in the wardrobe and the case has been pushed under the bed so only its wheels are showing.

He thanks me when I place the tray on the bedside table and I fight the urge to bow and shuffle backwards out of the door, *Downton Abbey*-style. Storm is right. Having a random bloke in the house, in Alice's bedroom, is weird.

Ten minutes later, Jacques comes downstairs carrying the tray and finds me waiting in the hallway. It's probably odd to wait in the hallway like I'm the local retainer or something but I can't settle to anything else.

'Shall we go for our walk?' he asks. 'I would enjoy some fresh air.'

He's just handed me the tray when the front door opens and in bowls Storm. She's wearing the clumpy Doc Martens bought with money from her mum that she insists on wearing whatever the weather.

'Penzance was rammed with tourists stinking of sun cream and—' she stops when she catches sight of Jacques and gives him a very obvious once-over.

'This is my sister, Storm, who lives here with me,' I say, hardly daring to breathe. 'And this is Monsieur Bouton – Jacques – who's staying here for a few days as we discussed.'

Storms glances at me before wiping her hand down her jeans and thrusting it towards our visitor. 'How do you do?' she says in a very posh voice.

Blimey, it's a miracle – though I've got a horrible feeling she's taking the mick. Jacques takes hold of her hand while I send up a silent prayer that he won't kiss it. Or her. If he goes in for a cheek-kiss this time we're in big trouble. But Jacques merely gives her hand a brief shake. 'It's good to meet you. I have not heard the name Storm before.'

'Huh,' Storm sighs and contemplates the name she hates. 'That's probably 'cos it's so sh—' She checks herself and smiles. 'It is rather unusual, yes. Now if you'd please excuse me I have shopping to put away.'

She brushes past Jacques and gives me a grin. 'Good to see you've got the best china out,' she mutters, before nodding at the sugar tongs and smirking. 'Fancy!'

'What a charming young lady.' Jacques holds the front door wide open so I can go out ahead of him. 'I think I'm going to like Salt Bay.'

'Charming' appears to be Jacques' favourite word. The church and its squat tower are charming, as is the village green with its intricate metal lamp post, and the view across the village from the rising fields that edge it. He doesn't know the English word for 'valley' but I don't know the French word for it either, so fair dues.

During our walk, he tells me he's about to retire from the bakery business he set up more than thirty years ago. I assumed he had a boulangerie or two in a Parisian suburb but it turns out that Monsieur Bouton is a big French cheese who runs loads of top-end pâtisseries in the city. He's obviously loaded so quite why he's opted to stay with us is a mystery and what on earth will he make of our shabby-chic house? A man like him must frequent five star hotels in swishy French resorts and he's already name-dropped his friend François Hollande.

'So you've never been to Salt Bay before then?' I ask, steering him through the low door of the Whistling Wave.

'Never. Actually, I have never been to Cornwall but I've heard it's beautiful and that's true.'

He ducks to avoid bashing his head on the beam above the doorway and follows me to the bar, cooing appreciatively at the thick bumpy walls and worn flagstone floors.

'So this must be Rupert.'

He nods at Roger, who's pulling a pint. There's sweat on his brow and he wipes his beefy arm across his forehead before lumbering over.

'It's Roger, mate. And you must be the French bloke. Good to meet you.' He holds out his sweaty hand and I catch the slightest of shudders from Jacques before he gives it the limpest of shakes.

'Is Annie looking after you then? She's taken the week off work specially to settle you in.'

'She is very hospitable,' says Jacques, leaning across the bar to inspect the gleaming beer taps.

'What would you like to drink?' I ask, pulling out my purse. I'm desperate for our B&B venture to succeed and if that requires bribing the guests with alcohol, so be it.

'That's very kind but do allow me to buy you a drink, Annie,' says my guest, who's pretty damn charming himself, especially when he says my name with a slight French accent – *Annee*. 'I will have a pint of that one please, Rupert.'

He indicates the St Austell's Tribute tap and Roger is halfway through pulling the pint when he glances over my shoulder and nods at someone behind me.

'Is it that time already? Be with you in just a minute so don't get arsey about waiting.'

'There's no need to be crude, Roger,' says a familiar voice. I turn and grin at Jennifer, who closes her newsagents at one o'clock on the dot every day and has an orange juice and sandwich in the pub before heading back for the afternoon shift.

'Jennifer, can I introduce you to our guest who's staying with us at Tregavara House for a few days.'

'It's good to meet you,' says Jennifer, patting her blonde back-combed hair. She gives a welcoming smile but her face freezes in a rictus grin when Jacques turns around.

'Bonjour, *Jennee*,' murmurs my guest quietly. '*Il est merveilleux de te revoir.*'

Jennifer's mouth drops open and then snaps shut as a flush rises across her cheeks. Roger has stopped concentrating on the pint he's pulling and liquid starts flowing over the top of the glass and slopping down his legs.

'Hell's teeth,' he grumbles, grabbing a cloth and mopping his knees. 'These were clean on today.'

But no one cares about his drenched trousers. Everyone in the pub is staring at Jennifer, who turns on her heel without a word and flees. What on earth is going on? Roger slams the pint down in front of Jacques and makes no attempt to wipe the glass clean when creamy froth trickles down the outside and pools on the polished-wood bar. Then he glares at me as though it's my fault that Monsieur Bouton has come to Salt Bay.

Jacques picks up his slippery pint without a word and carries it to a table near the blackened stone fireplace.

'What the hell was that all about?' demands Roger, pouring me a lemonade. 'I can't be doing with outsiders upsetting the locals. Jennifer can be tricky at times and she's got a mouth on her but she's a good woman and a Salt Bay stalwart.'

'I have absolutely no idea what's going on.' I fish about in my purse for a fiver because Jacques' offer to buy me a drink has been forgotten in the kerfuffle.

When I take a seat opposite Jacques, he carries on studying his pint with his head bent.

'Um, have you met Jennifer before then?'

'Yes, but it was a long time ago.'

Jacques sips his beer in silence after that and I don't feel able to pry although I'm desperately curious. Thank goodness Kayla's not working today or he'd be getting the third degree.

After downing half the frothy pint, Jacques suddenly scrapes his chair back across the flagstones and rises to his feet. 'Thank you for the tour but I must go back to your house because I have work to do.'

'If you need to be online, you'll be better off working in here where there's decent Wi-Fi. I'm sure Roger won't mind.'

I glance at Roger, who's glaring at Jacques with a face like thunder.

'That's a good idea but I have a financial report to complete which will not necessitate usage of the Internet.' Blimey, his English is brilliant! 'Perhaps you would be good enough to escort me home and allow me to use your dining room table.'

There's no sign of Jennifer when we come out of the pub and I take Jacques the long way home so we avoid walking past her shop. That'll lessen the risk of her spotting us and going all weird again.

Mind you, Jacques is being plenty weird enough on his own. He walks along beside me, making polite conversation as though nothing has happened and even starts telling jokes. They're not very good – the humour presumably lost in translation – but I laugh politely and wonder how long he's planning on staying. All I wanted was to try out our B&B idea, to see if it might work and help us to save Tregavara House. It sounded so simple, but it seems our first ever guest isn't quite all he seems.

Chapter Nineteen

The next morning I'm due to drive Storm to the station first thing so Emily is on breakfast duty. It's all arranged that Storm will spend a week with her mum and half-sisters in London and she spent yesterday evening packing. But ten minutes before we're supposed to be leaving, she stomps into the kitchen without her suitcase.

'Are you ready to go?' asks Emily as she slides a stack of pancakes into the Aga to keep warm. She's taking breakfast duty very seriously and Jacques will have a mini-feast awaiting him when he appears.

'Not going,' grumps Storm, dropping onto a chair and yanking petals off the wild flowers Emily's arranged in a vase on the table.

'Why not?'

Emily moves the flowers out of Storm's reach and brushes purple petals off the table into her hand.

'My mother rang on the landline a few minutes ago and said Perfect Pia's argued with her boyfriend and come back early from her holiday so there's no room for me.'

'Who's Perfect Pia?' I ask, shoving my car keys into my jeans pocket.

'Their perfectly stupid au pair from Croatia or Slovenia or somewhere. I sleep in her room while she's away and the walls are covered in Peter Andre posters.'

'Can't you sleep on the sofa so you can still go?'

Storm's been moaning non-stop about spending time with her half-sisters Poppy and Eugenie but it's all for show. I know she was looking forward to seeing her mother today. She hasn't seen her in weeks.

'I said I was used to sofa-surfing but Amanda told me their sofa is handmade in Italy and very precious so not for sleeping on. She thinks, or rather Simple Simon thinks, I'll drool over it in my sleep.'

I'd have thought a daughter was rather more precious than a piece of furniture but I hold my tongue. 'Mum' has become 'Amanda' so Storm must be very upset indeed.

'Could you go next week instead?' says Emily, putting a plate of bacon, egg and beans in front of Storm, who never says no to a full English.

'They're going to their villa in Tuscany for a fortnight.'

'You can go with them then. That'll be amazing.'

'No room.' Storm pushes a rasher of crispy bacon around her plate. 'They're going with some poncey friends and can't take me too. I won't fit in apparently.'

Whether she won't fit in the villa or fit in with Amanda's posh friends, she doesn't say. And it doesn't really matter because, either way, it hurts.

'But I didn't want to go to sad London or Tuscany anyway so it's not a problem,' says Storm, standing up so quickly her chair falls backwards onto the kitchen tiles. Without stopping to pick it up, she runs into the hallway and we hear the front door slam shut behind her.

'That is totally out of order,' huffs Emily, dropping a pan into the deep enamel sink. 'My mum's a pain sometimes but at least she's always pleased to see me.'

Steam curls up from the sink towards the ceiling as I pick up the chair and push it back under the table. Poor old Storm. Having a dysfunctional family sucks but at least when my mum was absent it was because she was ill and stuck in her own head, rather than living miles away with some toffee-nosed banker in Richmond.

Absent-mindedly, I spear the bacon on Storm's abandoned plate with a fork, dip the rasher into her runny egg yolk and take a bite. It's cooked to perfection but my head is filled with Storm's problems and I hardly taste it.

'You'd better go and talk to her, Annie, because she'll listen to you. Ooh, here he is.'

Emily plasters on a smile when the door opens and Jacques steps into the kitchen. He's wearing smart grey cord trousers today and a white polo shirt with a discreet gold logo that I don't recognise.

'Good morning, Jacques. Did you sleep well?' asks Emily, dipping slightly like she's curtseying.

'As you say, like a topping,' smiles Jacques, making a rare faux pas with his English.

'And did you enjoy your evening?' Jacques drove into Penzance late afternoon after finishing his report and didn't return until bedtime.

'I did, thank you. I looked around the town and found a pleasant restaurant for my evening meal. Though I would have eaten less If I'd known what you would serve me for breakfast.' He nods at the food mountain that Emily's currently building on his plate and smiles. 'This looks delicious – a traditional English breakfast.'

Emily blushes with pleasure and piles another rasher onto Jacques' loaded plate, determined to kill our B&B guests with kindness and cook away our profits.

Jacques takes a seat at the table and tucks his serviette into the neck of his shirt to catch egg drips. 'I saw Storm leaving the house and she looked a little upset.'

Eek! Rule number one of running a successful B&B business must surely be: *Never involve your guests in family traumas.*

'She's fine,' I assure him, 'though I really ought to go and find her if you're OK here with Emily?'

Jacques nods with his mouth full of baked beans as Emily stands over him with a plate of toast in one hand and a pan of scrambled egg in the other.

Leaving Jacques with Cornwall's answer to Mary Berry, I rush along the garden path but hesitate when I reach the gate. Where has Storm gone? She doesn't 'get' exercise so won't have taken the cliff path but she might have headed for the Whistling Wave's Wi-Fi to slag off her mum on social media. Or maybe she's gone to see Jennifer. The two of them have struck up an unlikely friendship since Storm started working for her – the fifty-something shopkeeper and the stroppy teenager. It's hardly a match made in heaven but it seems to work.

Ah! I suddenly realise where Storm will be.

After fastening the latch on the gate, I wander towards the harbour where Storm can often be found stroking the stray black cat that stretches out on the sand at low tide. Like me, she finds solace in this gorgeous part of the village where the land disappears and the ocean goes on forever.

I spot Storm straight away, sitting on the harbour wall dangling her legs towards the lapping waves. The sea is grey today and mirrors high grey cloud that's blocking the sun but will have burned away by mid-morning.

Storm continues gazing across the water as I get closer and doesn't move when I sit next to her on the cold stone. Ahead of us, seagulls are bobbing about on the waves and brightly coloured boats are specks on the horizon.

'I'm really sorry you're not off to London later.'

'Why, do you want me out of the house while Jacques is around?'

'You know that's not what I mean.'

Storm shrugs, eyes still fixed on the undulating sea. 'It's not really London anyway because there's too much countryside.'

She's such a city snob when it comes to Richmond, which lies on the very south-western edge of the capital.

'Richmond definitely has far too much fresh air,' I agree, taking a deep breath of a salty Cornish breeze. 'I guess it's difficult for your mum if Pia's come home earlier than expected.'

Storm's head whips round. 'Are you taking Amanda's side?'

'No, I'm just trying to make you feel better.'

'Well, you're doing a rubbish job and there's no need 'cos I'm fine.'

The muscles in her jaw have tightened so much, her mouth is hardly moving. She's very much like Josh when trying to suppress emotion and it breaks my heart. Josh is coming out of his shell now, thanks to lots of encouragement from me, and Storm is too – or at least she was until the mother who abandoned her dropped this latest bombshell.

We both sit in silence while a grey seal swims into the harbour. Its sleek grey head bobs above the water as it watches two humans drumming their heels against the wall.

After a minute or two, Storm pulls up her feet and tucks her legs under her. 'I know your mum was a bit' – she pauses – 'different, but she cared about you, didn't she?'

'She cared about me and for me as much as she could in the circumstances, when she wasn't too unwell.'

'Yeah, I know she was a bit mad.' Storm catches my eye and a flush spreads across her cheeks. 'Mentally ill. Sorry. But at least she never ran off with a dickhead and left you on your own.'

'But you weren't on your own. You had Barry.' When Storm winces, I have to laugh. 'OK, that's probably not the best thing to say but it's true and Barry might be hopeless at times but he does love you.'

It's the first time I've used the L-word when talking about our father and Storm's lower lip wobbles. 'I s'pose he does though he's away most of the time now with his new band.'

'They're going to be famous, don't you know.'

'Of course they are. Especially now his song's being played on the radio.' Storm snorts and wipes her nose up and down her sleeve until I pass her a tissue.

'He was still going on about that song when he rang last week to see how we were all doing.'

'That's 'cos he's like totally deluded. A couple of years ago he reckoned Robbie Williams was copying him when he wore leather trousers on telly just after Barry saw him on the King's Road. Like one of the most famous pop stars in the world is going to take fashion tips from a washed-up wannabe he spots in the street. But at least Barry likes seeing me.'

She scrubs at her eyes and rests against me when I snake my arm around her shoulders. Poor old Storm. It's bad enough being a hormonal teenager without the double whammy of feeling unwanted as well. At the moment, I'm doing a better job of being her mum than Amanda is – and I haven't got a freaking clue.

When Storm mumbles something into my shoulder, I bend my head towards hers. 'What did you say?'

'I said you won't leave me, will you?'

My heart melts and I hug my awkward, difficult sister tight. 'Nah, I'm afraid you're stuck with me and Josh.'

'And I won't have to leave this daft village either. Promise me.'

'I promise that I'll do my very best,' I say, feeling the ton-weight of responsibility that's sitting on my head get a little heavier.

'Good.' Storm relaxes into me and we sit like that for a while, gazing across the ever-changing sea while seagulls screech overhead. Sisters united against the big scary world outside Salt Bay.

Chapter Twenty

After persuading Storm to visit Josh's sister Serena – the thought of her moping about all day is unbearable – I head into the village because there's something else to sort out. Our mysterious visitor had a strange effect on Jennifer yesterday and I want to check she's OK.

I'm also eaten up with curiosity and imagining all kinds of unlikely Jennifer-Jacques scenarios. But mostly I'm feeling a tad responsible for the upset seeing as Jacques is staying with us. The last thing I want is to introduce problems and instability to this wonderful village that's given me a new life.

Jennifer glances up when the bell above her shop door pings but goes back to arranging magazines on the shelf above the newspapers.

'The delivery van got stuck in a traffic jam on the A30 so it was late again this morning. Flaming emmets! They turn Cornwall into a car park every summer.'

'They also buy an indecent amount of ice cream from your shop so it's not all bad.'

'Huh,' harrumphs Jennifer, popping *Cornwall Life* in pride of place at the front of the shelf. She slowly gets up off her knees and stretches out her back. 'You're on your own then.'

'Yeah, just me. Josh is teaching summer school, Storm's in Trecald-with with Serena and our B&B guest is probably still having his breakfast. Emily's force-feeding him a full English.'

'How nice,' mumbles Jennifer who's looking more soignée than usual for a Tuesday morning. She's swapped her trademark M&S skirt and blouse combo for a flattering mink-coloured dress, and her blonde, viciously backcombed hair is held in place with a diamante clip. Curiouser and curiouser.

Now, I could beat about the bush and get to the point via lots of small talk but, to be honest, I can't be bothered. And if there's one thing coming to Salt Bay has taught me it's that secrets are best shared. So I go straight for the jugular.

'What's going on between you and Jacques?'

'I have no idea what you mean,' says Jennifer. She turns her back on me and makes a great show of tidying up the chocolate selection that's already pretty tidy.

'You know exactly what I mean.' Pulling up Jennifer's stool, I plonk myself on it and fold my arms. 'Look, you don't have to tell me anything you don't want to but is it going to be a problem if Jacques stays with us for a few more days?'

A wave of emotion flits across Jennifer's face and her fingers tighten around the tube of Munchies she's clutching. 'I suppose everyone in the village is talking about me? It's a shame they haven't anything better to do.'

'Don't worry, I haven't said anything to anyone and I don't think Roger would have either.'

Jennifer thinks for a moment while the Munchies get ever-more squidged. 'No, he probably wouldn't. Did Monsieur Bouton tell you anything?' When I shake my head, she leans against the counter and folds her arms beneath her generous bosom. 'Monsieur Bouton – Jacques – and I know each other.'

'I'd gathered that much.'

'You're very nosey, aren't you,' tuts Jennifer, the nosiest woman in Salt Bay. Then she gives a little sigh as though she's come to a decision. 'I knew Jacques a long time ago when I was studying in France as a young woman. Have I told you that I studied music in Paris?'

Only like a million times. I bite my lip to help me keep a straight face. 'You have mentioned it in passing, yes.'

'Well, that's when I first met Jacques. His business was taking off, I got a part-time job in one of his pâtisseries and we had a—' She stops and nods at me, willing me to end her sentence. What does she expect me to say – a friendship, a laugh, a shag?

'A relationship?' I venture.

'Yes, absolutely, a relationship. It was very intense – my first love affair after a sheltered and often unhappy upbringing in Cornwall.' She gazes into the distance for a moment. 'But he was—' She stops again and looks at me, opening her eyes wide.

'Older?'

'Yes.' She nods her head impatiently. 'And—'

This really isn't any fun. I hold out my hands, palms to the ceiling, and shrug.

'And married,' she says crossly. 'Obviously.'

Blimey! Jennifer, who calls local Laura a hussy for having it away with a married fisherman from Perrigan Bay, had a torrid affair with a sexy French bloke who was married at the time.

'There, so now you know.' Bright pink spots are flaring in Jennifer's cheeks. 'Are you disappointed in me?'

'Of course not, this isn't the 1850s, Jennifer. I'm just surprised.'

'Me too because I'm a different person now. The years have changed me. You're different as well.'

'Me? Different in what way?'

'Different from the brittle person you were when you first arrived in Salt Bay. Experiences change us. They either chip away at our defences or build them up. You've softened whereas I've got harder.'

She waves her hand when I go to protest and the Munchies clatter onto the counter. 'No, it's true. What happened in Paris made me a different person but that's fine. I like who I am now.' She gives a short laugh. 'Mostly.'

'The affair didn't last then?'

'Obviously not,' says Jennifer sharply, then she sighs. 'It was the usual story – he kept promising to leave his wife and I was naïve and foolish enough to believe him until—'

She bites her lip as I shift uncomfortably on my stool feeling like a voyeur into long-buried pain.

'It's OK, Jennifer. I shouldn't have been so nosey, and you don't have to tell me anything else.'

'It's strange but I really want to tell you. I haven't talked about it for such a long time.'

Jennifer walks to the shop door and flicks the latch across so we won't be disturbed. Outside three young children in shorts and T-shirts run screaming towards the harbour without a care in the world.

'I got pregnant. Contraception wasn't so good in those days and it was a mistake. But once I got over the shock, I thought it might encourage Jacques to leave his wife. He told me their relationship was loveless and she didn't understand him. I was very naïve back then.' She smiles, softer somehow. 'Anyway, surprise, surprise, he didn't leave his wife, who turned out to be pregnant herself and I found myself alone and pregnant in Paris with no support from my family. I lost the baby with the stress of it all which was probably for the best. Single mothers had a hard time back then.'

She shrugs but her eyes are full of pain. 'After all that I became quite unwell' –she winces and whispers the next word – 'mentally. So I abandoned my studies and Paris for good and came back to Cornwall.'

She sucks in air and breathes out slowly. 'I have shocked you now. I'm not the perfect person you thought I was.'

Slipping off my stool, I walk over to her feeling profoundly sad. Life is hard and we're all damaged by traumas that remain buried within us.

'You're as perfect to me as you ever were,' I say diplomatically, putting my arms around her and pulling her in for a hug. Jennifer is one hundred per cent not a huggy person but it's the only appropriate response to what she's just told me.

Jennifer allows herself to be held for a few moments. She smells of gardenias and there's what feels like an industrial grade girdle underneath her dress. Then she pulls away and purses her lips. 'Everything I've just said is between you and me, all right? So there's no telling that young man of yours or blabbermouth Kayla and definitely no word of it to Storm. She's put me on a pedestal and I don't want to crush her. Promise me.'

'Of course I promise.'

It's the second promise I've made today but one I'm happy to keep. How awful to carry such heartache in silence for almost forty years.

'Good. It's a shame in one way because I'd have made a good mother,' muses Jennifer, flinging open the door when a small child presses her face against the shop window. 'Oy,' she bellows, 'unless you're willing to clean that window, get your nose off the glass!'

The girl scuttles off as I imagine Jennifer with a child of her own. Maybe motherhood would have smoothed her sharp edges and made her less spikey. But knowing Jennifer's story still doesn't explain one thing.

'So why do you think Jacques is here now?'

'I have absolutely no idea. We haven't been in touch since I left Paris all those years ago and him turning up out of the blue has unsettled me. I can't help wondering how my life would have been if I'd stayed in France. I like it here well enough but it's only human to wonder "what if".'

'I know but we'd miss you if you weren't here keeping us all in check.'

'Well, someone has to do it. There's a serious lack of discipline in this village which isn't helped by Roger allowing all kinds of drunken behaviour in his establishment. Oh, no!'

Jennifer is staring through the window and I follow her gaze. Striding towards the shop in a blue blazer and dapper Panama hat is Jacques.

'I don't want to see him,' blurts out Jennifer. 'Why did you let him stay in the first place?'

'I had no idea who he was. We were just giving the B&B idea a dry run.'

'Which is ridiculous because the village doesn't need a B&B establishment and lots of locals are saying the same thing,' barks Jennifer, moving away from the window so she won't be spotted from outside. 'Why can't you leave Tregavara House as it is? Alice wouldn't approve of you inviting strangers into her home.'

I let that go because Jennifer is about to self-combust. Usually under control to the point of coldness, she keeps swallowing and twisting her hands together so tightly her knuckles are white ridges.

Poor woman! We think our lives are under control but all it takes is a face from the past to blast our fragile defences to smithereens.

'I'll lock the door again.' Jennifer dives towards the latch but it's too late. The bell tinkles as Jacques steps inside, takes off his hat and gives me a small nod. His cologne smells of lemons warming under a sun-bleached sky and drifts across the space between us.

'Good morning, ladies. I don't mean to ambush you, Jenny, but I was told you work here.'

'I don't *work* here. The shop belongs to me and I know it's only small, but we can't all own fancy businesses across Paris.'

'That's true but your shop is charming.'

I'm sidling towards the door and have almost reached it when Jennifer jabs her finger at me: 'And where exactly do you think you're going?'

'Home. I've got things to do.'

'They can wait. Get back on that stool!' When I hesitate, she gives me a wobbly smile. 'Please.'

'It's fine to stay, Annie,' says Jacques. 'I have a feeling you are at the heart of the village.'

At the heart of a village that disapproves of my efforts to save my home – and if the fall-out caused by our first guest is anything to go by, they've got a point. I scuttle back to the stool like the biggest gooseberry ever.

Jacques takes off his hat and places it on top of the rearranged confectionery. 'It's good to see you again, Jennifer. I have often wondered how you are.'

'And now you've seen that I'm still alive and kicking so you don't need to stay,' says Jennifer, giving her magnificent bouffant hairstyle a pat.

'But I've come all this way and would like to catch up with an old friend. Tell me, did you continue with your music studies elsewhere?'

'No, I didn't but I'm doing just fine in retail, thank you very much.'

'That's such a shame because you had great musical talent.'

'Had? I still have great musical talent and sing with a choir which recently won a prestigious award thanks to me and my vocal skills. Isn't that right, Annie?'

That's over-egging it a bit – though Salt Bay Choral Society did win the Kernow Choral Crown, so I nod.

'Congratulations. And do you have a husband these days?' Jacques hesitates. 'And children?'

'No, it's just me.'

A tremor of emotion flickers across Jacques' handsome face. 'It's hard to believe there's no husband when you're looking so well. I can still see the young girl.'

When Jennifer looks up at Jacques from under her lashes, I can see it too. She's not an unattractive woman now but she must have been prettier then, with her high cheekbones and bright eyes. Before years of loneliness and dissing other people scored lines across her forehead and around her pursed lips.

She sighs: 'Why are you here, Jacques, after all these years?'

Her former lover pauses a moment while I shrink down on the stool. Being size twelve with no super-powers means invisibility just ain't gonna happen, but I'm acutely uncomfortable about being here. *EastEnders* has come to Salt Bay but this is painful real life rather than TV soap opera.

Jacques leans against the piled-up windbreaks. 'I started thinking about the past now I'm on my own and I have some regrets about my behaviour.'

'Did you finally leave your wife then?'

'She left me, actually. She died a year ago.'

'Oh.' Jennifer stumbles over her next words. 'I'm very sorry to hear that.'

'Me too. She had a lot to put up with. But her death has made me think about how I've lived my life.'

'So are you here trying to make amends?' Eek! I didn't mean to put my oar in, but the question just slipped out. An invisibility cloak would be wasted on me.

Jacques gives another Gallic shrug. 'Maybe. I didn't treat you well all those years ago, Jennifer, and I wanted to make sure you're all right.'

'As you can see, I'm absolutely fine so you can push off back to France with a clear conscience.' Jennifer folds her arms across her chest. 'How did you find me anyway?'

'I thought you might still be in Cornwall. You always told me how much you loved the place and I knew you would still be singing. You always had such a beautiful voice.'

'Still has,' I pipe up. Jeez, I seem determined to get involved in this when I've got quite enough going on in my life at the moment. Fortunately, both Jennifer and Jacques ignore me.

'So you found me through the choir?'

'I found your photo online when your choir won that competition last Christmas. I saw the picture and recognised you straight away. Rupert was there too and Annie and Storm.'

'Rupert?' Jennifer looks at me, puzzled.

'He means Roger.'

'I see. Well, you've found me, Jacques and I'm a successful retailer so you can go back home with your conscience eased and get on with your life.'

'I'll be returning to Paris very soon but I'm happy to see you and would like to talk about the old days, if you're willing. Perhaps you would meet me in the pub at lunchtime? I would like to find out what you've done with your life. I never forgot you, Jennifer.'

Ooh, it's still really awkward, sitting here watching the drama play out. But I'm agog about what Jennifer will decide. Will she accept an invitation from a former lover to reminisce or will she tell him to sling his hook? *Bam bam-bam bam-bam ba-ba-ba-ba!* The *EastEnders* theme tune starts playing in my head.

Jennifer looks around at her little Salt Bay empire. Newspapers and magazines, beach balls and sunglasses, headache pills and diarrhoea tablets. Then she gives a tight nod.

'One o'clock, the Whistling Wave. And I'll buy my own drinks, thank you very much.'

Jacques grabs Jennifer's hand, raises it to his lips and plants a soft kiss on her skin. 'How do you say it? It's a deal.'

Chapter Twenty-One

Storm is mooching about when I get home.

'Where have you *beeeeeen*?' she whines, pulling off my denim jacket and throwing it at the coatstand. She misses and it crumples down the back of the radiator.

'I went to Jennifer's and then had a walk across the cliffs. It's gorgeous up there. You ought to try it sometime.'

'What, walking?' Storm shudders. 'I don't think so. It sucks that there's nothing like the Tube round here but why would I walk more than I have to?'

'Exercise. Fresh air. Pleasure.'

Storm gives a 'does not compute' frown and propels me into the kitchen, which is spotless with piles of gleaming washed pots on the drainer. Emily's been busy.

'Whatever. I was worried Jacques would get back before you and it would just be the two of us in the house 'cos Emily's out.'

'I thought you were out too with Serena and you don't need to be worried about Jacques anyway,' I say confidently, though there's a slight niggle at the back of my mind.

Is it irresponsible to have a stranger in the house? I know very little about him – apart from the fact he was once an adulterer who seduced foreign students. Which really doesn't help.

'Serena's going out to see some old friend of her mum's who's down here on holiday from Derby or Dundee or somewhere.' She grimaces because if it's north of London it doesn't exist. 'They invited me along but I didn't fancy it. Having lunch with old ladies isn't much fun and someone from school might see me. Anyway, I thought you could take me to the pub for lunch. To cheer me up. I need chips.'

'Gee, thanks, Storm. That's very kind of you to allow me to buy you lunch.'

'Yeah, I think so too.' Storm grabs her ginormous plastic sunglasses from the kitchen table and flings open the back door. 'Come on then. I didn't have any breakfast 'cos I was so, like, traumatised and now I'm getting hangry.'

Hungry plus angry is a toxic mix when it comes to Storm so I grab my keys and usher her outside.

To be honest, it's nice going out with Storm, even when I'm merely viewed as a meal ticket. But maybe the pub isn't such a good idea this lunchtime.

'Let's go to Maureen's instead,' I suggest when we get closer to her tea shop, which is looking jaunty in the sunshine. Striped red and blue bunting is pinned above the door and tourists are chatting at tables covered in red gingham cloths.

'Nah, you're all right. I'd rather go to the pub.'

'You can have a sundae at Maureen's with clotted cream and chocolate sprinkles.'

Some mother substitute I am, tempting Storm to get stuck into a mountain of sugar. But she keeps on walking.

'Nah, I need lots of chips. It's definitely a carbs kind of day when your own mother doesn't want to see you.'

Sighing, I catch up with my half-sister and follow her towards the whitewashed pub. Maybe I'm feeling awkward unnecessarily and Jennifer will give Jacques the brush off, just like he let her down almost forty years ago.

The Whistling Wave is heaving with even more people than usual on an August afternoon and I don't recognise half of them. They'll be holidaymakers spending a week away in gorgeous Cornwall before heading home to the rat race. I get a sudden pang for the buzz and excitement of London but ignore it.

'Why is this place so rammed?' complains Storm, trying to hurry up a young man and woman who are leaving their table by standing uncomfortably close.

'Let them have some space.'

I give the back of Storm's T-shirt a gentle tug and she steps back a millimetre while the tourists hurriedly grab their bags and leave.

'Well, that worked.' Storm sinks onto the woman's chair and puts her elbows on the table that's littered with salt specks, sauce splatters and breadcrumbs. 'Ooh, this table's disgusting! Did they get any food in their mouths?'

'It's mad in here today,' says Kayla, suddenly appearing with a cloth and knocking all the table detritus onto the uneven flagstones. 'Are you eating? Specials are on the board.' She reels them off by heart without an ounce of enthusiasm.

'What would you recommend?' I ask her.

'Definitely not the boeuf bourguignon 'cos Dan's getting it out of a tin. He's filling in for Frank, who's off sick, and let's just say that cooking isn't his forte. Sadly, watching *The Great British Bake Off* doesn't turn you into a chef. The crab salad's all right 'cos there's not a lot that he can do to spoil that.'

'Can he cook chips?' Storm is so worried, she stops texting for a second.

'Even Dipshit Dan can manage the deep fat fryer though I wouldn't want to be near that today. It's so hot in the kitchen during the summer, I can't be doing with being in there.'

'But you're from Australia. You should be used to soaring temperatures.'

'Yeah, but in Oz we have a nifty little invention called air conditioning.' Kayla pants and blows her fringe off her forehead. 'I'm going to take a break in a min so order your food at the bar and I'll come and join you.'

By the time I've fought my way to the bar and placed our orders, Kayla has clocked off for lunch and comes to sit with us.

'Don't you think Roger needs a hand?'

Roger has damp patches under his armpits and his sparse, grey hair is sticking up like grass.

'He had a break a while back so it's my turn. What's going on with those two then? Roger says he's your B&B bloke.'

She takes a slurp of lemonade and tilts the glass towards a table at the back where Jennifer and Jacques are talking, heads bent together. She did turn up then. While I'm staring, Jennifer glances up and catches my eye. Oh, great! She'll think I'm in here spying on them.

'I have no idea what those two are doing. None at all. Why should I know? No one tells me anything. It's a complete mystery.'

Oops, I'm talking too much. Taking a huge swig of my sickly sweet orange juice, I pretend to be studying the desserts menu, but Kayla narrows her green eyes.

'You'd tell me if you did know, wouldn't you, Sunshine?'

'Of course I would.'

I give a little laugh as though I'd rather gouge out my own eyeballs than keep a secret from my blabbermouth Aussie friend.

'Hhmm. It all looks a bit intimate to me. Do you think they're on a date?'

'What?' Storm snorts so hard, Coke dribbles down her nose and she blots at it with a tissue. 'Those two on a date? They're both, like, ancient.'

'I hate to break it to you, Storm mate, but even old people go on dates. Sometimes they even have sexual intercourse.'

'Eew, that is disgusting.' Storm pulls a face and slams her drink down on the table. Sugary liquid slops over the glass and dribbles across the wood.

'Hey, watch it. I'm the sucker who's got to mop that up. What's the matter with you today, anyway? You've got a face like a bulldog chewing a wasp.'

'Nothing,' mutters Storm, arms folded and strop-face on.

'Weren't you supposed to be going up to London today, to see your mum?'

Storm shakes her head.

'Storm's trip had to be cancelled at the last minute because the situation at her mum's house changed.'

'That's a shame.' Kayla wiggles her eyebrows at me but doesn't pursue it, thank goodness. The last thing I need is Storm going off on one in a packed pub while Jacques is watching. 'So what's happening with running the B&B then, Annie? Can you see yourself doing it long-term?'

'Maybe, as long as the roof repair holds. But what do the locals think about having a B&B in the village? Jennifer was a bit iffy.'

'Jennifer's always a bit iffy but it's your house and no one can tell you what to do with it. Not everyone liked the thought of you reviving the choral society but now half of them claim it was their idea. And anyway, Alice left the house to you and not to them.'

Now Kayla is talking too much. 'So what you're saying is that people have been kicking up a fuss about it.'

'A few, maybe. But they're just set in their ways round here. And who cares what people think anyway?'

'I do. Salt Bay's my home and I don't want to upset the people who live here.'

'Pah!' exclaims Kayla. 'They'll be far more upset if you sell the house to Toby and he turns it into holiday flats, especially if he rents them out to his posh idiot friends.'

'You what?' Storm's head jerks up from her Twitter feed.

'Nice one, blabbermouth.'

'How was I supposed to know you hadn't told her?' whines Kayla, rubbing her shin where I've just kicked her.

'There's nothing to tell because nothing's been decided. It's just a possibility.'

'And they don't tell me anything anyway 'cos they think I'm just a kid.'

'We don't think that but we don't want to worry you.'

'Barry used to say that but all it means is I worry all the time that there's stuff no one's telling me. And I get that you're short of cash, Annie, but if you sell the place to Toby and he mucks it about, the old lady will come back and haunt you.'

Cheers, Storm. My sister goes back to tweeting in a right old huff while Jennifer and Jacques continue their conversation in the corner. One event changed the course of Jennifer's life forever and I'm at a fork in the road too. One way leads to Salt Bay and possible penury while the other leads to who knows where.

'Here you are – bon appetit!'

Dan slams down a crab salad in front of me and a plate piled high with chips in front of Storm. The fish I insisted Storm order with her chips is almost hidden beneath a mound of deep-fried potato.

'How's it going, Dan. Busy day today?'

It's a rhetorical question but I feel sorry for the poor bloke who looks like he's on fire, from the tip of his scarlet nose to the ends of his pillar-box-red ears.

'It's manic, the fryer keeps going on the blink and I'm going to tell Roger he owes me double-time for coming in on my day off.'

'Good luck with that,' murmurs Kayla, glancing at her boss, who's scolding an emmet for resting his feet on a chair. He spots Dan talking to us and gestures for him to get back into the kitchen.

'Unbe-feckin-lievable after I've done him a favour!'

Dan stalks off in a fug of sweaty pique while Storm gets stuck into her chips and I take a mouthful of crab salad. Ugh, Dan hasn't washed the lettuce too well and it's gritty. I start forlornly pushing the salad around my plate with a fork.

'Look at the three of us!' Kayla leans back in her chair and stretches her arms out wide. 'Here we are in one of the most beautiful places in the world – Cornwall, that is, not the pub – on a gloriously sunny day. But I'm hideously overworked' – she says that last bit extra loudly for Roger's benefit– 'you, Storm, are miserable 'cos your holiday's off for some strange reason I haven't got to the bottom of and you, Annabella, are worried sick about money and property. Come on, live a little. I mean, you're getting married to a lovely man. He's not my type – far too glowery. But you make a lovely couple. We so need to cheer ourselves up.'

She drums her fingers on the table and then her face breaks into a huge grin. 'I know exactly what'll do the trick. We can go wedding dress shopping on Saturday afternoon. There's that new shop in Trecaldwith that's down near the bank.'

'That sounds lovely, Kayla, but being worried sick about money means I can't buy wedding dresses from posh, expensive shops.'

'We don't have to buy them, silly. Just try loads on, have a giggle and get some ideas for when we hit the high street, which had better be soon 'cos you're getting married in just over a month. And Storm can try on some bridesmaids' dresses.'

Storm pauses with a chip halfway from plate to mouth. 'You've gotta be kidding, right? There's no way I'm dressing up in some sugar-pink frilly thing with bows or I might do a Serena and refuse to be a bridesmaid at all.'

I can imagine Storm in a sugar-pink frilly thing with bows. She'd look rather lovely, with her scowl. Like the grumpy, foul-mouthed princess of South Cornwall.

'You'd better come with us on Saturday and try some dresses on then so you can point us away from the frilly pink meringues,' says Kayla, giving me a wink. 'We could always have lunch afterwards at KFC.'

'Hhmm.' Storm is more interested now there's the possibility of a Bargain Bucket. 'I suppose I could come, seeing as I've already arranged with Jennifer to have this Saturday off. Talking of which' – she glances at her boss, who's listening attentively to her former lover – 'that is so lame.'

'What is?'

'Old people getting it on when it's far too late and they should know better. You and Josh are bad enough kissing all over the place.'

She wrinkles her nose and contemplates a better world where no one over the age of thirty is allowed any physical contact on pain of public humiliation. What a miserable world that would be.

The scrum at the bar has thinned out and Roger ambles over with a grubby cloth that he's using to mop his brow.

'Phew, that was a busy half hour. The trouble with coach parties is they all pitch up at the same time and expect immediate service. They were heading for Land's End but the driver got lost. I mean, all you have to do is head for the end of Cornwall. How hard can that be?'

He huffs and puffs and wipes the sweaty cloth across our table while I wince. Roger isn't the hottest on hygiene. His kitchen's not too bad and the pub is dust-free but his personal hygiene leaves a lot to be desired. His belly is busting out of his beer-spattered T-shirt, and greying bristles are sprouting from his chin. I give a little sniff. Yep. Roger definitely has a whiff of chip fat about him.

'What's the score with those two, Rog?' asks Kayla.

'Monsieur Bouton is someone from her past.' Roger sighs and stuffs the cloth into his trouser pocket.

'Really? I can't imagine Jennifer with a racy past. Are you sure?'

'I asked her when she was buying their drinks. She said she knows him from her time in Paris, when she was studying music at that fancy-arse place. Then she told me to stop being so nosey which is rich coming from her.'

He gestures for me to shuffle along the window seat and wallops his backside down next to me. 'Do you think she'll go back with him?'

'What, to France?' Kayla laughs. 'Why on earth would she? They're only talking and it's not like they were lovers or anything.'

She glances at me and starts bouncing up and down. 'Ooh, they were! OMG! Go, Jennifer!'

Damn my stupid face which is hopeless at keeping secrets. Storm does a mock retch and goes back to her tweeting.

'Shush, Kayla. It's Jennifer's business so let's leave it that way. And you're leaping ahead, Roger. They're only catching up.'

'You're right,' he says firmly. 'Jennifer would never desert Salt Bay and give up all that this village has to offer.'

Kayla stretches her arms above her head and yawns. 'Nah, of course not. She'd never leave behind an empty bed and early morning starts in a village that smells of fish for a posh house with Monsieur Smoothy Chops in the chic French capital.'

She giggles and nicks a chip from Storm's plate but Roger's beefy shoulders slump.

'Huh! What's so special about Paris?'

'The Louvre,' says Kayla helpfully. 'And the Seine. And the Eiffel Tower and Montmartre. Plus brilliant food – better than Dan can manage.' She prods my limp lettuce which is definitely gritty.

'There's no way sensible Jennifer will run off with that smarmy French bloke who's not so hot compared to Cornish men. What's he got that I haven't?' asks Roger rather unwisely, puffing out his chest.

'Nothing, apart from a sense of humour, Gallic good looks and a thirty-two-inch waist,' sniggers Kayla but she stops when I kick her again under the table. Roger blusters and grumps his way through life but right now he looks vulnerable and upset. He stares at the floor and breathes out heavily.

'Just joking, mate,' says Kayla. 'You're not bad for a Cornish bloke in his sixties.'

'Fifties,' mutters Roger.

'Yeah, that's what I meant. Fifties.' Kayla winces at me and shrugs.

'Would you be upset if Jennifer did leave?' I ask Roger gently.

'I dunno. Probably. Yeah. I've never thought of it before because I reckoned she'd always be around. But me and Jennifer go way back, and the place wouldn't be the same without her.'

'I'm sure you're leaping to all sorts of wrong conclusions. And whatever may or may not have happened between them in the past, Jennifer's not the type of woman to go ga-ga over an old suitor.'

As I finish speaking, Jennifer lets out a high-pitched tinkly laugh that carries across the pub. I've never heard her do tinkly before and it's slightly disturbing. Roger closes his eyes and sighs. 'I have a bad feeling about this.'

Chapter Twenty-Two

The wedding shop in Trecaldwith is nothing like the flash bridal stores I've walked past in London. Their chic, minimalist shop fronts showcase sleek oyster dresses scattered with tasteful Swarovski crystals glinting under discreet lighting. *Buy me, look gorgeous on your big day and live happily ever after*, they scream. Quietly.

In contrast, the shop window of Wendy's Wowzer Weddings is crammed with frothy, chalk-white creations. Huge rhinestones are catching the sun and blinding passers-by. Ruffles and frills are vying for attention in a riot of satin and lace.

'There is no way on earth I'm going in there,' says Storm, folding her arms across her Killers T-shirt. She glances around anxiously in case anyone she knows has spotted her within spitting distance of the naffest shop in the world.

'No probs. We can choose you something. Maybe that one.' Kayla points at a pale peach bridesmaid dress in the window, which is uber ruffled around the neck and waist and has fat, puffed sleeves edged with lace.

Storm blanches, shoves the shop door open and hurtles inside.

'Nice one,' murmurs Emily, who's almost beside herself with excitement about our pre-wedding try-on session. Even though I've warned her that we won't be buying anything today.

'Reverse psychology.' Kayla taps her head and purses her lips because she thinks it makes her look wise. 'Works every damn time.'

When we follow Storm into the store, a tall woman in an emerald green trouser suit rushes over. The chunky metal necklace she's wearing bangs up and down with every step.

'Come in, and welcome,' she gushes. 'My name is Maria and I'm at your service today. Which one of you lovely ladies is the blushing bride-to-be?'

'Yuk,' mutters Storm.

'That'll be me. We're just having a look at dresses today, if that's all right. We won't necessarily be buying.'

Kayla rolls her eyes at my honesty, but it doesn't seem right to raise Maria's hopes of commission.

If she's disappointed, Maria doesn't show it. 'Of course.' She smiles. 'You need to choose carefully for the most important day of your life and it's a decision that can't be rushed. When exactly is the Big Day?'

'September the 22nd,' says Kayla, running her fingers across a veil that's thickly encrusted with crystals.

'September the 22nd this year? And you haven't got your dress yet? Gosh, you're leaving it rather late. Unless the wedding is rather… spontaneous.'

Her eyes, topped by a bright slick of pearly green eyeshadow, travel down my body and come to rest on my stomach.

'She's not up the duff. Just getting on a bit,' declares Storm, who's standing right in the middle of the store as though she's scared that the dresses will contaminate her.

'And are you a bridesmaid, dear? I'm sure we can find a dress that will make you feel like a million dollars,' says Maria, blissfully unaware of the massive and, quite frankly, dangerous challenge she's taking on. 'What colour are you thinking of?'

'Black,' says Storm with a scowl.

Maria doesn't miss a beat. 'We don't have much demand for black, however we do have midnight blue for the more, um, assertive bridesmaid. Why don't you all take a look around while I have a word with the lady who's just come in.'

She scuttles off gratefully to talk to her new customer while Kayla, Emily and I start working our way through the rails of dresses lined up along the walls of Wendy's wowzer establishment.

There are some simpler, sleeker designs if you delve beneath the froth and Kayla soon pulls out a beautiful, understated dress in off-white silk that's cut on the bias.

'Try this one, Annie. It'll really suit you.' She presses it into my hands and shoves me towards the changing room. 'Maria won't mind, will you, Maria.'

The large carpeted changing room has a button-back pink chair in one corner and a floor to ceiling mirror on one wall. Ugh, if there's one thing I hate in well-lit changing rooms it's a floor to ceiling mirror that shows every bump and bulge.

'Strip down to your underwear,' orders Maria, who appears to have followed me in.

Carefully avoiding my undies-clad reflection, I stand obediently while Maria manoeuvres metres of soft silk over my head. The dress drapes down and settles across my stomach and hips.

It's more off-the-shoulder than I'd realised but breath catches in my throat when I risk looking in the mirror. The dress is absolutely gorgeous and Kayla's right, it does suit me. I can imagine myself in this swooshing down the aisle towards my lovely Josh in his dark suit waiting for me at the altar. He'd be so proud of me in this fabulous dress.

'Lovely, darling,' says Maria, opening the door of the changing room and propelling me into the shop.

Emily stops running her fingers over a satin dress in sugar-plum pink and her mouth drops open. 'Wow, you look well lush in that.'

'You look gorgeous, mate,' says Kayla. 'Ooh, I think I'm coming over all tearful. What do you reckon, Storm?'

She ferrets about in her handbag for a tissue as Storm gives me a cursory glance.

'Yeah, not bad. How much is it?'

Ah yes, in all the excitement that's the most important thing I haven't checked out. Maria turns over the tag that's hanging from the back of the dress and squints at it underneath her gold-framed glasses.

'This one is £950 but I can give you a five per cent discount.'

Eek! Even with the discount, that's around £900 that needs to go towards keeping Tregavara House afloat.

'Crikey, that's a bit steep,' says Kayla.

Maria's scarlet lips draw into a tight pout. 'It's a very reasonable price for a dress of this exquisite quality. We do have a slightly less expensive range over here for the bride on a budget.'

She points at a rail dripping with frothy creations. The more ruffles, the cheaper the dress, apparently.

'You could treat yourself, Annie.' Kayla walks around me slowly with her hands on her hips. 'Maybe you could put it on your credit card?'

But my credit card is already maxed out with boring day-to-day stuff and I can't justify spending so much money on a dress I'll wear once. Even if that once is my wedding. I run my hand along the smooth silk before heading for the budget section. It's either that or I *will* be wearing a bin bag to go up the aisle.

Maria is very patient but trying on a costly, to-die-for dress before heading for the bargain rail was such a mistake – it's like swapping a sexy weekend with Aidan Turner in a five-star hotel for a snog behind the bike sheds with the local letch. The cheaper dresses just don't measure up and after a while I give up and climb back into my jeans.

Emily and Kayla have better luck with a floor-length green dress which makes Kayla's red hair look amazing. But Storm steadfastly refuses to try on anything, claiming she'll look 'like, totally sad.' Eventually, with the help of some KFC bribery, I persuade her to try on a simple blue dress that cinches at the waist and falls in soft waves to the ground.

'You look fabulous,' breathes Emily when my sister stomps out of the changing room. And she does, even when she hitches up the dress to reveal her Doc Martens underneath. But she refuses to let me take a photo on my phone to show Barry.

'No way,' she hisses, heading back to the changing room at full speed. 'Barry would put it on Twitter and if it went viral I'd have to stay in until I died of old age.'

So, with our heads full of ideas but not enough money to make them happen, we leave Maria with no shopping bags and feeling rather glum.

I've never hankered after beautiful things – money was tight growing up so I quickly learned there was no point asking for the latest must-have toys or trainers. And since starting work I've hardly ever shelled out on costly shoes and clothes or expensive face creams. Clarks, Primark and Superdrug are my stores of choice.

But I'd love to look good on my special day and I'm not sure a bin bag is going to cut it.

We're heading for KFC because a promise is a promise when Tom lollops into sight ahead of us. His stride falters when he spots Emily but then he walks resolutely towards us.

'Hello, everyone.' It's hard to see his face because his long, dark fringe is swinging in front of it like a shield.

'Hey, Tom. Are you here on your own?' asks Kayla.

'Nope, I'm here with my mum who's gone into the fishmonger's,' he mumbles. 'Hi there, Emily.'

'Hey, Tom.' Emily smiles but continues fiddling with her phone which has just beeped with a message. It's always a novelty when we're away from black-hole Tregavara House and texts pile in thick and fast.

'We've been trying on wedding and bridesmaid dresses, preparing for the big day,' says Kayla.

'That's nice. I bet you all looked really nice.'

And he stares at Emily with such longing, I want to give him a hug. Unrequited love can be an absolute bugger.

When Emily carries on staring at her phone, Tom starts fidgeting from foot to foot and pulls at the rapidly descending waistband of his baggy jeans. 'I'd better go back and collect Mum then. See you at choir, Emily.'

When Emily nods absentmindedly, I could shake her.

Storm watches Tom slouch off into the distance with a thoughtful look on her face. 'You do know that he's kinda mad for you, don't you, Em? You can be a bit of an airhead about stuff like that.'

'He's just a friend,' asserts Emily, shoving her phone into the pocket of her cardigan.

'Believe me, he'd like to be more than that, mate,' says Kayla.

'Do you think? It doesn't matter even if he would because I'm off all men.'

'What, forever?' snorts Storm.

'Maybe. They're too much trouble.'

'Not all men are like Jay,' I tell her. 'Tom is kind and gentle and he's nice looking. Not as boy-bandy as Jay but he's sweet.'

Storm nods. 'Yeah, he's pretty fit if you're into that nerdy emo "kiss me or I'll cry" look.'

'He looks all right but I don't care. Men just aren't worth the effort,' says Emily with a toss of the head as though she's worked her way through a battalion's worth of scoundrels. 'Though I appreciate that I might change my mind one day, when I get as old as Annie.'

Nice!

'Well, I think you're doing the right thing,' says Storm.

'Do you?' Emily glows at Storm's approval.

'Yeah, I admire you for sticking to your feminist principles.'

Being a feminist didn't mean crying off all men the last time I checked but what the hell. There's no way I'm arguing the specifics of feminism with a stroppy teenager so I make do with an eye-roll at Kayla, who giggles and leads the way towards our lunch.

When you're feeling low, there's nothing like a bucket of fried chicken to boost those good endorphins. And after filling our faces, we're ready to hit the high street in Penzance, which is where I find a perfectly nice knee-length dress that'll do just fine. It's made of cream satin and lace with a fitted bodice and full skirt – and it's in the Monsoon sale which helps me like it even more.

'It makes your boobs look perky,' is Kayla's opinion. Which has got to be a good thing.

And Emily gives me a thumbs up after she's walked around me to inspect the dress from all angles. 'It fits you well and you look nice,' she says with a grin. 'Really nice.'

Really nice rather than well lush but I buy it anyway.

'Only a couple of shopping bags? It's a miracle,' laughs Josh, poking his head out of the sitting room when we trudge into the hallway. He's been coating the shed with weather-proof paint all morning and there are flecks of green in his thick dark hair.

'There was nothing to buy 'cos Cornwall's full of rubbish shops,' declares Storm, throwing her jacket in the vague direction of the coatstand and heading for the stairs.

'Annie tried on a gorgeous wedding dress. It was oyster silk and' – Emily stops and bites her lip – 'is it all right to say 'cos you're the groom? I wouldn't want it to be bad luck or anything.'

'It's fine, Emily, because I didn't buy it. I bought this one instead.' I wave my Monsoon bag at Josh and hide it behind my back when he tries to look inside.

'Yeah and you look great in that one too. I just meant you looked beautiful in the silk dress – like a proper princess. The one you bought is lovely, it's just a bit less… wedding-y. Although you'll still look amazing on the day and regal and…'

Kind, gentle Emily tails off, horrified that she might be saying the wrong thing. And she makes a dash for the kitchen after I reassure her that I know what she means.

'Freya would approve of the silk dress seeing as she already thinks you're a member of the royal family,' says Josh, beckoning me into the sitting room.

It's a standing joke in his family that Freya mistook me for a princess when we first met because of my unusually bright blue eyes. He puts his arms around my waist and pulls my hips against his. 'Why didn't you buy it, if it was just right?'

'It was around £900, even with a discount.'

'Wow, that's steep. But you could have bought it and we'd have managed. I want this to be your special day.'

'Josh, it would have cost just about every penny we've got to cover the whole wedding and we're trying to put money away for the roof as well. So buying it would have been completely daft and totally unfair.'

'Unfair to who?' he asks, nuzzling his nose against my neck.

'Unfair to everyone who's relying on us to keep a roof over their head. And Emily's exaggerating anyway 'cos the dress wasn't that great whereas the one I bought makes me look the spitting image of Elizabeth Taylor circa the early 1960s.'

Josh laughs and crushes me against his chest. 'I love you, Miss Trebarwith, but are you sure? I'd buy you an expensive engagement ring and a snazzy silk wedding dress if we didn't live in this money pit.'

'I don't need those things,' I tell him, looping my arms around his neck and standing on tiptoe so we're almost nose to nose. 'I've got more than I ever thought possible – a proper home, a family and you. I don't need anything else.'

Yuk! I sound like the kind of schmaltzy greetings card I'd never send anyone in case they thought I'd lost it. But it's true and I'll do whatever's best to keep my home and my family safe. If only I knew exactly what that was.

Josh kisses me and I sink into it, only slightly distracted by my inner voice whispering: *Sell the money pit, Trebarwith, buy the dress and live happily ever after. In Trecaldwith.*

Chapter Twenty-Three

There's no sign of Jacques heading back to Paris over the next few days. He and Jennifer have rekindled their friendship and he spends most of his time on the stool in her shop, charming the women who call in. And there seem to be a lot of them all of a sudden. Maureen, Florence and even Fiona appear to have fallen for Jacques' Gallic charm and go giddy in his presence. He doesn't do it for me but maybe it's more a menopausal thing.

His charisma is definitely not having the same effect on Roger, who stops short when he spots Jacques sitting at the back of the church before the weekly choir rehearsal.

'What's old matey boy doing here?' he hisses.

'I expect he's come to listen to Jennifer sing.'

'Well, it's not right, stalking her like that,' harrumphs Roger, scratching his belly. 'And she's following him round like a lovesick puppy.'

'That's a bit harsh,' I say, but Jennifer spoils things by giving Jacques a girly wave from the soprano section.

'See. She's lost her mind,' mutters Roger, slouching off to find his seat before the rehearsal begins.

Emily and Storm are already in their seats and nudge one another when Jacques leaps to his feet and kisses Florence on both cheeks when she walks up the aisle. She giggles and blushes to the roots of her grey perm while Roger slowly shakes his head. Poor old soul. The village is suddenly awash with oestrogen and he can't understand it.

After everyone's arrived and settled down, Josh stands on a crate so we can all see him while he's conducting and we start to sing. Wow, Salt Bay Choral Society are in good voice as we practise pieces for Josie Pardew's sixtieth birthday party at the end of September. And Jacques looks enthralled – his elbows are on the pew in front, his chin is resting on his hands and he's giving us his full attention.

Our reputation and confidence have grown since we won the Kernow Choral Crown competition last Christmas and now we're booked to sing at events in the villages nearby. We even get paid – only a few pounds admittedly but enough to cover transport costs and chocolate biscuits in the break when hungry tourists have scoffed all Maureen's cakes.

We're halfway through singing 'Any Dream Will Do' – Josie's favourite song, apparently – when my attention strays to Pippa, who's wincing. At first I think it's because she's standing near Ollie, whose determination to reach the top notes is enough to make anyone cringe. But she carries on wincing even when the singing stops.

'Are you OK, Pippa?' calls Josh.

'I'm fine,' she puffs. 'It's just a spot of indigestion.'

'Are you sure, dear? We don't want any babies arriving mid-song,' says Florence, patting Pippa's swollen belly like it's public property.

'I've been getting a lot of indigestion recently but it's nothing to bother about. There's no need to worry, Charlie.'

She glances at her sweet husband, who's a stalwart of our tenor section and gives him a reassuring smile but he frowns. 'Are you sure, Pips?'

'Absolutely and anyway it's stopped now. Please carry on with the rehearsal 'cos the baby loves the music and starts dancing – it's probably its Gangnam moves that are making me so uncomfortable.' She lovingly caresses her bump. 'Anyway, the baby always settles down when Jennifer does her solo.'

'Did you hear that, Jennifer?' calls Roger. 'Even the unborn think your lovely singing voice is soporific.'

Which is Roger's cack-handed attempt at a compliment, but it doesn't go down too well with our star singer, who shoots him a filthy look.

Pippa seems fine now but, all the same, we make her sit out the rest of the rehearsal. We've almost finished anyway – all that's left to practise is the solo that Jennifer will be performing at the party.

Since arriving in Salt Bay, I've heard Jennifer sing loads of times and she's always the first to put up her hand when a solo's needed. But when she runs through her piece with accompaniment from Michaela, her voice has never sounded more glorious. Crystal-clear soprano notes soar to the apex of the arch above the altar and her extra-welly vibrato bouncing off the ancient stone makes me shiver.

Jacques closes his eyes as she hits a perfect top A and I wonder if he's pondering on the fallout from their affair and feeling guilty that Jennifer's talent has been wasted. Maybe, because he applauds loudly when her final note dies away and shouts 'bravo' while she blushes and gives a tiny curtsy. Roger's face twists into an ugly scowl.

After the rehearsal, we all head for the pub as usual and I sit next to Pippa while Josh and Charlie are getting our drinks at the bar.

'Are you looking forward to the baby?' I ask her, wondering how it feels to have a real, live human growing inside you.

'Not the birth. I'm nervous about that but we can't wait to meet him. Oops' – she face-palms – 'I'm not supposed to let on we're having a boy but my head's full of cotton wool today. I think I've got nappy brain. Please don't tell anyone.'

'Of course I won't. There's no way I'd spoil the surprise but congratulations on the imminent arrival of your son. I can't wait to meet him.'

'Me too. Ooh, ow-ow-ow.' Pippa grabs her huge stomach, pretty face pinched and pale against her blonde hair.

'Indigestion again?'

'Yeah, I've been getting it on and off over the last few weeks and the midwife said it was nothing to worry about, but today it keeps coming and going and I can't get rid of it. It's my own fault for bolting down my tea so I could get to choir on time.'

'When you say coming and going?'

'It grumbles about a bit and then disappears.' Pippa shifts uncomfortably in her chair. 'But it feels like indigestion and backache and Henry moving about… Oh no, I've told you his name now.'

Pippa's latest slip hardly registers because alarm bells are ringing in my head. I've never had children, but my mum enjoyed giving me a contraction by contraction account of the painful hours she spent having me, in a dingy Ealing flat.

'Perhaps you should go to hospital, Pippa, to be checked out. It's best to be on the safe side though I'm sure it's just trapped wind. My pregnant friend Maura suffers with that. Do you, um…?'

Nope, there's no good way of asking someone if they fart a lot so I leave the question unasked.

Panic has stirred in Pippa's pale eyes. 'Maybe I should go to hospital. I'll get Charlie.' She hauls herself to her feet but sits down again straight away. Now she looks terrified.

'I – I think' – her teeth are chattering and she can hardly get the words out – 'my waters just broke. Either that or I've wet myself which is totally embarrassing.'

'Charlie!' I yell across the pub, heart pounding. Jeez, I'd be useless in a crisis because I'm already panicking big-time. Josh's head snaps up at the tone of my voice and he hurries across with his pint.

'What's up?'

'We need Charlie. Now.' I gesture at Pippa, who's groaning as a sudden wave of pain washes over her. Josh blanches and slams his drink onto the table. 'He's gone to the loo. Hold on and I'll get him.'

We have to get Pippa to hospital. That's the best place for her. But when I try to help her to her feet so we can get to the car, she groans and sinks back onto the chair.

'Exactly how long have you had this indigestion, Pippa?'

'All day, on and off,' she says through gritted teeth.

'And how often is the pain coming now, dear?' asks Florence, who's wandered over and is staring at Pippa with her hands on her hips.

'All the bloody time,' shouts Pippa, pushing herself up onto her feet and giving a loud scream that silences everyone in the pub. 'Gosh, I do apologise,' she pants, clasping the table with her head bent so a long curtain of blonde hair swishes across her face. 'I don't usually swear but it's suddenly got very painful and, ooh… it's happening again!'

She sinks towards the floor, her face twisted in agony, and I put my arms under her elbows to support her. But it turns out that a heavily pregnant woman in free-fall weighs a ton and we both end up sitting on the floor, with my legs spread around her hips and her back against me.

'Oh. My. God. What's happening?' yells Charlie, hurdling over a stool as he hurtles across the pub. He crouches down beside his wife.

'I think you're having a baby, mate. Though preferably not on my floor.' Roger cracks his knuckles. 'Kayla, get my car ready outside with the engine running. Looks like I need to make another mercy dash to hospital.'

Poor Pippa will never stand the strain of Roger's Formula One driving. She'll end up giving birth in the backseat while Roger's screeching the wrong way round roundabouts on two wheels.

'Josh can drive,' I yell, trying to avoid being head-butted by Pippa, who's jerking backwards and forwards in pain. Charlie tries to stroke her hair but she pushes him away with a snarl.

'No way,' huffs Roger. 'I reckon I can shave a couple of minutes off my Alice time if I don't stop at any junctions or traffic lights. Observing the highway code was where I went wrong last time.'

'It really is best if I drive, Roger,' insists Josh, pulling the keys to his Mini from his jeans pocket. But Florence shakes her head.

'Whoever drives, you'll never get her to hospital in time. Not when everywhere's clogged with emmets and there's still temporary traffic lights on the top road. Not that you ever see anyone doing any road repairs. Those lights have been there for ages and I've never seen a single workman.'

'Me neither,' huffs Arthur, who's watching what's going on with his pint nursed against his chest. 'I'm going to report them to the highways agency for—'

'For fuck's sake!' hollers Pippa, gripping my thighs and digging her nails in. 'Stop blathering on about bloody workmen and do something useful 'cos this baby is coming fast. Ooh, I want to sodding push now.'

'OK, dear.' Florence winces and pats Pippa's head. 'For someone who doesn't usually swear, you're certainly making up for lost time. Roger, you'd better call an ambulance and get her upstairs pronto.'

'Ambo's on its way already,' shouts Kayla from behind the bar while Charlie helps Josh pull Pippa to her feet and half-drag, half-carry her towards the back of the bar.

'What if the baby comes before the ambulance?' calls Charlie over his shoulder, his face rigid with fear.

Farmer's wife Florence rolls up her sleeves. 'That won't be a problem 'cos I've overseen lambing season enough times and I've pulled plenty of lambs out by their legs so I can cope if your baby's breech. How different can it be?'

'Do you need towels and hot water?' asks Kayla, skidding in Pippa's amniotic fluid when she races over. 'I can put the kettle on and grab a load of towels from the airing cupboard. I have no idea what you do with them but that's what they always shout for when someone's sprogging on TV.'

'Yes, towels and hot water. Ooh, and tongs,' Florence shouts at Kayla, who's already heading for the kitchen. 'My Andrew was a forceps delivery so it's best to be prepared.'

'I'm scared,' wails Pippa, who's being hauled up the backstairs towards Roger's bedroom.

Scared? I'd be terrified at the thought of Florence approaching my nether regions with barbecue tongs. And as no one else is leaping forward and offering to deliver Pippa's baby, I'm going to have to step in and lend a hand. I can hardly leave Charlie and Josh up there alone while Florence channels *Countryfile* meets *Call the Midwife*. If only I wasn't such a wuss when it comes to childbirth. At school, they made us watch a film of some poor woman going through it, but I kept my eyes firmly shut.

'Perhaps I can be of assistance.' Jacques has appeared at my side with Jennifer just behind him. He's a beacon of calm compared to the panicked huddle of choir members around me. 'I don't like to intrude but I assisted the obstetrician in delivering my two daughters.'

'Of course you did,' says Roger glumly. 'You'd better follow me then, Jack.'

As it turns out, no towels or tongs are needed because an ambulance is diverted from a sprained ankle in Trecaldwith and turns up quickly. Two paramedics decide they can blue-light Pippa to hospital before the baby arrives and she's carried out on a stretcher, gulping down gas and air as if her life depends on it.

'Good grief, that was intense. Has it put you off having kids?' asks Josh. He sighs with relief when the ambulance pulls away from the pub with an ashen-faced Charlie inside.

'Maybe a bit,' I say, crossing my legs and watching the lights disappear into the distance. And when I glance along the line of women waving the ambulance off, we're all doing the same. All except Florence, who's standing legs astride and tongs in hand, looking disappointed.

'It's typical,' moans Roger ten minutes later. Josh and I are propping up the bar and I've just ordered a double G&T after all the excitement. If only I could share it with Pippa, who could probably do with mainlining alcohol right now.

'What's typical? What are you talking about?' Kayla's taking advantage of a lull in customers and is leaning against the bar with her arms folded.

'That Jack bloke not only owns a string of businesses and speaks with a romantic French accent, he can also deliver babies. Jennifer will definitely go back with him to Paris.'

'They're just good friends catching up on old times,' I assure him, but he shakes his head.

'Arthur reckons he saw them holding hands yesterday on the coast path near Perrigan Bay. Her head's been turned and it's not surprising. I've been thinking about what you said, Kayla, and I don't suppose Salt Bay has much to offer compared to the capital of a foreign country. I don't suppose I have either.'

'Nah, don't put yourself down. You Brits do it all the time and it's not good. True, you're packing a few pounds of extra weight.' Kayla eyes Roger's belly, which looks a lot like Pippa's. 'But you've still got a bit of hair and you've got nice eyes.'

Roger *has* got nice eyes. He blinks at me from behind his old-man specs.

'But you need to do something about your clothes. Ooh, I've just had a brilliant idea!' She starts jumping up and down. 'Me and Annie can give you a makeover like they do on the telly. You know the sort of programme – from right old minger to super cool in a month. No offence, Rog.'

'Super cool would look ridiculous behind the bar of a small Cornish pub. There's no way you're turning me into George Clooney.'

'No risk of that, mate. But it'll be fun and you can show Jennifer a different side. The suave, handsome, devil-may-care side that you keep well-hidden – buried, in fact. Jennifer's used to seeing you every day and familiarity breeds contempt so we need to make her sit up and take notice of what's under her nose. What do you reckon?'

'I reckon you're barking mad and it would never work.'

'It might!'

Roger's jowls wobble back and forth when he shakes his head. 'What do you think of her ridiculous scheme, Annie?'

'Yeah, what do you think, Annie?' demands Kayla, folding her arms and giving me her best 'you'd better agree with me, or else…' glare. No pressure, then. When I touch Josh's arm for support, the corners of his mouth twitch but he keeps staring into his pint. Swine!

'I think if Jennifer really matters to you, Roger, maybe it's worth a try.'

Roger looks at Jacques, who's surrounded by locals listening to his tales of French midwifery, and sighs. 'OK, I'll give it a go. But there's no way I'm bleaching my teeth or waxing my chest.'

'Excellent.' Kayla grabs the crisp that Roger is about to stuff into his mouth. 'Your makeover had better kick off with a diet and it might as well start now.'

Chapter Twenty-Four

When Kayla decides to do something, she really goes for it. And, sadly for Roger, she's decided to do him. Sprucing up the landlord of the Whistling Wave is her latest project and she's not about to fail.

First of all, she drastically limits his food intake and switches him from chips and beer to salad and low-calorie soft drinks.

'A rabbit would starve on this,' grumbles Roger a couple of days later, holding up a piece of limp lettuce and shaking it in Kayla's face. 'I'm hauling beer barrels about so a few chips wouldn't go amiss.'

'Does Jacques ever order chips?'

'What, old miracle baby deliverer?' Roger whistles through his teeth. 'I bet he's never had a pomme flipping frite in his life.'

'And what does Jacques usually order?' asks Kayla in a sing-song voice as though she's talking to a child.

'Salad,' sighs Roger. He shoves the lettuce into his mouth, chews and swallows.

I don't mention the bread and chips that Jacques is devouring at our house because I don't think it would help. Emily has taken pity on our guest and started inviting him to have dinner with us. She doesn't seem to have fully grasped the concept of bed and breakfast although the clue's in the name.

Kayla's also dragged Roger into Trecaldwith to have what's left of his hair cut and she's planning a trip to help him choose some new clothes and glasses.

'What's wrong with this?' moans Roger, stroking his beloved pewter-grey sweatshirt that's gone bobbly in the wash. But he shuts up when Kayla points at Jacques, who's looking particularly dapper today in beige chinos, pale blue polo shirt and navy blue blazer. He and Jennifer are still spending every lunchtime in the pub.

'That's the look you're going for, mate. Understated and confident with a touch of class rather than your just-fell-out-of-bed vibe.'

'That man has such style,' says smitten Florence, breezing past on her way to the ladies'. 'You can tell he's French just by looking at him. What a gent.'

Jacques is being treated like the hero of the hour even though he didn't actually deliver Pippa's baby. She gave birth to a gorgeous seven pounds two ounces baby boy ten minutes after arriving at the maternity unit and is now back home with Charlie. But everyone still seems very taken with our French guest.

Everyone except Storm, who corners me in the kitchen the next morning while I'm shovelling toast into my mouth before leaving for work. I'm trying not to cry after finding Alice's half-eaten jar of marmalade at the back of the fridge, which is making swallowing toast rather tricky.

'What do you think of him then?' she asks, sitting on the kitchen table in her dressing gown and swinging her legs while I wait for the kettle to boil.

Flicking off the kettle which is belching steam, I force down another mouthful of bread and perch on a chair.

'I presume you mean Jacques? I like him well enough.'

'But we don't really know what he's like, even though he does nothing but talk about himself.'

Which is true enough. Jacques is gregarious and charming, but he does enjoy talking about his business successes, and he's never once mentioned Jennifer since I played gooseberry during their first catch-up.

'He can be a little self-obsessed but what do *you* think of him?'

Storm wipes the back of her hand across her pale, make-up free face. 'I think he's a dick and he's not nice to Jennifer.'

'He seems very fond of Jennifer and they're always together these days.'

'Yeah, too fond if you ask me. It's a bit creepy and he's very controlling.'

When I raise my eyebrows, Storm drums on the table leg with her heels. 'He is. I hear things when I'm working in the shop and I'm behind a shelf and they don't know I'm there. Or when I happen to be standing near the stockroom door and they're talking outside. Or when my shoelaces come undone near them in the pub and I have to stop to do them up. I can't help overhearing.'

Storm's overhearing sounds more stalky than accidental but I want to know what our guest has been saying.

'He's always telling her what to do. He reckons she's stocking the wrong stuff in the shop, which she is but that's not the point 'cos it's not his business. And he told her to get changed the other day 'cos he didn't like her wearing trousers.'

'Crikey, and did she get changed?'

Storm nods, which surprises me because only a brave man or a fool would comment on Jennifer's outfit. She once told Roger she thought her bum looked big in cords and boycotted the pub for a month when he agreed with her.

'She huffed about a bit, but she went and put a dress on. And pukey pink eyeshadow that made her look like she'd been punched in the face. To be honest, she's gone ga-ga. It's like he's her leader or something. I'm never going to be like that with any man. I might go lesbian instead 'cos women are less trouble.'

She glances at me for my reaction but I nod and smile. Good luck to anyone, male or female, who takes on my sister and tries to tell her what to do.

'Maybe Jennifer just likes Jacques, Storm. I know you think they're both ancient, but it does happen.'

'Yeah but you can like someone without making them change for you. If he really likes Jennifer, he should be happy with her the way she is.'

Which is a damn fine point and I get a sudden urge to hug my sister for being so insightful. Though I don't, obviously, because she'd only think I've gone ga-ga too. I'm also tempted to confess that I've sent a wedding invitation to her mum and am already regretting it, but I chicken out.

'Plus, he said stuff about our choir,' says Storm with a sideways look at me.

Her heels continue to kick hell out of the table leg until I gently tap my hand against her shins. 'What sort of stuff?'

'He told Jennifer she was wasted in such a silly amateur choir and she should sing with a more professional choir in Paris. Then he laughed and said our choir was something weird. It sounded like nully?'

'Did he, indeed?'

French lessons at school are a bit of a blur; a jumble of vocab and declensions and being sent to the Head for talking in class. But one phrase I do remember is 'être nul' which means 'to be no good'.

Salt Bay Choral Society can be pitchy at times and we're not professional – we'll take in anyone who loves music and wants to sing. But Jacques raved about our community choir and told me how brilliant it was for Jennifer to be a part of it. I wonder what the French word is for 'two-faced'?

'Hey, what's going on in here then?' booms Barry, slamming the door into the wall when he barges into the kitchen wearing just his underpants. He's paying us a fleeting visit while his band is in Plymouth and appears to have forgotten his pyjamas.

'My eyes! My eyes!' moans Storm. 'First it's Josh with his top off and now Barry with his bits hanging out. I could report you to social services.'

'Stop being such a drama queen. Where's that French bloke?' asks Barry, scratching his chest, which is covered in tight greying curls.

'Fortunately, Jacques isn't here. He had an early breakfast and has gone out for an early morning constitutional on the cliffs.'

'You what?'

'A walk, Barry.'

'Oh, right.' My father yawns and adjusts his off-white baggy boxers. 'And what about you, Storm? What are you doing up at' – he peers at his watch – 'blimey! Quarter past eight in the school holidays. What's going on?'

'Nothing,' scowls Storm. 'I just wanted a word with Annie about Jacques.'

'Yeah, he's a funny one.' Barry grabs half a slice of cold toast from my plate, takes a bite and crumbs spray everywhere when he adds: 'I wouldn't trust him as far as I could throw him.'

'Why? What's he done to you?'

'Nothing. But he's a man who expects everything to go his way. He comes across as arrogant and he looks at me funny.'

Most people look at a fifty-something bloke funny when his paunch is overhanging his leather trousers and his hair is hanging loose to his shoulders. But Jacques' looks must have been extra funny for Barry to notice.

'Told you.' Storm folds her arms and starts drumming her heels again while I push the rest of my toast towards Barry. My long-lost father and sister seemed totally insensitive when they barged their way into my life last year but sometimes they pick up on things that others ignore.

Suddenly Barry leaps from his chair, lunges for the radio and rams the volume up to ear-bleedingly loud. 'That is most definitely my song!' he yells over a catchy tune that's juddering across the kitchen.

'Not again,' shouts Storm, slouching across the table and slamming her head down onto her splayed out arms. 'It's a stupid song that's high in the stupid charts and sung by a stupid boy band. But it's not *your* stupid song, Barry. You're getting dementia.'

'Yes, it is my song,' he yells back, 'My band performed it in the eighties at the Sunshine Festival which is where I got up close and personal with Joanna and Annie was conceived.'

Fantastic! Jacques will come back at any moment to find my father in his underpants yelling about impregnating my mother while a pop song is shaking the house's foundations.

'What the hell is going on?' shouts Josh, bowling in through the back door and flicking the radio off. 'I could hear that down by the harbour.' He does a double-take at Barry's underwear and raises his hands to the ceiling in defeat. It's happened! My outrageously dysfunctional family have defeated my lovely boyfriend.

'Isn't it about time the two of you got dressed?'

It's like talking to toddlers but sometimes that's the only way to get through to the father and sister I've been landed with.

'My eardrums are, like, totally screwed now, not that you'd care, Barry,' moans Storm, stumbling to her feet. And she carries on grumbling under her breath all the way up the stairs, with Barry slouching along behind her.

'Sorry, Josh. Are you rethinking the whole getting married thing?'

He laughs and holds out his arms. 'Come here. You look like you're in need of a hug.'

When I lay my cheek against Josh's chest, I can hear the beating of his heart even though my ears are still ringing.

'I apologise for having such a peculiar family when yours are so normal.'

'Normal? Mum's fine but Lucy can be a nightmare, Serena's just like Storm a lot of the time and Freya's hyperactive. So the wedding's still on as far as I'm concerned.'

'That's good because I'm working my way down the wedding to-do list and the freezer's already stuffed with prawn vol-au-vents.'

Snuggling up against the soft cotton of Josh's T-shirt, I can just see the list which is stuck to the fridge and topped by FOOD in capital letters. We're doing the wedding grub ourselves to save money and it'll only be a glorified buffet which still won't be cheap. But it's far less expensive than having outside caterers and our reception doesn't have to be perfect. It just has to be here.

In the hallway, I hear the front door open and heavy footsteps as Jacques heads upstairs. Please don't let him encounter a half-naked Barry on the landing.

'Josh, do you think it's fair on Storm and Emily bringing strangers into our home and running a B&B?'

'Whoah! Where did that come from?'

'Storm reckons Jacques is weird and has some sort of Svengali hold over Jennifer, Roger's upset that he's here at all, the locals are kicking off about our B&B idea and then there's the marmalade.'

Josh holds me at arm's length and narrows his eyes. 'What's that about marmalade?'

'I found Alice's marmalade in the fridge.'

'Ah. As Storm would say, that sucks big time.'

Josh wraps his arms around me and holds me while I snivel.

Chapter Twenty-Five

Thunder wakes me in the early hours of Saturday morning. The sky was a huge yellow bruise when we went to bed so we knew a storm was coming. But I hoped it might do a swerve and head for France instead.

I've got nothing against summer storms. Cornwall is awesome when the air's heavy with the tang of sulphur and lightning forks into a black sea. But it's the rain that's worrying me; the rain and Tregavara House's dodgy roof.

Slipping out of bed, I sit at the open window watching as the village is lit up by white flashes and thunder rolls around the valley. Behind me, Josh's legs are tangled in a crumpled sheet and his bare back gently rises and falls in time with his breathing. That man could sleep through anything after sharing a house with Freya when she was a baby.

A sudden gust of wind billows the curtains into my face and rain begins to fall. Oh, no. Fat drops splatter and burst on the garden path and the scent of baked earth drifts into the bedroom as I cross my fingers this is as bad as it gets.

Has the crossing fingers thing ever worked? I wonder, when there's a crash of thunder and rain begins to fall in torrents – proper torrents that scour the pavement and form dark rivulets where water meets the road. After a while, the rain starts bouncing off the stone window ledge onto my nightshirt and I'm pulling the window closed when there's an ear-curdling screech from the landing.

'What the hell?' Josh is sitting bolt upright in bed, rubbing his eyes. 'What's going on?'

Before I can answer, another screech echoes along the landing before being drowned out by a huge clap of thunder.

Josh leaps out of bed but I'm at the door before him. The landing is in darkness but illuminated every few seconds by flashes of lightning. The storm must be directly above us now because the thunder is deafening, and rain is smashing into the stained-glass window above the staircase.

I flick the light switch, but nothing happens. The power's out.

Another flash lights up Storm, standing in her long white T-shirt like a ghost.

'It's coming in,' she yells into the darkness.

'What is?' I trip and stumble over the shoes that Storm will insist on leaving in the middle of the landing.

'Water. I almost drowned in my sleep. There's water everywhere.'

Josh sprints past me, waving a torch, and rushes into Storm's room. He points the light at the ceiling, which is moving as though it's come to life. No, it's not the ceiling that's moving. It's water – a stream of water that's cascading onto Storm's bed. Josh waves his torch across the room and the beam picks up another stream flowing from the ceiling in the corner.

'This house is trying to kill me,' wails Storm as Jacques emerges from Alice's room in a striped dressing gown. He does a double-take at Emily, who's lit up by Josh's torch and looks like a giant rabbit in her fluffy onesie.

'Mon dieu! Qu'est-ce qui se passe?'

'Water's coming in through the roof,' shouts Josh above the thunder. 'I need to get into the attic.'

He illuminates the ceiling hatch that's halfway along the landing, pulls down the loft ladder and clambers up it, closely followed by Jacques.

'Not again!' moans Storm when a flash of lightning turns night to day and she gets an eyeful up Jacques' dressing gown. 'Social services would have a field day in this place.'

'Buckets and torches!' I yell, leading a charge for the kitchen.

Twenty minutes later, the storm has passed and the floor of Storm's bedroom is an obstacle course of buckets, bowls and anything else we could find to catch the water that's still dripping. I've stripped her bed and made up a new one for her in the small spare room that Barry and Toby use.

'We've done the best we can and patched up the roof with polythene,' says Josh, coming down the ladder ahead of Jacques while I shine my torch on the rungs.

'How bad is it?' I uncross my crossed fingers because what's the point?

'The repair held, ironically, but another part of the roof's letting in water now. I think the roof's completely knackered. Has the storm passed?'

'I think so. It's heading for Land's End.'

'Thank goodness for that.' Josh turns, his face ghostly in torch light, and shakes Jacques' hand. 'Thank you for your help and sorry about all of this. I don't suppose rain coming through the roof is what you expect from a B&B.'

'Not really but it's not a problem. I found it quite exciting actually.'

'Exciting?' mutters Storm. 'You'd have found it fricking terrifying if *Titanic* was being re-enacted in *your* bedroom.'

Jacques doesn't hear, or pretends not to, and bids us all *bonne nuit* before heading for his dry bed. Storm slouches off after him to the spare room and Emily gives me a brief hug before going back to her room.

'Can we get by with another repair to the roof?' I ask Josh once Emily's door has clicked shut.

'I expect so but it's just short-term, Annie. We can't put off sorting out the roof properly forever and it needs to be done before the winter storms set in or this house has had it.'

Darkness cloaks his lovely face when he lowers the torch and pulls me close against him. His chest is still damp from battling with the elements and several metres of polythene.

'I'm so sorry,' he murmurs into my hair. 'I know how much this house means to you.'

It means so much to me, I might have to let it go to save it.

Chapter Twenty-Six

The next morning, I wake up feeling groggy as though I've had a few too many in the Whistling Wave. And for one blissful moment before I open my eyes I think the night's happenings were a dream – but a trip to Storm's room quickly puts paid to that notion.

Water is still dripping slowly from the stained ceiling and the buckets and bowls are full of brown sludgy liquid. The rain picked up dirt while it was cascading through the attic and onto Storm's bed. Her room will need repairing and redecorating and as for the roof…

Rob from the roofing business comes out quickly, spends ages poking around under the eaves and climbs down the loft ladder looking grim.

'Just as I feared, your roof can't withstand a good old Cornish storm because it's compromised.' Which is presumably business speak for 'knackered'. He shoves his pencil behind his ear and scans the piece of paper he's been scribbling on.

'Can you repair it?'

'I can make it watertight again, but you'll be in the same position before too long if you don't replace the whole roof. And next time the rain comes in the damage to the interior of the house might be more severe. You got off quite lucky really with the storm passing over quickly. They often sit on the village for ages 'cos it's in a valley.'

Oh dear. My knees suddenly feel weak and Josh puts a steadying hand on my shoulder before taking over. 'You'd better make the roof watertight and we'll let you know about replacing it.'

Rob gives me a sympathetic smile. He can tell we're strapped for cash. 'Sure thing. But have a think about what I've said and I wouldn't leave it too long before you get back in touch. This is a gorgeous old house and I'd hate to see it spoiled.'

While Rob's banging about in the attic, I wander into Storm's soggy room and perch on the cold stone window sill.

'What are we going to do, Alice?' I whisper to the walls. 'We can't afford a new roof but the thought of Toby ripping the heart out of this gorgeous house is killing me. And what about the wedding? Am I daft getting married when we're skint? If it's no trouble, could you send me a sign? Please.'

I sit there waiting while Rob bangs about above my head, but nothing happens. There's no bolt from above, no vision of Alice with angel wings pointing me in the right direction, no flashing sign saying 'Sell up!' or 'Stay put!' Of course there isn't. Alice has gone.

The brown stain on the ceiling has spread like mud above Storm's bed and breath catches in my throat when I spot a brown line above the wardrobe in the corner. But it's only after I've pulled open the wardrobe doors that I know for sure. Filthy water has snaked inside, a musty smell hits me and there it is. My second-best but perfectly adequate wedding dress has huge, brown water marks running down the cream bodice and skirt. It's ruined.

I run my fingers across the ruined satin, which is still sopping wet and smells of wet dog.

'Blimey, Alice. That's one hell of a sign.'

I go in search of Josh who's been out for a run and find him getting dressed after his shower. So far, he's put on dark grey boxers and black socks and his wet hair is standing on end. Usually the sight of a half-naked Josh fills me with lust, though the socks are a bit of a passion killer, but today there's nothing. I'm so tired and fed up I don't even want to shag my boyfriend.

'Are you OK? Rob's doing a quick patch-up and the damage is quite extensive so it's going to be a bit pricey. But we'll sort something out.' He sits on our bed and pats the space beside him.

I sit next to him and take a really good look at Josh's lovely face. He's still gorgeous with a shadow of stubble across his strong jaw but there are dark circles under his eyes. He's getting married in three weeks' time and should be on top of the world but instead he's stressed and tired and scrabbling for every penny.

Suddenly everything clicks into place as though Alice has whispered the answer in my ear.

Turning towards Josh, I lace my fingers through his. 'This house deserves more than a succession of quick patch-ups. It needs someone who's got the cash for a new roof to keep the place going. It needs Toby.'

I'm expecting Josh to put up a bit of a fight and insist we should try selling to someone else. But he nods, as worn down by money worries as I am. 'You'll have to move out of Salt Bay.'

'That's all right. The locals don't like my B&B idea and I'll be persona non grata when they find out I'm selling to Toby. I'll be run out of the village anyway.'

Josh grins and squeezes my hand. 'What changed your mind?'

'A river running through Storm's bedroom was a bit of a wake-up call and I've realised what's most important.'

'Which is?'

'All of us. You and me, Storm and Emily. I've been so upset about losing Alice, I couldn't see what really matters. So let Toby have what he wants and we can all move on. I love this house and it'll break my heart to leave it but you all matter to me more. That's it.'

I shrug and breathe out slowly. 'Oh, and we shouldn't get married. Not this month anyway. The rain's ruined my dress and there'll be no money to replace it or buy food for the reception once we've paid Rob for the latest repair. And we need to save every penny in case the roof needs another repair before...' I gulp, 'before it goes to Toby.'

Eek, I was doing so well but now my eyes are filling with tears and Josh is stroking my arm which doesn't help. I blink rapidly and twist my silver engagement ring round and round on my finger.

'I'm so sorry about your dress, Annie, but we've already bought some food and could still do the wedding on the cheap.'

'We were already doing it on the cheap and we can't feed people on nothing but prawn vol-au-vents. Let's get real, Josh. We need to spend what we have on keeping the house watertight, so the wedding will have to wait for a while until we're living somewhere else and money's not such an issue.'

'I know it makes financial sense but you so wanted to have the reception at Tregavara House where you feel close to Alice.' Josh frowns. 'I suppose Toby might still let us have the reception here when he owns the place and before he carves it up into flats.'

'He might but there'll be strings attached because that's just the way he is and he doesn't like you.'

'He really doesn't like me,' agrees Josh.

'So it wouldn't be the same and I'd rather we did our own thing without having to tiptoe around Toby. Alice will be with me in my heart wherever we have our wedding.'

And I try to smile to show that I'm absolutely fine with our change of plan. But my mouth wobbling rather gives me away.

Chapter Twenty-Seven

Toby almost bites my hand off when I ring and tell him he can buy the place if he'd like. So that's it then. Tregavara House will be partitioned into flats and strangers will live here. But at least I'm passing it on to a Trebarwith and the house will survive – which is what Alice would want. If only I could shake off the niggling feeling that I'm still letting her and the house down.

Yep, the house! I've assigned a full gamut of feelings and emotions to a two-hundred-year-old heap of granite and mortar. But sometimes the house's groans in the early hours, as old walls are settling, sound like admonishments and I've started saying 'sorry' in reply. Really quietly so I don't wake Josh and tip him off that I'm quite possibly losing my mind.

I'm also bitterly disappointed that our wedding's off even though I keep telling myself that nothing important has changed. Not really. Josh and I still love each other and live together and we will get married one day. But right now, this wonderful house that's been in my family for generations has to be saved from my penury. Even though leaving will break my heart.

Jacques, on the other hand, has no qualms about saying farewell to a falling-down house and heads back to Paris the day after the storm. He does promise he'll be back as he climbs into his shiny Mercedes but I'm not sure whether he means it or he's just being his usual charming, two-faced self.

Jennifer doesn't look too upset when I call into her shop on the proviso of buying a newspaper but really to check how she's doing. In fact, she's looking good and appears to have ditched her trousers completely – these days, she's never seen without a nice dress, full slap make-up and blonde hair backcombed to within an inch of its life. Her bouffant hairstyle is so magnificent, Kayla keeps threatening to set it up with its own Twitter account.

'Did Jacques get off on time yesterday?' she asks, on her knees adjusting bottles of sun cream so the prices are more visible. 'And I'm so sorry about the rain coming through your roof. That's the trouble with these old houses.'

Then she goes back to her sun cream without giving me the third degree about what damage was done and the cost of repairs. Storm was right. Jennifer isn't quite herself.

'I don't mean to pry but I wondered how you're feeling about Jacques leaving?'

'Sounds like prying to me.' Jennifer staggers to her feet and wipes her hands down her overly snug dress. 'I feel fine, thank you very much, and Jacques is coming back for your wedding – he'll be my plus-one if that's all right. I didn't think you'd mind seeing as it's your fault he was here in the first place.'

I nod, keeping my face as neutral as possible because I want to tell Kayla first about our change in wedding plans and selling to Toby. She'll go ballistic so I've been putting it off. Storm and Emily didn't take it too well at first but are coming round.

'He's giving me some space to consider his offer,' says Jennifer, settling down on the stool behind the counter. 'You might be surprised to learn that he's invited me to live rent-free in a flat he owns in Paris and he'll pay for singing lessons and set me up with some work opportunities.'

'Wow, that's some offer. What are you going to do?'

'I'm considering it. Leaving this business that I've built up over the years would be hard but he's offering a lot.'

'He certainly is but...' I hesitate, not sure how to word my next question. 'What would he expect in return?'

'Are you alluding to sex, Annie?'

OK, I wasn't expecting that. 'I just wondered... I mean, I didn't mean to imply...'

'We're just old friends, though I wouldn't rule out becoming – how do young people put it these days? – *friends with benefits* in the future. But it's the singing that particularly interests me and the chance to do what I should have done forty years ago. Before... well, you know what happened.' She gazes into the distance and her face hardens. 'Anyway, that's my news and I'd be grateful if you didn't bandy it about. You've proved yourself to be a reliable confidante.'

'I won't say anything if you don't want me to and it is an amazing opportunity, Jennifer. But how do you feel about leaving everyone in Salt Bay, people like Roger?'

'Roger is behaving very oddly at the moment. He's obviously imbibing rather too much of his merchandise. But I'd miss him and everyone here, including you. That's why I'm taking time to consider Jacques' offer. But how often do people get second chances, Annie?'

'I got my second chance when I left London for Salt Bay and met Alice.'

And my third chance, I guess, will be when Tregavara House is sold and we move to Trecaldwith. That's my fork in the road all decided and almost done and dusted while Jennifer is still hesitating at the crossroads.

There's a smudge of pink lipstick on Jennifer's top teeth when she smiles. 'This village has been good for you, Annie, and you've been good for the village in return. My second chance will mean leaving Salt Bay but the village can't stay the same forever.'

I'm so tempted to let it all spill out – about us leaving the village too and Toby having the house and our wedding being postponed and my heart hurting even though I know I'm doing the right thing. But Jennifer would only tell the whole world so I keep my mouth shut.

The bell over the shop door clangs and Jennifer slides off the stool. 'Linda, how lovely to see you up and about after your operation. Are you here for your magazines? I've kept them for you under the counter.'

I slip away, leaving Jennifer to deal with her customer and make up her mind about the path her life will take.

Chapter Twenty-Eight

News that our wedding is off spreads around the village like wildfire once I've told Kayla. And I get used to people approaching me in the street, doing an 'aw' face, patting me on the arm and walking off without a word. They obviously don't know about Toby yet – I made Kayla keep that bombshell quiet – or their pats might be punches.

I'm expecting the same mute sympathy at the next choir rehearsal but there's an air of fevered excitement when I arrive on the dot of seven-thirty. Josh, Emily and Storm went on ahead while I finished clearing up the tea things. Normally they help but they all ate their food and bolted. Weird.

'You're here at last! Come with me,' insists Maureen, putting her hand on the small of my back and propelling me towards the altar. She has dark smudges down her blouse and there's a pile of oozing chocolate cupcakes on the front pew. Fabulous! Breaktime will be a bonanza of buttercream.

The choir are sitting silently in their seats and Josh is standing near the piano with Michaela. Everyone here's except for Jennifer and they all smile at me when I reach the crate cum podium. Which, again, is weird. Usually I have to raise my voice to get their attention first thing.

'What's going on?' Everyone's still staring at me and I run my tongue across my teeth for any stray teatime spinach.

Lovely Mary levers herself to her feet using the back of the chair in front of her. 'We have something to tell you.'

'O-K.' I laugh nervously because, in my experience, when people have 'something to tell you' it's often bad news: Mum disclosing she had cancer, Alice confirming her health was deteriorating, Barry turning up on my doorstep and announcing he was my long-lost father. Though that last one turned out to be a good thing in the end.

'The thing is,' says Mary, her white curled hair shining under the lights, 'we were upset to hear that you and Josh have had to postpone your wedding because finances are tight. Especially as it was your last chance to have the reception at Tregavara House.'

'Yeah, seeing as we hear it's going to toffee-nosed Toby, who'll ruin the place and never fit in round here,' grumbles Roger, who's slimmer and smarter than usual.

'Kayla, you told them?'

She holds up her hands, palms towards me. 'It wasn't me, Sunshine. You wanna tell that brooding fiancé of yours to keep a lid on things.'

Has Josh been blabbing? He doesn't look particularly guilty.

'Shush,' shouts Arthur. 'Let Mary finish – though can I first register my disquiet at your cousin becoming the owner of prime property in Salt Bay.'

Mary tuts softly. 'Disquiet noted, thank you, Arthur. Anyway, we've all been talking to Josh about the situation you're both in and the thing is, you *can* get married.'

'And we will once we've found somewhere else to live and we've got enough money for a reception and you'll all be re-invited. It would be lovely to have the reception at Tregavara House but it really doesn't matter,' I say brightly, to cover up that it does matter very much.

'What Mary means is that the Salt Bay Choral Society is going to save your wedding,' butts in Maureen, jumping to her feet. 'We're going to give you the best reception and send-off that Salt Bay's ever seen. Well,' she backtracks, 'it won't be anything too posh, I'm afraid, but we'll all bring a dish to share and chip in for the booze.'

'Which I can get at cost price,' adds Roger.

'We can sort out tables and decorations and flowers too,' says Fiona. 'So what do you think?'

I think I'm going to cry and the muscles in Josh's jaw are working overtime.

'What you're suggesting is amazing and wonderful, but we can't let you go to all that trouble.'

'It's no trouble,' says Cyril from the back row of the tenors. 'You've done so much for us and for the village. So this is our wedding present to you both.' His cheeks go pink and his chin drops to his chest.

'Well said, Cyril,' calls Gerald. 'You're one of us now, Annie, and we help our own. So the wedding's going ahead, right?'

'But I've cancelled the ceremony.'

'That's all right because I've had a word with Hilary this evening and un-cancelled it,' says Josh with a grin. How long has he known about this?

I look around me at the strange ragbag of people I've come to love over the last nineteen months. People who've accepted an incomer from London and made her a part of this close-knit community.

'If you're sure,' I gulp. 'That would be the most fantastic wedding present ever. Thank you so much.'

Everyone cheers when Josh strides forward, circles my waist with his strong arms and swings me round.

'Did you organise this?' I whisper into his ear as his thick dark hair tickles my nose.

'Nope, it's all their idea. Gerald sounded me out about it this morning and you deserve it because you're always doing so much for other people. Anyway, I can't wait any longer to make you Mrs Pasco.'

'Ms Trebarwith.'

'Whatever you want to call yourself. I don't care as long as you marry me this month.' And he kisses me on the lips while everyone claps.

During the break, I sit alone at the back of the church gathering my thoughts. I'll be walking down this aisle in less than three weeks' time thanks to my lovely choir, who are currently clustered round the chocolate cupcakes.

The only sour note of the evening is Jennifer's absence. Is she starting to cut her ties with us in anticipation of her move to Paris? The village will be devastated if she leaves, especially Roger, who's shoving a whole cupcake into his gob while Kayla's back is turned.

Who'd have guessed he was holding a candle for our star soprano? Not even Roger, it seems, and now he's realised when it's probably too late. That's tough. But at least he'll be slim and smart as well as sad in the crisp new shirts that Kayla's made him buy.

Aargh! Covering my face with my hands, I rock gently back and forth in the pew.

It's all very well organising the reception so my wedding can go ahead but what the hell am I going to wear? I picture the satin dress still hanging stained and bedraggled in the wardrobe because I haven't had the heart to chuck it out.

'Are you all right, dear? Have you got a headache?' calls Florence, marching up the aisle. 'I need a quick chat with you if possible.'

'Of course. What's the problem?'

'Not here when he's about.' She glances at Josh, who's chatting with Tom and Ollie. 'In the vestry. Follow me.'

She scuttles off down the aisle, does a swerve past the cake scoffers and shoots into the vestry with me following her. After pushing the door to, she pulls out a large suit carrier stashed behind a cupboard.

'I didn't want your fiancé to see this. He told Gerald that the rain coming through your roof ruined the dress that you were going to wear for your wedding, which is a terrible shame.'

She starts unzipping the carrier. Uh-oh, I have a horrible idea where this is going. I swallow and nod.

'So I brought this in for you to wear. It's the dress I wore when I married my Bob and it should fit you because I was a lot skinnier in those days. But feel free to alter it if need be. It would be a great honour if you'd wear it on your wedding day. There's no need to thank me.'

She beams and pulls back the black nylon cover.

Oh my. It's so kind of Florence to let me wear her wedding dress. I'm touched beyond belief at her thoughtfulness and kindness. But Florence's dress is absolutely hideous. Huge looping swathes of lace and shiny chalk-white satin festoon the creation, which has a deep ruffled neckline and puffed sleeves edged with a flurry of more ruffles. And there appears to be a hoop underneath the full skirt.

'Wow, Florence, I really don't know what to say!' I exclaim as Kayla barrels into the room holding a plastic cup of orange squash.

'Here you are!' She gasps at the dress, open-mouthed. 'What – is – that?'

'It's Florence's beautiful wedding dress which she has extremely generously said I can wear on my wedding day.'

Kayla looks at me in horror but clamps her mouth shut when I widen my eyes at her.

'Well' – she swallows – 'that is indeed very generous of you, Florence. Annie will look a right picture in it.'

Florence beams even more widely and smooths down one of the many lace swags on her precious dress. 'I'll leave it with you, dear, and I'll be so proud when you wear it down the aisle. Right, I'm off to grab one of Maureen's cupcakes before Roger has another one.'

'Another one?' scowls Kayla. 'He promised me he hadn't had any.'

'What a scamp. He's had at least two that I've seen.'

The second the door closes behind Florence, Kayla starts shaking with laughter. 'That is a million times worse than any of the dresses at Wendy's Wowzer Weddings.' She's shaking so much, orange squash is splashing in all directions.

'Shush, Kayla, I don't want Florence to hear you and don't get your drink on the satin or she'll kill you. It's incredibly kind of her to lend me such a special dress.'

Kayla snorts. 'You say special. I say hideous. Have you noticed the hoop? You'll look like Little Bo Peep walking up the aisle in that and Josh will definitely do a runner. All you need is a crook on your arm and a couple of sheep for bridesmaids. The photos will be priceless.'

'I know. But how can I not wear it without upsetting Florence?'

'Just tell her you'd rather walk into church stark naked. You need to stop thinking about everyone else, Sunshine. You're the one getting married so you get to be selfish for the whole day.'

'OK but it's not as though I've got anything else to wear.'

'Anything else – and I mean *anything* – would be better than that,' chortles Kayla before collapsing into more fits of giggles which is no help whatsoever.

After the rehearsal, Josh, Emily and Storm go to the pub but I'm tired and walk home with Florence's dress over my arm. It weighs a ton – it must be all those ruffles.

The house is eerily quiet when I let myself in and switch on the lamp in the sitting room. It's still light outside but the lamp casts a golden glow over Alice's favourite chair where she'd sit when a storm blew in and watch sea spray plume into the air. Our windows are always streaked with salt on blowy days.

Alice would know what to do about Florence's dress and how to avoid hurting her feelings. She knew everything about everyone in the village though she wasn't always the most tactful of souls. Roger reckons she once told him he resembled one of his beer barrels from the side.

After carefully laying the dress across the back of the sofa, I sink onto the soft cushions and sit for a while thinking about my wedding. My lovely choir will never know how much their rescue plan means to me – and how pleased Alice would be with my last hurrah before leaving Salt Bay.

When the house is silent like this, I can almost feel her presence. Not her spirit, because all that supernatural stuff is too woo-woo for me. If ghosts were real, Mum would be haunting me right now and accusing me of 'submitting to the patriarchy' by getting married – though I know she'd like Josh.

Alice's presence is more ethereal as though her vitality has leached into the stones of Tregavara House and she's become part of the building. I just hope she'll still be here after Toby has taken a sledgehammer to the place.

Chapter Twenty-Nine

In the end, I hang Florence's dress next to my ruined one, close the wardrobe door and try to forget it. At some point I'll have to break the news that I'm not going to wear it, but procrastination is hugely underrated.

Over the next couple of days I decide that the pretty maxi dress I wore to Maura's wedding in London will do for getting married in. Wearing pale lemon cotton isn't how I imagined myself going up the aisle but it seems shallow to get hung up about clothes when it's only thanks to people's kindness that we're getting married at all.

Seeing as I've gone off piste with the dress, I've told my bridesmaids they can wear what they like on the big day so we're going to look a right ragbag going up the aisle. Me in a summer frock, Kayla done up to the nines in a slinky body-con from her wardrobe, Emily in something frilly and frumpy and Storm in Doc Martens and jeans. It'll certainly be a wedding that Salt Bay will never forget.

Talking of unforgettable, Roger's doing his best to make himself irresistible to Jennifer by sticking to Kayla's regime, which he describes as boot camp. It's early days but it's already starting to pay off.

He's definitely looking more svelte when I nip into the pub after leaving work early on Friday afternoon. He's slimmed off slightly around the neck and belly, he's got new specs, and he's wearing a moss green T-shirt that suits his colouring better. Best of all, the ubiquitous summer damp patches under his arms have disappeared.

'I made him change his deodorant,' says Kayla when I mention it. 'I should have done it ages ago 'cos now the bar's far more fragrant. I've also culled the pub's CD collection by telling him Jennifer hates pan pipes. He threw all his pipes CDs in the bin straight away. Result! You customers owe me a debt of gratitude.' She clenches her fist and punches the air.

'Does she hate pan pipes?'

'She must do. No one in their right mind can stand the damn things. They're far too… cheerful. I told him she loves Radiohead so he's ordered a job-lot of their CDs from Amazon. My wiles are legendary.'

She wanders off looking pleased with herself while I sip at my lemonade. I've only nipped into the pub to escape Rob, who's doing another evaluation of the roof's condition for Toby. My cousin wants to double-check what he'll be paying out once the house is his which is fair enough. But I can't face a conversation with Rob about a roof that soon won't be mine.

Fortunately Rob's van has gone when I get home and it's blissfully quiet because everyone else is out. I'm planning on having a cup of tea in the sitting room but first I head to my bedroom for a cardigan. The hot weather has returned and emmets are out in force but the temperature noticeably drops inside the house's thick stone walls.

On the landing, a large steamer trunk is blocking the way and I spot a scrawled note on top.

Found this in corner of attic and have brought down so it won't get wet when rain comes in again.

When rain comes in again… Toby had better pull his finger out and get this house purchase finalised.

I run my hand along the top of the trunk, which is bound by thick wooden bands and covered in dust. I've never seen it before but then again I've hardly ever been in the attic.

There's a pile of junk up there plus loads of spiders so I only ventured up the loft ladder once and came right back down again when a web brushed my face. Flood, bereavement and cancelled weddings, I can cope with. Eight-legged arachnids with hairy bodies – not so much.

Two heavy metal clasps on front of the trunk give a satisfying clunk when I unfasten them and push open the heavy domed lid. Piles of photos and yellowing papers are stacked up inside.

Sitting back on my heels, I pull out a handful of pictures. Most are black and white, but some are in colour though the colours are fading to brown. These are amazing! A few of the photos are more recent and include two shots of my mum as a young woman with her long fair hair. They must have been taken just before she left Salt Bay for good.

But most of the photos show people in old-fashioned clothes. One particularly striking picture is of a middle-aged couple sitting near a huge fern in an enamelled planter. The woman is wearing a high-necked blouse and dark jacket over a belted full skirt. The man standing behind her with his hand on her shoulder is in a smart suit with a watch chain looping from his waistcoat pocket.

Neither of them are smiling. In fact, they look terrifyingly severe but they probably weren't allowed to move for ages while the picture was taken on a Box Brownie. It was a big deal back then. Not like nowadays when people are always shoving iPhones in your face.

Spidery black writing is scratched across the back of the picture which is mounted on thick card: *Benjamin and Charlotte Trebarwith.* They must be ancestors of mine. My DNA and theirs are linked. Do

I look like them? I study the shape of their mouths and the angle of their cheekbones and shiver. The thought of looking like people so long gone is weird.

Putting the pile of photos to one side, I pull out a large bible from the trunk, which is bound in mottled brown leather with gold lettering. The tissue-thin leaves are loose when I carefully open up the book and there, written out in blue ink on the inside cover, is the Trebarwith family tree.

This is brilliant! It's like being on *Who Do You Think You Are?* and striking gold at the end of the programme. So Danny Dyer can trace his roots back to William the Conqueror? Well, I can now trace mine back to – I run my finger along the main branch of the family tree – Jeremiah Trebarwith, born in Cornwall in 1638. Amazing!

My mum's name, Joanna, lies beneath the names of my grandparents Samuel and Sheila and under her there's a question mark. That must be me. I was nothing but a question mark to the Trebarwith family for ages but now I belong.

After carefully placing the bible on the landing carpet, I delve into the trunk and pull out a small parcel wrapped in tissue paper. The paper was probably once white but has yellowed with time and, when I peel it back, I stop breathing. Nestled in the fragile parcel are children's clothes.

There's a Babygro made of white flannelling and tiny baby shoes in soft beige leather. Underneath lie a pair of small grey shorts and what looks like a school tie. A striped child's top is wrapped around a silver frame which holds a family photo. Three people are smiling at the camera – a young woman I immediately recognise as Alice, a handsome dark-haired man whose eyes crinkle at the edges and, between them, a small boy in grey shorts with a mischievous grin.

'Hello, Freddie. How marvellous to see you at last,' I whisper, tracing the outline of his face with my finger. I can only imagine the devastation soon after this photo was taken when Freddie caught measles and died from complications. No wonder Alice hid away this cruel reminder of what she'd lost.

Children are playing outside on the harbour sand and their shouts drift through the open windows as I cry for lost Freddie and lost Alice. How could she bear to go on without her beloved son?

I sit snivelling for a while, afraid to delve further into the trunk that's unlocking pain from the past and pulling it into the present. Though maybe Alice would be glad it's out in the open at last.

'You've come this far, Trebarwith, so get a grip and keep going,' I say out loud, my words echoing down the stairs.

Next out of the trunk is a pile of old school reports dating back to the early 1930s and below them there's a double layer of tissue. My fingers push around the tissue and touch fabric – smooth fabric that's heavy when I pull it from the trunk and gasp. I'm holding a beautiful wedding dress made of cream silk that's nipped in at the waist with a long full skirt. It's Alice's, I'm sure of it, because her wedding photo from the 1960s was on her bedside table. But the lace overlay across the bodice and shoulders is delicate and the style suggests it's from two decades earlier.

Whenever it was made, the dress is absolutely gorgeous. Stripping off on the landing, I pull the dress over my head and it rustles down over me. The fabric smells slightly fusty but the dress fits, more or less. It's too long and bunches around my feet but wearing high heels would fix that. Josh is over six feet tall so towering heels won't be a problem – just so long as I practise walking in them first. Literally tripping up the aisle isn't great on your wedding day.

But I'm getting ahead of myself. Gathering up the skirt in both hands, I walk slowly into Alice's bedroom and stand in front of the floor-length mirror propped up against the wall.

Yay! I don't look half-bad. In fact, I'd go so far as to say I look pretty damn decent. The creamy colour of the silk complements my bright blue eyes and brown hair and warms my pale colouring. In fact, my face seems to glow. The only thing that spoils the effect are the mascara trails on my cheeks from all that snivelling.

'Thank you, Alice,' I say in the room that's still full of her. 'Is this the ideal wedding gift you told Josh you had for me?'

The front door slams and I start panicking in case it's Josh but thundering footsteps coming up the stairs announce Storm's arrival.

'What's all this crap?' she grumbles, spotting the trunk and its contents strewn across the landing.

'Storm, can you come here for a minute?'

'Where are you?' She clumps along the landing and comes to an abrupt halt at the bedroom door.

'What the hell are you wearing?'

She's hot and flustered and holding her blonde-streaked hair up off the back of her neck.

'It's a wedding dress.'

'Well, duh! You're hardly going to do the gardening in it, are you? Is that the dress Florence got married in? Only she must have been a lot less fat then.'

'No, this is Alice's wedding dress. I found it in the trunk that's on the landing. What do you think?'

'Hhmm.' Storm walks all round me with her hands on her hips like she's inspecting an ancient monument. 'It's not bad at all,' she finally declares which in sulky teenage lingo means, 'you look amazing'.

I smile and the skirt swishes around my legs when I do a twirl. 'I don't think Alice would mind if I wore this on my big day.'

'I think the old lady would probably be all right with it. It'll be like a bit of her is here supporting you and your family should always support you. Mums especially should always support their children even if it happens to inconvenience them a bit.'

'Have you had a reply from your mum to the wedding invitation?'

'Yeah, to the wedding invitation that I said not to send her. Most of the time you don't tell me what the hell's going on and the rest of the time you're poking your nose into my business. Your behaviour is, like, totally inappropriate.'

I apologise while she stomps around the room to demonstrate how totally inappropriate my behaviour is. Then she fiddles with her phone and thrusts it under my nose so I can see recent text messages between her and her mum.

The last one from Amanda reads: *Thanks for invite. You being a bridesmaid – really? Cornwall is a long way and invite bit last minute so afraid I won't make it. Hope it goes well. Send me pic of you in a dress or Poppy and Eugenie will never believe me x*

'That's disappointing, Storm. I only got involved because I wanted you to see your mum but Cornwall is a long way for her to travel.'

I'm making excuses for Amanda, who's a right cow for not going out of her way to support her daughter. But I want to make my sister feel better.

'Yeah, I know,' she says, thrusting her phone back into her jeans pocket. 'Salt Bay is at the end of the freaking world, but it wouldn't be any different if you were getting hitched in Hackney. Amanda's always got other stuff to do because she's a very busy person. But that's fine. I didn't really want her here anyway, as you well know, and we only invited her to be polite.'

Storm never does anything to be polite, but I nod. 'We'll still have a fantastic day.'

'Yeah, but I don't have to wear some sad dress now you're wearing that, do I?'

'You can still wear what you like.'

'Cool. And it *will* be a fantastic day.' She lowers her chin and mumbles so I can hardly hear what she's saying. 'And even though you're inappropriate, you still do a better job than Amanda.'

Without warning, she hurls herself into my arms and gives me a huge hug. Which is lovely but there are strawberry lolly stains round her mouth and strawberry juice and cream silk don't mix. Patting her back, I force myself not to pull away when she squeezes me tight. To misquote Oscar Wilde: to lose one wedding dress may be regarded as a misfortune; to lose two looks like the universe screaming 'Don't get married!'

But I'll always be here for Storm when her own mother isn't. I hug her close and breathe a sigh of relief when her mouth brushes my hair and not Alice's beautiful dress.

Chapter Thirty

The next few days are a scurry of getting ready for the wedding, which will happen at half past eleven this coming Saturday. The choir are organising everything for the reception which is a huge weight off our minds and they won't let us get involved. But there's still a house to clean and a garden to tidy up and lots of last-minute things to sort out.

I've taken the week off work and Josh and I are scrubbing kitchen tiles together – aw, *so* romantic – when we hear a car pull up and there's a knock on the front door.

Leaving Josh scrubbing, I dodge past the bits and pieces piled in the hall that need to go upstairs before Saturday and pull the door open. Immediately, Freya charges at me and clamps her chubby arms around my thighs. She's wearing yellow shorts and a pink T-shirt and her jet-black hair which reminds me of Josh is tumbling down her back.

'Hello, sweetheart. What on earth are you doing here?'

'Toby's taking me to the beach,' she mumbles into my legs, scuffing at the doorstep in her pretty sandals.

'Where is Toby?'

'I'm here.' My cousin steps into view from behind the rampant honeysuckle that's growing up the front of the house like a Triffid. His arms are wrapped around a picnic basket – one of those posh wicker ones with leather straps that's large enough to hold three courses for a dozen people. 'Sorry to spring it on you but we thought you might like to come to the beach with us.'

Really? We've only communicated by text and email since I agreed to sell the house and now he's here expecting me to play happy families and go off on a jolly. Two days before my wedding.

'I'm afraid I'm rather busy at the moment.'

'Just for a couple of hours.'

'I don't think so.'

'Please,' says Toby quietly. 'I'd really appreciate it.'

Freya giggles when I stroke her soft cheek. 'Why don't you see if you can find Uncle Josh. He might be in the kitchen.'

'Uncle Josh!' yells Freya, unfastening herself from my thighs and hurtling through the hallway.

When she's disappeared through the kitchen door, I step blinking into the garden. The sun is blazing from a flawless blue sky and everything seems extra bright.

'What's going on, Toby? You don't need to come round schmoozing up to me any more because you've won and you're getting the house.'

'It wasn't a competition and I'm paying you good money for it. Better than anyone else would with a rubbish roof.' Toby stops, tightens his grip on the picnic hamper and exhales slowly. 'Look, I could just do with your company and your advice. Oh, here we go.'

I recognise the sound of Josh's long stride on the hall tiles before he steps into the garden with Freya following behind

'What's going on?'

'Good morning to you too, Pasco. I'm hoping Annie will come with Freya and me to the beach. What do you say, Annie?'

I'm about to say no because there's a wedding to be organised and a morning on the beach with Toby isn't my idea of fun. But Freya slips her hand into mine and stares up at me with eyes as dark as coal. 'Please come with us, Auntie Annie. I'd 'preciate it.'

'I don't know, Toby. Perrigan Bay will be packed with tourists at this time of year.'

'Which is why we're not going there, because the last thing I want to do is mix with emmets. We're going to Salt Bay beach instead.'

'You're going down the cliff path with a six-year-old and a… is that a hamper?' snorts Josh. 'That's not a good idea, Toby.'

Hell's bells, it's a terrible idea and Toby will totally wet himself if he's scared of heights. I almost did the first and only time I scrambled down the Path of Doom. Cut into the cliff, the path is utterly terrifying and hardly used these days because it's become even more treacherous over the last few months. It's certainly not suitable for a child.

'I have no intention of taking the cliff path, Pasco. I'm not a complete idiot. I've paid a local fisherman to take us round to the beach in his rowing boat.'

'We're going in a boat!' squeals Freya, jumping up and down on my toes.

'Is Lucy aware that you're taking Freya out in a boat?' asks Josh.

'Does your sister know where Freya's father is taking his own daughter? Yes, she does, thanks very much.'

'And she's OK with it?'

'She is as long as Annie comes too.'

Cheers, Lucy. There's nothing I'd enjoy more than being stuck in a tiny rowing boat with my tricky cousin, a boisterous six-year-old and a hamper the size of a small car.

When I hesitate, Toby leans forward. 'You said I should spend more quality time with Freya which is why I'm taking her to the beach I played on as a child. I'm just following your advice.'

Josh's arm snakes round my waist and he pulls me into the hall where Toby can't overhear us.

'Why doesn't he just keep out of our lives? That man is such a pain in the neck.'

'I know. But he's our pain in the neck because he's related to me and to Freya and soon he'll own this house. So what are we going to do about this beach trip?'

'This ridiculous beach trip.'

'It sounds like he's got it all planned and I guess it's quite sweet that he wants Freya to enjoy the beach he went to as a child.'

Ugh, I so wish I would stop standing up for Toby. It's becoming a habit – an embarrassing tic that just won't go away.

'I just don't trust him to take care of Freya near deep water and, I know it's a pain, but I'd feel easier if you were with them.'

'I don't suppose you fancy coming along too?'

Josh grimaces. 'I'm not sure that me and Toby marooned on the same patch of wet sand for a couple of hours would be a good idea. There's only so long I can resist the urge to punch him in the face.'

He's right. Freya doesn't need to witness her father and uncle having a ruckus round the rock pools. But the thought of being stuck with Toby for hours is grim.

'Pleeeze Auntie Annie,' calls Freya. She pops her head around the open front door and gives me a gorgeous grin. 'My bucket's got princesses on it.' Toby appears behind her, waving the bright green bucket and a matching spade.

'All right, Toby. I can spare a couple of hours but that's all.'

'The beach! The beach!' yells Freya, whirling round in a circle with her arms spread out wide. Toby's been feeding her sweets if the open packet stuffed into his trouser pocket is anything to go by and she's high on sugar and E-numbers. Wowzers, this boat trip is going to be fun.

As it turns out, the boat trip is fabulous. Peter Seegrass rows us in his blue boat with a burgundy stripe around the harbour wall that juts into the ocean. The water is smooth as glass near the shore but there's a swell beyond the sheltering wall and Freya chuckles with delight as the boat bobs up and down. Rowing looks like hard work but Peter whistles in time with the strokes of the oars, completely at ease after a lifetime working on the sea.

He manoeuvres round the headland, keeping his distance from the waves crashing onto rocks and rows towards the bay. Ahead of us lies a perfect semi-circle of golden sand littered with granite boulders and rock pools. Towering cliffs rise up from the back of the beach and at the side there's the opening to a deep cave. The beach is totally deserted.

'Here you go, me 'andsomes,' says Peter in his soft Cornish burr, drawing close to the sand. 'Hop out here and I'll be back to collect you before the tide turns and the beach disappears.'

'Make sure that you are.'

Toby struggles out of the boat with the hamper and carries it further up the sand while Freya and I stand hand in hand waving to Peter as his boat disappears out of sight.

'He'll be back before long, Freya, so start having fun now,' barks Toby, who really doesn't have a clue about being a dad. His trousers are still rolled up to his knees and he made a right old fuss about having to wade the last few metres to shore.

'Whee!' yells Freya, running full pelt towards a rock pool that's dripping with brown seaweed. 'I want to find a mermaid.'

I join Toby at the back of the beach and we settle down on a thick picnic rug he pulls from the hamper. Then he takes out a red gingham tablecloth which he spreads across the sand and lays out two wine glasses and three china plates.

The hamper is bulging with packets and boxes and tins and some of them have 'Fortnum & Mason' on the side.

'Blimey, Toby, how much food did you bring?'

'There's no point in starving and I wanted to make it special.' He spoons out a tub of pâté into a silver-rimmed bowl. 'Do you like Gorgonzola?'

'I do but it'll be too strong for Freya. Have you brought anything along that she might like?'

'There's guacamole and foie gras and shrimps,' says Toby, holding his glass of wine up to the sun to inspect it. 'I was hardly going to pack chicken nuggets. She'll eat hummus, won't she?'

'Maybe.' I ferret about in my handbag for a flapjack because Freya is a fussy eater. Sometimes it's all we can do to get a jam sandwich down her.

Toby sighs when I pull the flapjack from my bag. 'Is that what she eats? See, I'm rubbish at this parenting stuff and don't know why I put myself through it. I've been trying for ages and I still get it wrong every time. I'm not parent material.'

He slams the hamper lid shut and pouts. And in spite of his tidy goatee beard and the furrows on his forehead, he reminds me of an upset child. His lack of parenting skills are really bothering him.

'Don't be too hard on yourself, Toby. You're doing the best you can and I'm a sort of stand-in mum for Storm so I know how tricky it can be.'

'Your sister? She's practically feral. But my efforts with Freya aren't much better. You insinuated I was trying to buy my way into Freya's affections and you were right. At work I clinch deals worth hundreds of thousands of pounds without breaking a sweat, but I have no idea how to deal with a six-year-old. It's rather pathetic.'

'A trip to the beach isn't pathetic. Sharing with Freya what you did as a child is a lovely way of making joint memories. Look, she's having a wonderful time.'

Freya is paddling in a rock pool, happy as Larry, and scooping tiny fish into her bucket.

'But if I can't even get her food right perhaps I've left this whole fatherhood thing too late.'

I'm tempted to point out it's entirely his fault that he only got to know Freya a few months ago but that would be mean. And I'm still finding it hard to be mean to Toby even though he's a git. It's very annoying.

'Don't worry, Toby, it's just food and I'm sure Freya will eat those, um, what are they?'

'Organic oat cakes from the Highlands embedded with salmon flakes,' he mutters, grabbing one of the cakes and sinking his teeth into it.

'You never know, she might love them. But why is being a good dad so important to you all of a sudden?'

Toby carefully places the remainder of his oatcake on the gingham cloth. 'She's family and I don't have much family left.'

'So why, if family means so much to you, did you want to bulldoze Tregavara House, which holds so much of our family's history? Turning it into flats is one thing but destroying it? How could you even contemplate doing that? Alice cared about you and always stood up for you, but she'd be so disappointed in you for this.'

'Oh, lighten up. It was just a passing thought and never likely to get past ridiculous planning regulations, but holiday flats will be a nice little earner if I market them to the right audience. And there's no need to give me the evil eye. You can sell the house to someone else if you're so against my plans.'

'Who's going to agree to a quick sale on a house that needs a whole new roof before the winter? You know you've got us over a barrel. Freya's waving at us.'

Toby gives his daughter a stiff wave in return and she goes back to searching out mermaids.

'Look, Annie, I do like the house. It holds lots of happy memories for me and I'm well aware of the fact that it's been in our family for generations. But the fact is I love a good business proposition more and, at the end of the day, it's just bricks and mortar. I don't have the same connection to the place as you which is ironic really – I've been visiting that house my whole life and you've only been there, what, eighteen months or so? Yet you can feel it – that pull to past generations whereas I just don't get it. I wish I did but I don't.'

'You feel a connection to the painting Alice left you or you'd have sold it by now.'

Toby shrugs. 'Sorry to disappoint you but that's a business decision too. Some idiot in Scarborough found an undiscovered stash of Van Teels in an attic – dozens of the buggers – so the market's flooded at the moment. I'm waiting until they're more scarce and prices go up again. Where's Freya gone, by the way?'

He jumps up and scans the beach with his hands on his hips but Freya's nowhere to be seen. Tiny waves are breaking on the sand but, only a few metres out into deeper water, the current is swirling around two rock-stacks and forming mini whirlpools. Surely Freya wouldn't have gone into the sea.

I rush to the water's edge, panic rising in my throat. Seagulls are white flecks bobbing on the waves but there's no sign of Freya's dark head or her pink T-shirt.

'Is she in the cave?' yells Toby, sprinting for its gaping black mouth.

I turn and desperately scan the empty beach. We were in charge of a six-year-old girl and we've lost her. Our lives are beginning to shift and change course. There will be a 'before Freya went to the beach' and an 'after'.

Suddenly my attention's caught by a flash of colour on the narrow path that winds up the cliff face. It's Freya! Icy cold relief zaps through me until I realise how high up she is.

'Toby!' I shout, and his eyes follow my pointing finger.

'Thank God!' Toby rushes over, his face ashen and his jaw stretched tight. 'How the hell did she get up there? It's almost vertical.'

'She must have scrambled up the path behind us when we weren't looking.'

'Freya!' shouts Toby. 'Come down here now.'

'No, stay there!' I yell when Freya moves and stones cascade down the cliff-face and bounce off the rocks below. 'She's halfway up the cliff already so coming down will be dangerous. I think she's stuck anyway.'

High above us, Freya is huddled down on the treacherous path and whimpering.

'Christ, I'm going to have to go up there or she'll fall off.' Toby is pacing up and down and sweating. Full-on, shiny-faced, leaky armpits sweating. He's terrified, poor bloke.

'I can do it. I know you hate heights so I'll get her.'

What am I saying? I hate the Path of Doom. In my nightmares I slide down the bumpy track and fall to my death on the hard, jagged rocks. But what the hell – life without Freya wouldn't be worth living anyway.

'Right, I'm going up.'

I'm checking that the laces on my trainers are properly fastened when Toby hurtles past me and starts scrabbling up the cliff path on all fours. Stones shower out in all directions as he pulls himself higher.

'Toby, what the hell are you doing?'

'Saving my daughter,' he yells, backside bobbing up and down in time with his frantic scrabbles. 'Don't worry, Freya. Daddy's coming.'

Toby might be a whizz at selling art, making money from property and putting all sentiment to one side, but his climbing technique leaves a lot to be desired. He favours fast and frantic rather than slow and steady which means he's in far more danger of falling right now than Freya. There's nothing for it; I'm going to have to climb up too.

Taking a deep breath, I push fear from my mind and start making my way up what will hereafter be known as the Track of Terror because Path of Doom doesn't do it justice. Warm weather has dried out the rock, loosening stones that slide under my feet and scuff the palms of my hands. And Toby's scrambling has dislodged half the cliff which is raining down on my head.

But at last I reach Freya, who's crouched down against Toby. He gives her a cuddle.

'I've told Freya there's nothing to worry about and we're going to get her down. Or up,' says Toby, glancing at the rest of the cliff towering above us and blanching. 'I don't suppose you've got a phone signal, have you?'

Very carefully I pull my phone from my jeans pocket and wave it around my head. 'No signal as usual. How long until Peter comes back for us?'

'A couple of hours.'

We both look at Freya, whose head is buried in Toby's chest. She's shaking with fear and needs to get off this cliff as quickly as possible. If she starts panicking and moving, she'll fall and it's a long way down. For the first time since I started climbing, I take a peek at the beach far below and the rocks which are dark shapes in the yellow sand.

'I'd better keep climbing, Toby, and get help. I'll be as quick as I can.'

'No, I'll go. She's my daughter and I should have been keeping an eye on her.'

Toby's face is white with fear and anguish.

'So should I and you're not the best climber.'

'I know but Freya will be calmer with you and your wedding's on Saturday. Pasco will kill me slowly if anything happens to you. So I insist.'

He gives a wobbly grin and slowly unpeels Freya's arms. She whimpers and grabs hold of my legs until I slide down beside her.

'We have to be really brave.' I say softly in her ear. 'Your dad's going to get help so all we have to do is sit here and be really still. Can you manage that?'

Freya's button nose, all snotty from crying, slides across my T-shirt when she nods. 'Sorry, Auntie Annie. I wanted to get high but I got stuck,' she mumbles.

I put my arms around her and pull her face into my chest. She really doesn't need to see her father scrabbling terrified up the cliff or – I can hardly bear think about it – hurtling past her if he loses his footing. I'm not that keen on witnessing it either but looking up is better than looking down.

Toby starts climbing, more slowly and measured this time but with lots of huffing and puffing and the occasional half-scream when his feet slide. My heart's in my mouth as he gets higher and higher but, give him his due, for a man who's terrified of heights, Toby's doing a bang-on job.

After what seems an age, he reaches the top and manoeuvres the last tricky bit over the lip of land that pokes out beyond the rock face. All I can see are his legs sticking out when he collapses on the grass. Then he scrambles to his feet, yells 'I'll be back with help', and disappears.

Seagulls wheel above and below us while Freya and I wait for the Salt Bay cavalry to arrive. She's stopped shaking but is sucking her thumb for comfort. I'm quite tempted to shove my thumb into my mouth, but a strange thing happens while we're sitting with our backs to the hard rock.

A deep sense of peace descends and I'm able to appreciate the vista in front of me – the grassy headland jutting out into deep-blue water, white-crested waves rolling into shore and tiny red flowers growing out of the cliff-face. If this is my last ever view, at least it's a magnificent one in gorgeous Cornwall and so much better than dropping dead one day in a grimy London backstreet.

I've lost all track of time when Josh's worried face appears over the edge of the cliff.

'Are you both OK? Peter and Toby are going to hold the rope and I'm coming down.'

'OK but please be careful.'

Stones tumble past us when Josh walks backwards off the cliff edge with nothing but a thick rope tied around his waist. And all calm deserts me as the man I love – the man I'm supposed to be marrying in forty-eight hours' time – hangs suspended in thin air. I've stopped breathing and Freya's tiny fingers are digging into my arm.

Bit by bit, Josh abseils down the cliff, his long legs banging against rock when he scrabbles for a foothold. And at last he arrives on the ledge where Freya and I are sheltering.

'Are you all right, sweetheart?'

He might mean me. He might mean his niece. But we both nod.

'Now, Freya,' he says, stooping down beside her. 'I need you to be really brave and put your arms around my neck and your legs around my waist so I can get you up the cliff. Can you do that?'

Freya nods again and throws her arms around his neck, making him wobble alarmingly.

'Whoah!' shout Peter and Toby way above us, pulling on the rope to make it taut.

Josh secures Freya to him by tying another piece of rope around his waist and hers. Then my gorgeous brave fiancé loops his arm around my shoulder.

'I'll come back for you. I promise. So don't move,' he says, kissing me hard on the lips. He feels so solid and reassuring and I don't want him to go but he pushes his feet against the rock, steadies himself against the taut rope and starts climbing. Freya clings to him like a limpet all the way up, her head on his shoulder and her eyes firmly closed.

When they reach the top, Josh hands Freya into Toby's outstretched arms before starting to descend again towards me. Great, it's my turn.

I don't like being stuck halfway up a cliff. It's pants, to be honest, even with a view to die for – though I'd rather not. But it's got to be better than climbing the cliff and I'm too heavy to be carried.

'Are you ready?' Josh is back on the ledge and unfastening the rope around his waist. He loops it around mine and ties it tight. 'You need to take it slowly 'cos the path is so slippery. Heaven knows how Toby made it without breaking his neck. But the rope will stop you from falling so you'll be fine.'

He pulls me so close my thighs are tight against his. 'Don't look down and just keep thinking of the wedding. On Saturday you'll be walking up the aisle and looking beautiful.'

'Yeah, it's amazing how attractive a p-p-plaster cast can look these days.'

My teeth are chattering with fear even though I never knew that could actually properly happen.

Josh cups my face in his warm hands and smiles. 'Listen to me, sweetheart, it'll be fine. But you need to go now. Thinking about it will just make it worse.'

So I signal to Toby and Peter that I'm coming up and I step into space.

It isn't fine. It's utterly terrifying but the rope keeps me from tumbling to my death while I'm scrambling my way to the top. At last, I climb over the lip of land and collapse face-first on the grass.

'Auntie Annie!' Freya launches on top of me, knocking all the air from my lungs.

'Give her a minute, lass,' says Peter, lifting Freya off me and untying the rope around my waist with hands gnarled by years of salt water. He throws it down to Josh before helping me to my feet and stands back when Toby pulls me into an awkward hug.

Toby isn't soft and warm like Josh. He's rigid and embarrassed and smells of stale sweat but he sounds like he means it when he says quietly: 'Thank goodness you're all right.'

'Come on, Toby,' calls Peter, poised at the cliff's edge. 'There's still Josh to come up yet so grab the rope and brace yourself.'

I've never been so pleased to see Josh in my whole life when his lanky frame appears at the cliff edge. He hoists himself feet-first onto the grass and I throw my arms around his waist from behind and snuggle into his back while he shakes Peter's hand. Then he and Toby hesitate slightly before brushing hands for the briefest handshake ever.

Peter saunters off back to his boat while Toby starts coiling up the thick rope that came from our shed. He keeps stealing glances at Josh and finally blurts out: 'This would never have happened if I'd kept a better eye on Freya. So go on, Pasco, let me know what you think about my appalling parenting skills. You know you want to.'

Josh hesitates and a range of emotions flit across his face – anger, dislike, years-long enmity. Then he shrugs his broad shoulders. 'Kids wander off, these things happen and climbing that cliff to get help for Freya and Annie was pretty brave when you're petrified of heights.'

'Hardly petrified,' bristles Toby, who presumably considers the word un-manly, 'but I was apprehensive, to be honest.'

'Apprehensive? I'd have been terrified without a rope to keep me from falling.'

'Would you?' Toby puffs out his chest, manliness restored. 'I didn't have any choice because Annie's the only Trebarwith family I've got left and I'm Freya's father. I couldn't let my fear put my daughter's life at risk.'

'And that, Toby, is why you *are* a good parent when it really matters,' I say, stroking Freya's hair. 'Don't you think so, Josh?'

Oops, this might be an affirmation too far, but Josh gives a grudging nod. 'You did all right this afternoon.'

'Thanks, I appreciate that.' Toby hands the coiled rope to Josh and holds out his hand to his daughter. 'I'd better get her back home to her mum, who I don't suppose will be as understanding about our little adventure. Though we don't necessarily have to tell her what happened, do we, Freya.'

'I got stuck on a cliff higher than the birds and Uncle Josh came down on a big rope and saved me,' squeals his daughter, pushing her tiny hand into Toby's.

'I see. I'd better take her home and face the music then. This parenting thing takes a lot of practise.' Father and daughter amble off together but Toby stops and turns when they reach the low white wall of the cemetery. 'By the way, I'd be grateful if you don't gossip about what happened this afternoon. The locals will only blame me for not keeping a better eye on Freya and my reputation around here is already shot to pieces. Have a good wedding on Saturday.'

'Why don't you come?' I ask him without properly thinking it through.

'I wasn't invited.'

'I never thought you'd want to be there with all the fuss going on about the house.'

Toby shrugs. 'You don't want me at your nuptials, do you, Pasco?'

Josh and Toby's eyes lock together and they stare at one another in silence. Above them, midges swarm and seagulls swoop but neither man moves. It's like the climax of a Western where the sheriff and outlaw are seeing who'll draw a gun first and blast the other one to death.

Josh is the first to speak. 'You might as well come. Freya's being a flower girl and I expect you'd like to see her.'

'I would.' Toby swallows and ruffles the top of his daughter's hair. 'Thanks. I'll be there.'

Chapter Thirty-One

After the stressful day I've had, all I'm planning when Josh nips to the pub is a long soak in the bath until I resemble a prune, followed by an early night. You can keep your cocktail bars and night clubs and cultural evenings at the theatre. All I need is peace and quiet, hot water and my comfiest PJs – I'm a woman of simple tastes.

So I run a bath, pour in a frankly obscene amount of scented oil and I've just stripped naked and put my toe in the water when there's a tremendous commotion downstairs.

Tremendous commotions aren't that unusual with Storm around so I stand frozen, like a Roman statue with a cocked leg, hoping that it – whatever it might be – will die down. But no such luck.

'Annie! Are you in there?' yells Storm, galloping up the stairs and hammering on the bathroom door. 'Kayla's downstairs and going proper mental so you'd better sort it out. Emily's getting her a cup of tea – like that's gonna help!'

She snorts at the very idea of caffeinated comfort and stomps off along the landing to her bedroom.

Please don't slam the door.

Storm's door crashes shut and the film of amber oil on top of the bathwater sloshes up the side of the enamel.

Fantastic! I spend two long hours with Toby, almost die on a vertical cliff-face and now I have to talk down a bonkers Australian. This is turning into a right pigging pain of a day.

Shrugging on my long cotton dressing-gown, I venture downstairs and discover Kayla with swollen red eyes in the sitting room. She's sitting slumped in Alice's chair while Emily flaps around trying to force-feed her tea.

'Don't worry, Em. I'll make sure she drinks it.'

Emily mouths 'thank you' at me when I take the steaming cup and backs out of the room at speed.

'It's all terrible,' wails Kayla the second Emily has disappeared from view. 'Ollie and I had a terrible argument and he's leaving me.'

'What sort of leaving you?'

'Leaving me to go to the stupid Lake District.'

'Is that all? I thought you meant that you'd split up for good.'

'We might as well have. He'll be up there and I'll be down here.'

'But you knew he was going.'

A draught is whistling up my dressing gown, my bath water is rapidly cooling, and I'm starting to lose my patience.

Kayla leans forward and rubs the back of her hand across her nose. 'I know. But I didn't *know* know. Not for sure. I still thought he'd change his mind.'

'He took you on a mini-break to the Lake District where he'll be living and he's been looking for flats.'

'That's all true but I still never thought he'd really go and leave me. I think I've been in denial.'

Which is exactly what I've been telling her for weeks, but I find her a tissue in my dressing-gown pocket and do my best to look sympathetic.

'What's changed today then? Why do you suddenly know this move is for real?'

'A lettings agency rang while Ollie was in the loo so I took the call. And it turns out he's paid a deposit on a flat and the first month's rent. He's really going and breaking up with me. What a bastard!'

She suddenly jumps up and starts jabbing her finger at the window. 'Oh no, he's here.'

'You what?'

'He's here. He must have followed me like a stalker.'

'Or like a man who's in love with you. I can't see him anywhere.'

There's no one in the garden when I peer through the glass or standing at the front door waiting to be let in.

Oh, no. Please don't come in through the kitchen, Ollie, because I need time to run upstairs and put on some pants.

Too late.

Ollie bursts into the sitting room, red-faced and panting.

'Kayla, there you are! Um, hi, Annie.'

'Hi, Ollie.' I give a little wave and pull the V-neck of my dressing gown closed. Underneath this thin covering of cotton I'm completely naked and – I glance down – yep, my flaming nipples are showing.

I start edging towards the door while Kayla and Ollie launch into what's best described as an intense discussion. And I've just wrapped my fingers around the door handle when Kayla demands: 'What do you think, Annie?'

Aargh, so close!

'What do I think about what?'

'About Ollie breaking up with me?'

'For the millionth time, Kayla!' Mild, gentle Ollie is shouting. 'I am not breaking up with you. I'd love you to come to the Lake

District with me but if you won't we'll have to try a long-distance relationship.'

'But you love Cornwall so why are you going?'

'Because I'm good at my job and want to be promoted but also because of you. You're always telling me about your adventures abroad and it's made me realise there's a big, wide world out there beyond Cornwall. Keswick's not exactly Kathmandu but it's a big deal for me. A big, exciting deal and I want to give it a try.' He pushes both hands into his blonde hair, which is standing on end. 'Oh, whatever.'

With a final tut of despair and frustration, he does a magnificent sweep out of the room. I swear he's been taking lessons from Josh, who was a serial sweeper before he settled down with me and became less angry at life.

Kayla settles back on the sofa, totally spent, and I join her to demonstrate sisterly solidarity although I've no idea what to say.

'Sorry,' she murmurs after a couple of minutes. 'You're getting married on Saturday and don't need all of this drama.'

'Don't worry about it. My whole day's been kind of dramatic so it doesn't matter.'

'What kind of dramatic?'

'Nothing important.' My bath is calling and Kayla's not in the mood for tales of daring cliff rescues. She'd only call Toby an idiot for letting Freya wander off in the first place – and that was my fault too. 'Do you want to stay here tonight?'

Kayla's still staring at her lap. 'No, thanks. I've ruined enough of your evening. I'll go home, grab a few things and stay at the pub so I can have a proper think. Roger won't mind.'

'Look, whether you decide to leave with Ollie, stay here or go globe-trotting again is up to you but, if it helps, I used to be terrified of commitment and here I am about to get married.'

Kayla sniffs. 'That's different 'cos you're much older than me and you're less adventurous.'

Which I'm pretty sure means more boring.

Chapter Thirty-Two

Cornwall weather gives new meaning to the word 'unpredictable'. It can be gloriously sunny first thing but pouring down an hour later, and it varies widely from coast to coast.

Salt Bay lies on the thin strip of land that leads to Land's End. We're on the east coast and the west coast is only half an hour's drive away – but some days they might as well be different countries. Nip over to the other coast if you wake up in Salt Bay to grey skies and mizzle, and often as not you'll find sun sparkling on blue seas.

Fortunately, I wake on Saturday to bright sunshine. Sunbeams are pouring through the open curtains of our bedroom and coating the wooden floorboards in light. I often sleep with the curtains open because falling asleep looking at the stars is awesome. They were hidden by light pollution in London but here the stars are scattered like brilliant diamonds across the inky sky.

Yawning, I push my legs across the bed but there's no familiar shape of Josh. It's daft because we live together but tradition decreed he spend the night at his mum's so we won't see each other until we meet in church. When I walk up the aisle in Alice's dress which he's never seen.

I've woken ahead of the alarm so I lie under the covers for a few more minutes, thinking of Alice and Mum. Two women who've had a huge effect on me and should be here to see me marry the love of my life.

Today is going to be bitter-sweet. But mostly sweet, I tell myself firmly, swinging my legs out of bed and pushing my feet into my slippers. There's been too much sadness and uncertainty in this house lately. Today we'll redress the balance with love and joy and happy ever after. Mum and Alice would approve.

I'm brushing my hair and wondering if Emily's already had a shower when there's a tap-tap at the door and she pokes her head into the room. She blinks at me from behind her thick-framed glasses and grins.

'Brilliant, you're up! Happy Wedding Day, Annie. Is it OK if I come in?'

'Of course. Is everything all right?'

'Yeah, I just wanted a quick word before it all goes mad later. There's already six people in the back garden putting up tables but you're not allowed to look 'cos it's a surprise.'

It certainly is. Heaven knows what the choir's got planned because Josh and I were told in no uncertain terms to butt out when we tried to get involved. 'We've got this covered,' said Gerald, putting his hands on my shoulders and ushering me out of the pub when I accidentally wandered into the choir's planning meeting. And even Kayla's been tight-lipped about it.

When I sit on the bed and pat the cover, Emily sits down beside me. She's still in her bunny onesie with tousled bed-hair.

'I just wanted to say thank you again for taking me in and looking after me and trusting me with your B&B idea which would have so been a go-er if you hadn't run out of money.'

'I've told you that you don't have to keep thanking us because we're not doing you a favour. You're part of our family now and you'll come with us to Trecaldwith. Did you see the details of the house that Josh brought back?'

'It looks nice.'

I nod because the house we're planning on renting while we decide what to do next *is* nice. It's smaller than Tregavara House and quite modern and it doesn't have a view of the sea but it's close to a parade of shops and Josh's school. I wish I could feel more enthusiastic about living there but I expect that will come.

Emily sucks her lower lip between her teeth. There's something else bothering her but I can't worry about that today. Or mourn Alice and my mum and leaving Tregavara House. Or flap about whether Barry will turn up on time to walk me up the aisle. Or, indeed, at all. His band's tour is over but, the last I heard, he was carrying out some errand in London that couldn't wait. I sigh. Nope. Today is a day to forget all troubles and heartaches. Today is a day for celebration and love.

'I'm getting married to Josh Pasco in exactly' – I peer at my bedside clock – 'three hours and fifty-two minutes.' I wrap my arms around my body as excitement fizzes through me.

'And I can't wait to be your bridesmaid. I've never been one before. It's just…' Her words trail off and she bites her lip. It seems there's no escape, not even on my wedding day.

'It's just what?'

She looks up at me with huge eyes. 'I'm a traitor,' she whispers. 'A traitor to the feminist cause.'

Oh, Lordy.

'Would this have anything to do with Tom?'

She nods. 'I think I like him.'

'And not like a gay best friend?'

'No, more than that. I've been feeling a bit weird about him for a while, but I ignored it 'cos I'm off all men. But he's so kind and he seems different these days. More grown-up and more…'

'Fit?'

So it's a bit blunt but I'd really like to get back to my wedding day.

'Yeah, exactly. But what will Storm think if I sell out my principles and me and Tom get it on?'

'Storm will probably make a few wisecracks and then she'll find something else to focus on. Going out with a boy you like isn't selling out your principles, Emily. It's just having fun.' I put my arm around her shoulders. 'You should try it sometime.'

Before Emily can reply, the door flies open and bashes into the wall.

'Here comes the bride!' sings Kayla at the top of her lungs as she hauls a suitcase onto the bed. 'Come on' – she physically pulls me and Emily apart – 'you haven't got time for any of this kissy-kissy business 'cos you're getting married in exactly' – she consults her watch – 'three hours and fifty minutes' time.'

She opens the case and starts rooting inside while Emily scurries off to bag the shower first.

'Is everything between you and Ollie OK?'

'Yep,' says Kayla. 'And I don't want to talk about it now 'cos there's loads to do.'

She studies my sleepy face and winces. 'I've brought everything with me – make-up, curling tongs, blister patches, industrial grade anti-perspirant. Operation Get Annie To The Church On Time is on!'

Kayla is as good as her word. I'm 'beautified' (her term) to within an inch of my life, though I draw the line at false eyelashes. And once Kayla's worked her magic I must admit I look far less *meh* than usual. It's still me staring back in the mirror but a better version of me. A me that can be bothered to use blusher and lip liner. And when I put on Alice's dress, I can hardly believe the transformation.

'You look brilliant, mate,' gulps Kayla. 'I'd marry you myself if Josh hadn't got there first. You're missing something though.'

She points at my shoulder-length hair, curling gently around my face.

'I don't have a veil. I'm not too keen on them, really – all that covering your face on the way in and uncovering it when you're a respectable married woman seems a bit archaic.'

'You don't need a veil,' agrees Kayla, 'but this might help.' She delves into her suitcase that's more a Mary Poppins bag full of endless surprises. 'I bought you this 'cos I thought it would complete your wedding vibe.'

She thrusts a small silver box at me. Inside, nestled on black tissue paper, is a gorgeous, glittering tiara.

'It's absolutely beautiful. Thank you so much.'

After Kayla's fixed it into my hair, I turn my head this way and that in the mirror. The tiara catches the light and adds a touch of bling that's just the right side of tasteful.

'Wow!' Freya has just arrived with Marion, her ebony hair already set into ringlets that cascade across her tiny shoulders.

'Wow is the right word. You look wonderful, Annie.' Marion has started crying and Kayla fishes out a box of tissues from her magic bag. My soon to be mum-in-law is looking pretty wonderful herself in a fitted purple dress that complements the silver streaks in her dark hair.

'Did Josh sleep all right?' I ask her.

'He was up very early because he's nervous but looking forward to today. We all are.' Marion dabs at her cheeks with the tissue and sniffs. 'You've made my son very happy, Annie, and I wish you both all the love and luck in the world.'

'Tissue?' Kayla hands one over in case I start blubbing too but my frantic blinking seems to be doing the trick.

'You look like one of the princesses on my bucket,' says Freya, peeping out from behind her grandmother.

'Yep, the Princess of Salt Bay – and it's time to go marry your prince, Sunshine,' says Kayla with a grin.

Kayla, Emily, Marion and Freya go ahead of me to the church. And Storm too, who nipped off without showing me what she's wearing. I can only hope she's ditched her jeans and boots for a few hours.

When they've gone, the house is eerily quiet and there's no noise from the back garden. I've solemnly promised not to look out there or to go into the kitchen, which was taken over by the choir earlier. So I pace up and down the hallway until the grandfather clock shows quarter past eleven. There's still no sign of Barry so I'll have to walk alone to the church and call on the services of my stand-in dad, Cyril.

'Thank you, house,' I murmur, pulling the front door closed behind me. 'I can't think of anywhere else I'd rather be married from.'

I've reached the garden gate when a car speeds along the road and screeches to a halt in a cloud of dust. What the hell? I step back, worried the dust will settle on my dress, as Barry clambers out from behind the wheel. He's flushed and flustered but wearing a smart suit and his shoulder-length hair is pulled into a tidy ponytail.

'I made it,' he gasps, slamming the door of the clapped-out Polo that's surely held together by rust and dirt. 'Gazzer let me borrow his car though I'm not insured for it. Mind you, I don't think he is either. Anyway, it got me here in time to give you away.' He winces. 'Oops, sorry, *walk you up the aisle* seeing as you've gone all feminist on me. I'd have been here earlier only I had something important to do in London. Hell's bells, Annie. You look a million dollars in that dress.'

'Thank you and I'm glad you got here but we have to go now. I don't want to keep Josh waiting.'

'That man of yours can wait a bit 'cos I want to give you your wedding present first.'

Barry starts fishing in the pocket of his waistcoat and pulls out a folded sheet of paper.

Oh no, he's written me another song. It's great that my dad enjoys composing music and he's good – the song he wrote for Salt Bay Choral Society bagged us the Kernow Choral Crown. But he'll sing my wedding song at the reception after having a few too many and Storm will totally go off on one.

My fingers tighten around his arm. 'That's lovely, Barry, but could you save it until after the ceremony? I'll be able to fully appreciate it then and if I don't get to the church soon, there won't be a wedding at all.'

Barry hesitates while the paper flutters in the breeze and then he shoves it back into his pocket. 'Righty-oh. This can wait. Let's get you to the church on time.'

It only takes a few minutes to walk to the church: me, holding up my dress to stop it trailing in the dust and Barry striding along beside me. Organising a lift was pointless for such a short journey and, anyway, I want to feel a Cornish wind on my face and taste salt in the air before stepping into the church. Before the ceremony begins and I marry the love of my life.

My bridesmaids and flower-girl are waiting for me outside the church porch – Emily and Kayla are wearing pretty mint-green maxi dresses they picked up in Topshop, Freya is gorgeous in a blue dress with a tutu-skirt, and Storm is a revelation. Her hair is up off her shoulders in a soft bun with tiny ringlets around her ears. And she's wearing a dress too! It's short and dark grey with silver studs across the tight bodice – not very bridesmaidy at all – but she looks wonderful. She tugs at the hem self-consciously when I get closer.

'I had no choice. They bullied me into it. You turned up then, Barry.'

'Sorry I'm late but I had something to sort out first. Something big and very important.'

'Yeah, course it was,' says Storm, rolling her eyes.

Cyril's near the church door and smiles when I do a twirl. 'You look beautiful, Annie.' He's in the old suit he wears for choir concerts, but his dark shoes are shining, his grey bristles have gone and he's had a haircut that's more of a head shave.

He spots me looking and rubs his hands across his scalp.

'Florence brought her clippers round and insisted on giving me a haircut. I think she's done some sheep shearing in her time. I was waiting out here in case I was needed but I see your real dad has turned up so I'm not wanted.'

And he looks so sad, I make a sudden executive decision.' You stay right there, Cyril. Why don't you both walk me down the aisle if you're up for that, Barry?'

My father nods. 'That's fine with me.'

But Cyril frowns. 'It's not very traditional. Jennifer will have something to say about it.'

'She can say whatever she likes! It's my wedding and the people in Salt Bay are my extended family so it's right that I have my dad on one arm and you on the other.'

Oh, crikey. I think Cyril's about to cry. His Adam's apple bobs up and down while he swallows hard but then he pulls himself tall and holds out his arm.' It would be an honour. You really are an unusual woman, Annabella Trebarwith – it's as though you've always been a part of Salt Bay.'

Which is the most wonderful compliment on my wedding day. I take a last look at the village spread out around me and, with Barry on one arm and Cyril on the other, I step into the church and my new life.

The tiny granite building is almost full of people and heavy with the scent of flowers. Salt Bay Choral Society have done us proud – colourful posies adorn the ends of every pew and two huge arrangements of verbena, agapanthus and valerian flank the altar. Light is flooding through the stained-glass windows casting streaks of brilliant blue, scarlet and gold across the flagstones.

The first chords from the organ bounce off ancient stone and everyone stands to watch me walk up the aisle. It's all a bit of a blur – Lucy's passing a tissue to Marion, who's welling up again, Jennifer in an enormous hat is hanging on to Jacques' arm, Fiona's dyed her greying hair ash-blonde in honour of the occasion and I glimpse Toby standing alone out of the corner of my eye.

But the only person I'm focused on is Josh. My Josh, who's waiting with Best Man Ollie at the altar. He's ridiculously handsome in his hired dark-grey suit and deep-red tie that matches my bouquet of roses from Mary's garden. But he's nervous. I can tell by the way he's shifting from foot to foot.

His eyes light up when he turns and sees me and he whispers: 'You look amazing!' when I reach his side and clasp his hand. He breathes out slowly and his shoulders relax. 'Let's do this.'

Reverend Hilary Baxham waits for Freya to sit on her mum's lap, gives us a very unvicar-like wink and the ceremony begins.

All's going well until Roger does a humongous sneeze and Kayla starts giggling. She's been threatening to disrupt the ceremony by shouting: 'Annie keeps a sex slave in the cellar at Tregavara House' and I'll kill her if she does anything daft. But her giggles are drowned out by the creaking of the church door, which is in urgent need of some WD40.

The loud noise echoes through the building as a short woman in an immaculate white trouser suit ushers in two small children dressed identically in plaid skirts and short-sleeved jumpers. She shuffles them into a back pew and, when she holds up her hand in apology, diamond rings on her long fingers split the light into a prism of colours.

'I don't believe it,' mutters Barry behind me but Storm is beaming. Proper full-on beaming like she's properly happy for once and not about to slip into sullen teenage silence.

'It's my mum,' she mouths at me. 'She came after all!'

Hilary gives a discreet cough. 'Is everything all right? Shall I carry on?'

'Yes please. It's a member of my family arriving late.' Josh raises his eyebrows at me. 'It's Storm's mum,' I whisper to him. 'I'm afraid my dysfunctional family just got bigger. Can you bear it?'

'Our dysfunctional family. What's yours is now mine and all that.'

'For better or for worse?'

'Definitely, though to be honest I'd prefer for better.' And he grins and squeezes my hand as Ollie ferrets in his waistcoat pocket for our wedding rings and Salt Bay Choral Society prepare to sing.

Everyone applauds when we walk up the aisle which doesn't seem very British, but it matches the celebratory mood in Salt Bay. I'm married! And though Mum and Alice aren't here, I know they'd be delighted for me and my new husband.

Josh and I emerge blinking into a Cornish September afternoon to a peal of church bells and the cheers of strangers. A little huddle of tourists has gathered by the church wall to see what all the excitement is about and they start snapping photos of us on their iPhones. Ooh, I feel like Amal Clooney in Venice after marrying gorgeous George.

Twenty minutes later and we've all decamped to the cliff top for our official wedding photos. It's not the most traditional of places for wedding pictures, and I don't suppose I looked very elegant slogging up the cliff path with skirt in hand and wellies on. But Tom is insistent the ocean backdrop will be amazing. He's been studying photography so was the best person to take on the role of official snapper – and, boy, is he taking it seriously.

His usual diffident manner has disappeared and he's ordering everyone around with gay abandon. Safe behind the lens, the real Tom is emerging and it suits him. He's more confident, more grown-up, more at ease in his own skin. He's even chatting easily with Emily in between shepherding us into position though presumably he's still unaware of her change of heart.

Tom takes several photos of me and Josh hand in hand with our backs to the sea, and when he shows me one of the pictures on his camera I can hardly believe it. We're laughing as a breeze whips back my hair and billows my skirt, revealing my wellies. And behind us, the land ends and the indigo ocean stretches to the horizon. Tom has a real talent.

Storm has done little more than wave at her mother so far but sidles up to her while Tom's trying to get a good shot of Ollie and Kayla together. Poor lad. The atmosphere's tense because they're still scratchy with each other so getting them to smile is hard work.

Amanda greets her daughter with a brief hug and stretches out her hand to me when I wander over.

'You're obviously Annie. I can tell from your resemblance to Storm and the gorgeous dress, of course. Is it vintage? You look absolutely wonderful. Congratulations.'

Her long, blood-red nails tickle my skin when she shakes my hand. My nails were like that once, when I lived in London and regularly visited the nail bar at Westfield shopping centre. Now they're short and practical though Emily insisted on painting them pearly-pink last night.

'Thank you so much for coming to my wedding.'

Amanda gives a tinkly laugh. 'Thank you for inviting us and I'm so sorry for turning up unannounced – and late.'

When she does an 'eek' face, her muscles hardly move. Her forehead is suspiciously unlined and the skin around her eyes is taut and smooth.

'I didn't think you were coming,' says Storm.

'Neither did I because Cornwall is such a long way from London. But then I realised we could combine the wedding with a few days in Padstow.

Simon's boss has a bolthole near Rick Stein's seafood restaurant and said we could borrow it. It's not ideal, actually – full of antiques so a bit of a nightmare with Poppy and Eugenie but they're being very good.' She smiles at the girls, who are sheltering behind her as though they've never met people like Salt Bay villagers before. 'But our trip gave me a chance to nip across to see you being a bridesmaid. Doesn't she look lovely, girls?'

Poppy and Eugenie nod and eye their half-sister warily.

'Simon didn't come with you then, Amanda?'

'No, I'm afraid he had some urgent business to attend to. He was very disappointed because he'd have loved to see his step-daughter. You don't mind, do you, Storm?'

Storm gives the slightest of eye rolls as she shrugs. 'It's fine. Are you coming to the reception?'

'Gosh, no. I've already gatecrashed Annie's wedding and wouldn't dream of imposing any further.'

'It's really not a problem,' I tell her. 'I'm sure we can make room for you and the girls. We're holding the reception in our garden and it's pretty informal.'

Amanda glances at the wellies peeping out from under my skirt and gives a puzzled smile. She's not the sort of woman to wear wellies to a wedding and especially not her own.

'I can't stay long but maybe we could come back for an hour or so. It would be lovely to spend some time with my daughter when she's looking so gorgeous.' She puts one arm around Storm's shoulders and uses her other hand to pull her phone from her tiny, shiny handbag. 'Talking of which, I must get a photo or Simon will never believe me. He's only ever seen Storm in jeans and Doc Martens.'

Storm stands awkwardly, one foot crossed in front of the other, while her mother snaps away.

'Smile, darling,' commands Amanda, taking another half dozen pictures. 'You look so much prettier when you're smiling.'

'Can you take one with Annie?' Storm beckons me over, puts her arm tightly around my waist and leans against me. Amanda takes another gazillion photos but suddenly glances past us and lowers her phone.

'Balls!' mutters Storm.

Barry is striding over to us, ponytail undone and hair blowing around his shoulders. He looks pretty rock-star cool actually with his suit on and huge mirrored shades covering half his face.

'Amanda.'

Barry nods at his ex-wife, who's fished her own sunglasses out of her bag and put them on.

'Barry.' She pushes her girls forward. 'I don't think you've met my daughters, Poppy and Eugenie. Girls, this is Storm's father.'

The girls stare open-mouthed at the strange man in front of them while Barry and Amanda eyeball each other from behind their sunglasses – Amanda's designed by Prada in Milan, Barry's bought from Superdrug in Kettering.

'Hello, girls,' says Barry, ruffling their hair. 'I don't think you've ever met my daughter, Annie, either.'

'From what I've heard, it's not that long since *you* met her,' snipes Amanda, but she clamps her lips tight when Storm groans.

Barry pulls back his hair that's being whipped by the wind. 'Simon not here then?'

'Working!' says Amanda, sharply.

'Of course he is. I know it's the weekend but I'm only taking a quick break from work myself.'

'Still busy in a band then?' Amanda's face looks weird. I think she's trying to wrinkle her nose but nothing's moving.

'Barry's doing really well,' butts in Storm. 'His band's touring all over the place. They were in Wales last week.'

'Wales? Heavens! You've really hit the big time at last, then, Barry.' If Amanda's eyebrow could move, she'd be raising it.

'Yeah, he's doing really well,' protests Storm but Barry places his hand on her shoulder.

'It doesn't matter, love. Leave it.'

I feel a sudden rush of affection for this odd little man who only pitched up in my life eleven months ago. How on earth did he and Amanda ever get it on? I can't help it. I'm imagining them kissing and cuddling and, ooh, I really don't want to go down that road. But they seem the most unlikely couple ever. Was Amanda ever a rock chick? She certainly isn't now. She's moved on, but Barry hasn't.

'My dad's doing brilliantly with his band and has been absolutely wonderful since we met. I don't know how we'd manage without him.'

I'm not quite sure why I said that because it's not strictly true. Barry drove me demented when he first arrived in Salt Bay with Storm in tow. But now's not the time for honesty; not when his ex-wife is being sneery.

'Thanks, babe. That means a lot,' says Barry, lifting up his sunglasses and giving me a wink.

Storm's mouth twitches into a half-smile and she lets Tom lead her away for yet another photo of my unusual bridesmaids against the magnificent backdrop of the roiling Atlantic.

Ten minutes later and we're all pretty much photo'd out but Tom is still angling for a group shot of everyone.

'Please all group together,' he shouts while Emily tries to round up stragglers spread out across the clifftop. It takes ages but at last everyone's huddled together facing the windswept cemetery where generations of Trebarwiths are buried. Everyone except Toby, who's hanging back.

He hasn't been mingling with the other guests and loneliness is coming off him in waves. Usually he's full of swagger but today he's muted as though someone's flicked his off switch.

Peter shuffles along from Jennifer, whose hat is trying to have his eye out, and holds out his hand. 'There's room here for you, Toby. Though you might not fancy getting too close to the cliff edge after your heroic climb.'

My heart sinks. In all the fuss of almost hurtling off the cliff and getting married, I totally forgot to ask Peter to keep the rescue quiet.

'Heroic climb by Toby? Why don't I know about this?' Jennifer's almost twitching with agitation at being out of the loop.

'Toby climbed the cliff without a rope to rescue his daughter and Annie,' says Peter. 'One of the bravest things I've ever seen.'

'Or most foolhardy,' insists Jennifer as my guests cluster round Toby asking him how he managed the climb without breaking his neck.

'Will you please all stop moving and get in place for a photo,' yells poor frustrated Tom, but no one's listening.

Chapter Thirty-Three

'Mind the dog poo!' says Maureen, steering me to one side and manoeuvring me through the garden gate at Tregavara House. My skirt brushes against the gate posts as I feel my way forward with Maureen hanging onto my arm.

She insisted I close my eyes when we reached the house so there's no risk of me getting an early glimpse of what's been organised for our reception.

'Keep them closed,' she orders, leading me through the front garden and around the side of the building. The grass feels springy under my feet and I can smell honeysuckle mingling with the fresh tang of the sea.

We stop, and Maureen lets go of my arm. 'Here we are. Open your eyes!'

The scene in front of me takes my breath away. It's glorious. Trestle tables are groaning under the weight of Cornish pasties, sausage rolls, bowls of brightly coloured salads and platters of cooked meats. Behind them are towering stands of iced cupcakes and, at the very back, a fabulous three-tiered wedding cake that's dripping with strawberries.

'It's chocolate sponge with chocolate chips and chocolate butter-cream,' says Maureen, laughing at my delight when I spot her creation. 'Jennifer told me how much you're addicted to the stuff.'

Oops, my daily Twix fix has not gone unnoticed.

Our guests are already seated on a variety of chairs – from dining room chairs and fold-up wooden seats to white plastic chairs plundered from villagers' gardens. Cream paper cloths have been Sellotaped to the tables and there are balloons and tiny vases of flowers everywhere. A white canopy has been erected over the top table in case of rain, soft music is wafting from a CD player, and dozens of glasses from the pub are lined up and sparkling in the sunshine.

'Wow. I'm speechless. I don't know what to say.' I swing round to Josh, who was led into the back garden just behind me.

'It's wonderful,' he splutters, as lost for words as I am.

'Can we eat now?' yells Roger, who's sitting as far away from Jennifer and Jacques as possible.

I was thinking we'd do speeches first – from Josh, Ollie and Barry, who'll probably take the opportunity to sing his wedding song. But who cares? There are no rules at our wedding – all that matters is that Josh and I are celebrating with people we care about in a house that we love. What a wonderful way to say goodbye to my beloved Salt Bay.

When I give Roger the nod, people fall on the spread like vultures and forego the seats to sit on the grass with their picnics. There's a glimpse of blue sea around the corner of Tregavara House and I can hear the whoosh of waves on wet sand. The cliffs behind me are casting shadows and seagulls are swooping overhead. It's an eclectic reception that wouldn't pass muster with my sophisticated London friends. But I wouldn't swap it for anything – not even a swanky do at The Ritz.

I wish Maura had been able to come – she's so heavily pregnant now she has to pee every two minutes and couldn't face a car or train journey. But Lesley and Gayle are here from work and Pippa and Charlie with adorable baby Henry, whose fists are the size of walnuts.

Amanda and her children have helped themselves to plates of food and are sitting with Storm near the azaleas that Alice planted after Tregavara House was flooded and the garden was swamped.

Amanda catches my eye a few times and comes over while I'm on my second dessert. My appetite disappeared just before the wedding but now it's back with a vengeance and Mary's home-made profiteroles are *so* good.

'The girls and I will have to head off in a minute or Simon will be wondering where we are, but could I have a quick word first?'

'Of course.' My dress rustles when I get to my feet and is definitely more snug in the waist area following my post-nuptial pig-out. Holding in my stomach, I swoosh my way to the sitting room and close the door behind me and Amanda.

She stands by the window, tapping her fingernails on the stone sill. 'Thank you so much for inviting me to your wedding and I wish you and your handsome new husband every happiness.'

Which is very nice and all that but nothing she couldn't have said to me in the garden. As I suspected, Amanda isn't finished. She clears her throat.

'You think I'm a terrible mother, don't you?'

Whoah! That came out of nowhere. When I don't respond, she ploughs on.

'I couldn't stay with Barry. You've seen what he's like – a nice enough man but a total dreamer. It was exciting at first when we were going from gig to gig and always on the brink of the big time. But after a few years it was just tedious and then I met Simon and he offered something different – stability and more than a hand-to-mouth existence. I wanted a change and I needed a change, but I didn't realise that *I* would have to change quite so much.'

She stares at the brightly coloured boats marooned on sand by the low tide before turning back to me.

'Simon didn't see Storm as part of the package. She could be prickly and difficult even back then. I could have insisted she came with me, I suppose, but I was desperate for a different life, and then there was Barry. He was devastated when I told him I was leaving and begged me not to take Storm away from him too. So I walked away from both of them and I'm not proud of it but I still think it was the right thing to do.'

She leans against the wall, ready for condemnation but I had quite enough of being judged as a child. There were always people who thought they knew best and looked down on me for being a council house kid with a 'mental' mother.

I give a small sigh. 'I think you did what you thought was best at the time. But I know Storm misses you.'

Amanda nibbles her plump bottom lip. 'She's not the easiest of daughters which is possibly mostly my fault, but I miss her too.'

'Then maybe you shouldn't cancel her visits at the last minute because your au pair has come home unexpectedly.' I say it gently, but it sounds like the accusation it is.

'Fair enough. Simon thought it would be too much having Storm and Pia in the house together, but I should have insisted. I will insist in future.' She gazes into the distance for a moment, lost in thought, and then shakes her head. 'But you must get back to your reception. I'm sorry to drag you away but I didn't know when I might next have the chance to speak to you and say thank you.'

'For what?'

'For letting Storm be your bridesmaid. For giving her a home. For loving her and being like a mother to her when I can't be.'

Her face collapses in grief and she turns away when the door is flung open.

'There you are,' says Storm, bowling in with a paper plate of crisps in her hand. 'Barry reckons he's going to make a speech and you need to tell him not to 'cos he'll just make a total tit of himself.' She glances between me and her mother. 'Is everything all right?'

'Everything's fine.' Amanda has regained her composure and steps forward. 'I was just wishing Annie all the best because the girls and I have to leave in a minute.'

'Yeah, I thought you'd soon be off.'

'We have to go but before I do let's sort out when you can visit us for a few days. Perhaps at half term? There's a punk exhibition at the V&A that Simon's not keen on going to but I thought maybe you could come with me?'

'Sounds interesting,' says Storm slowly. 'But won't your au pair be around?'

'I'm sure she can sort out a put-you-up in the girls' room for a few nights.'

'Simon won't approve.'

'Probably not but he'll have to put up with it for once. And before I leave I also want to tell you how proud I am of you.'

'Because I'm finally wearing a dress and looking' – Storm puts the next word in ironic air quotes – 'pretty?'

'No, because you're doing well at school and holding down a Saturday job and making a wonderful new life here in Salt Bay. Though, I must admit, it is good to see you out of those damned Doc Martens.'

Storm's face breaks into a slow smile. 'Yeah, well I might not stay in Salt Bay forever.'

'I don't suppose you will. I expect you'll go on to even bigger and better things.'

Storm walks forward as though she might hug her mother but side-steps her when Barry barges in.

'I wondered where you'd all gone. You're not in here slagging me off, are you?'

He eyes me suspiciously, but I shake my head and laugh. 'There's been no slagging off, Barry, and I hear you're about to make a speech.'

'That is so lame,' says Storm with a dramatic sigh. 'Come on then. Let's get it over with.'

'You can stay in here if you don't want to hear it.'

'Nope. You're marginally less likely to say something horribly embarrassing about me if I'm actually listening so I have no choice.'

After they've all trooped out, I gather up my skirt in both hands and rush upstairs for a quick loo break. Though doing anything too quickly in metres of silk is impossible unless you want to risk tripping or ripping the fabric or accidentally weeing on your wedding dress.

But if I don't soon get back to the garden, they'll be starting the speeches without me. Dress intact, I scurry downstairs and fling open the kitchen door but my way into the garden is blocked by Roger and Jacques, who appear to be squaring up around the kitchen table. Damn! I so should have used the front door.

'Are you two coming into the garden for the speeches?'

'We've got to sort this out first,' scowls Roger, who's looking dapper in a black suit and crisp white shirt with only minimal food staining.

Jacques groans. 'Sort out what exactly? Why have you trapped me in this room? Congratulations, by the way, Annie, on your marriage. I wish you and Josh much happiness.'

'Thank you. Roger, can you tell me why you've trapped Jacques in the kitchen on my wedding day?'

I say those last three words extra loudly in the hope they'll shame Roger into not being such an idiot. But they fall on deaf ears.

'I want to know his intentions regarding Jennifer.'

'Really, Roger?' I position myself directly in Roger's eyeline so he gets the full effect of the fabulous dress I'm wearing. 'You choose today of all days to have it out with Jacques?'

'Sorry, Annie, but this has been building up and has to be said. I need a word with you, Jacques, about how you're treating Jennifer, who's a very good friend of mine.'

'Not that it's any of your business but I've invited Jenny to live in Paris so she can pursue the singing career she deserves.'

'To live with you?' says Roger, his body language screaming defeat. 'Like your sexual plaything?'

Among the terms I never thought I'd hear Roger utter, 'sexual plaything' is way up there. And now my mind is filled with images of Jennifer in basque and fishnets, stretched out languorously on a chaise longue while she waits for Jacques to service her. And while I've nothing against older women getting their rocks off, it's not what you want to be picturing on your wedding day.

Jacques is shaking his head, a slight smile on his lips. 'Not to live with me but you English men are so repressed.'

'I'll show you repressed, mate,' bellows Roger, tearing off his jacket and rolling up his shirtsleeves.

Jacques' jacket comes off too and they start strutting round the kitchen table, chests out, jaws clenched and eyes narrowed.

When the strutting goes on for a while, I'm tempted to leave them to it. But Roger's panting, his face is lobster-pink and he'll go down like a sack of potatoes with one left hook.

'Come on, fellas, let's work this out in a civilised manner so we can go and hear the speeches.'

'Work what out?' Jennifer is framed in the back doorway, drink in one hand and Mrs Thatcher bag in the other. 'Are you two arguing? What on earth is going on?'

'Nothing,' mumble Roger and Jacques like naughty schoolboys.

'Hopefully I can get some sense out of you, Annie. Tell me exactly what's going on in here.'

I take a deep breath. 'Jacques is upset that Roger's asking about his intentions regarding you. Roger's upset that you might move to Paris and is worried Jacques will use you for sex. Roger doesn't want you to leave Salt Bay because he likes you a lot. He's trying to impress you which is why he's on a diet and looking generally spruced up though you haven't noticed.'

Jennifer, Jacques and Roger are all staring at me with their mouths open. But I'm through with secrets and half-truths and pussyfooting about. Tell it like it is, have it out and sort it out. That's my mantra from now on.

'I see.' Jennifer closes the back door very quietly, but her hands are shaking. 'Frankly, I don't appreciate being fought over like a piece of meat. Roger, my living arrangements in Paris are absolutely none of your business and it's outrageous that the two of you are arguing on Annie's wedding day.'

Yes! Thank you, Jennifer.

'But I have come to a decision,' she continues, 'and I may as well tell you now as later. Jacques, I've enjoyed seeing you again but tell me the truth, is all that you're offering – the singing opportunities and help with securing accommodation in Paris – fuelled by guilt?'

He shrugs. 'Not completely, because I care about you, Jenny. But I do feel guilty about the way I behaved when we were young and what you lost because of it. It's bothered me for years and I want to make amends.'

When Jennifer smiles, her pale blue eyes twinkle and the years fall away. 'What happened was a long time ago, Jacques, and you don't need to carry that guilt with you. I may have lost a great deal but I've gained in other ways. Salt Bay seems small and inconsequential to you but it's my home and I'm happy here because I love it and the people are' – she glances at Roger, who's staring at the table – 'loyal and caring and very dear to me. It's rather too late for me to change course.'

'So you're not leaving?' mutters Roger.

'No, I'm not, though it's none of your business. Jacques, would it help if I told you that I forgive you?'

'It would help a great deal.' Jacques raises Jennifer's hand to his lips and kisses it gently. 'Thank you. I hope we can stay in touch now we're friends again.'

'Christmas cards and birthday cards. That kind of thing?'

'Yes, that kind of thing.'

Jennifer smiles at the man who broke her heart forty years ago and pulls her hand away. She's decided which path to take and, unlike mine, it won't take her away from Salt Bay.

'If that's all done, we'd better get back into the garden for the speeches. Oh, and Roger,' she says quietly when she passes him at the table, 'I did notice.'

Chapter Thirty-Four

'Is everything all right? You were ages and Barry's itching to get on with the speeches though he's adamant he wants to go last for some reason,' says Josh when I slip into my seat next to him at the top table – which is actually Gerald's wallpapering tables laid end to end and covered in white crepe paper.

I nod, pushing a creamy mound of seagull droppings off the crepe with one of the serviettes Jennifer supplied. They must be left over stock from Christmas because tiny fir trees are picked out around the edges. But that's Jennifer for you – sensible and practical when it comes to money and matters of the heart. She, Roger and Jacques are sitting together near the bird bath and she raises her glass to me when our eyes meet.

Behind them, Amanda's being talked at by Florence, who must have nabbed her on the way to her car.

Florence, who's forgiven me for not wearing her wedding dress, gives me a wave as Emily and Tom walk past her, hand in hand.

'Ollie, did you want to say something first?' Josh leans across the table and gestures at his best man, who's sitting quietly on his own. Ollie slowly gets to his feet and tucks in his shirt which is hanging out over his trousers. His straw-blonde hair is so messy he looks like Cornwall's answer to Boris Johnson.

'I haven't got much to say really.' His hands are trembling slightly because he's nervous, bless him. 'Just that Josh is the best man I know. He's a true son of Cornwall and Annie is perfect for him even though she used to live in London and he hates the place. They've both changed each other as people, since they met, in ways too many to mention. Except that Josh isn't so grumpy these days and Annie isn't as scary.' He glows with pleasure when people laugh. 'What I mean is, they're perfect for each other so let's have a drink to celebrate their wedding.'

'Any excuse!' calls Arthur, downing half a glass of white in one gulp and wiping drips from his shirt.

'And Annie looks beautiful and so do the bridesmaids,' adds Ollie, who's already half sitting down. 'Lots of you already know that I'm leaving Salt Bay for a new job next month and I'm going to miss you all and especially Kayla who I—' he clamps his mouth shut and slumps into his plastic garden chair.

Kayla, who's been chucking it back for ages, leaps to her feet.

'Ah, I'm coming with you, you great arse. You'll be hopeless on your own and those lakes you showed me are pretty spectacular. They've got nothing on the great lakes of Australia, obviously. But they're pretty amazing, all the same. Just don't go getting any ideas about you and me settling down.'

A smile lights up Ollie's face. 'You're coming with me? Do you mean it?'

'Seeing as I've just said it in front of the whole freaking village, I can't back out. Is that all right with you, Rog?'

'Of course it is,' shouts Roger. 'I'm not your jailer. Personally I think you're mad to leave Cornwall and go up north. And I'll miss you, even though you're daft as a brush.'

Kayla swallows hard. 'I'll miss you too, you old curmudgeon, and you too, Annie. But we'll be down to visit loads. I feel like I'm abandoning you but you were right about the fear thing and you've got Josh now so you'll be fine. Won't you?'

I pull her into a hug and have a little cry because I'm so pleased she and Ollie will be together. And because everything's changing.

'I'll be fine and it's about time you started wandering again for the sake of those itchy feet. Josh and I haven't sorted out a honeymoon yet and I reckon the Lake District would be perfect.'

Kayla kisses me on the cheek before plonking herself in Ollie's lap. The plastic chair bows and bends but stays upright.

'If all the excitement is over, I think it's my turn.'

Josh puts down his glass of beer and gets to his feet. The sun is glinting on his ebony hair and sparking off the gold band on his fourth finger.

'I want to thank you all for being here to share our special day and for all pitching in to save our wedding. It's been wonderful and a huge thank you to everyone who's brought us to this time and place – to family who are here, those sadly no longer with us, and to our friends. I'm not much of a one for heart on sleeve stuff but' – he falters and his deep voice cracks – 'I'm so proud and happy to be Annie's husband. She completes me.'

There's an 'aw' from every woman in the garden and I dab at my eyes with a tissue. I'm sure you're not supposed to cry on your wedding day but Kayla and now Josh between them have scuppered my self-control. My lovely new husband snakes his arm around my waist and kisses me gently on the lips. It's rather a chaste kiss but he whispers 'I'll save the rest for later, Ms Trebarwith,' and gives me a slow, sexy wink.

'Is that it with the speeches then? Shall we cut the cake?' calls Maureen, waving a huge knife above her head.

'Hold your horses 'cos the father of the bride's got something to say,' shouts Barry. 'I'd like to propose a toast to my lovely daughter Annie and her handsome husband Josh. I would have written them a song but I've been rather busy so I'll save that for my first grandchild.'

Everyone cheers and I feel my cheeks getting hot. Give us a chance!

'My other lovely daughter, Storm, has threatened me with physical violence if I'm embarrassing so I'll keep it short. But Annie and Josh, I hope you'll be happy, far happier than I was during my marriage, which turned out to be absolute shite.'

Storm slowly lowers her forehead onto the table as Barry raises his pint of beer.

'To Annie and Josh.'

'To Annie and Josh.' Everyone throws back their drinks and applauds.

But Barry hasn't finished. He's just pulled out the sheet of paper he shoved into his waistcoat pocket when he first arrived this morning.

'This is my wedding present to Annie and Josh, which I was going to give them in private but what the hell. This is for the two of you because you both deserve it.'

He hands me the folded sheet and steps back, biting his lip. Is it the promise of a song when he's had the time to write it? Or tickets to his next gig? With my father, it could be anything. I open the paper and see the back of a cheque.

'You don't need to pay anything towards the wedding, Barry,' says Josh quietly. 'It's kind of you but you're as skint as we are and this is the twenty-first century.'

'Look at it,' commands Barry, a grin playing at the corners of his mouth.

When I turn the cheque over, blood rushes from my head and I come over all faint like a Regency heroine. I re-read it and push it under Josh's nose – there's Barry's signature and the amount he's scrawled: thirty thousand pounds.

'That's crazy, Barry,' I stutter. 'Is this a joke?'

'No joke,' says Barry, now grinning widely. 'You know that boy band song I kept hearing on the radio? Turns out I'm not senile and it really is one of mine. I wrote it with Weirdo Wayne, drummer with Va-Voom and the Vikings, who turns out to be the boy band's manager, lucky devil. The song's topped the charts and is about to feature in a TV ad which means mega-bucks. Anyway, Weirdo's apologised for not letting me know – he claims he thought I was dead – and now, after speaking with his lawyers, I'm getting royalties. I can prove we co-wrote the song and they don't want any scandal spoiling the squeaky clean image of the band.'

'But you can't give your money to me. You can't give us thirty thousand pounds.'

'Yes, I can because you're my daughter and I was never around to give you anything before.' He grabs hold of my hands, 'You can use it to mend the roof on this old place and get your B&B business going.'

'But what about Storm? She's your daughter too.'

'I'll find a bit of dosh for her and there's a condition attached to your money. You use it to mend the roof and, in return, Storm and I will always have a home here. I won't be here that much and I can sleep on the sofa when you've got B&B guests. But Storm needs a permanent base, somewhere she'll always be welcome and can call home. You might be stuck with her for a while 'cos she likes it here and she's happy. You've given her the home I never could, Annie, and I'll always love you for that.'

He shrugs. 'Anyway, that's it. Let's cut the cake.'

There's a hush over the garden and then it's pandemonium. I fling my arms around Barry's neck while Josh slaps him on the back, the crowd goes wild, and Storm cries on Emily's shoulder. At the back of the garden, Amanda gives Barry a thumbs up and slips away with her mute children in tow.

I plan on eating lots of cake. So much chocolate cake my stomach feels bloated and I won't care because my daft, annoying, lovely dad has come up trumps and I feel like celebrating. In practical terms, his hugely generous gift means we don't have to sell Tregavara House and leave Salt Bay. But it's also given me something less tangible that money can't buy – roots, continuity, happiness.

The only person not likely to be delighted is Toby but he doesn't look too upset when he corners us both after the cake-cutting. He's been having a good afternoon because news of his exploits on the cliff have spread and people are being nicer to him than they usually are.

'Do you want to put that knife down, Pasco? Better safe than sorry if we're about to have a conversation,' says Toby, tilting his head at the cream-covered blade in Josh's hand. 'I wanted to say best of luck with the marriage thing.'

'Thanks,' says my new husband. 'How are you after your cliff adventure?'

'A bit sore and achy but mostly surprised that I managed it.'

'It's surprising what you can manage when you put your mind to it,' I tell him, pointing at Freya, who's sugar-rush central after stuffing down her portion of cake. She's clambered onto a table and is jumping up and down while Lucy tries to coax her back onto firm ground.

Toby grimaces. 'She's a bit of a handful but I'm hoping I can be a good dad if I keep slogging on. I'm more confident after what happened, and apparently climbing a cliff to rescue a small child gets you brownie points so the locals don't think I'm the Antichrist any more. All in all, it's a win-win.'

'Have you had any flack about her being on the cliff in the first place?'

'No one's mentioned it. Only Lucy went mad but she calmed down eventually when she realised I'd sorted the situation out.' Toby accepts a slice of cake from Maureen, who's passing them out on paper plates, and gives it a sniff. 'Anyway, talking of paternal issues, I don't suppose you'll be selling me the house now your strange father's loaded.'

I glance at Josh, who grins at me and nods. 'I'm afraid not. Josh and I have had a chat and we're going to stay here because it's our home.'

'Well done. You win.'

'When you came round on Thursday and invited me to the beach you said it wasn't a competition.'

'I lied.' Toby pokes his finger into the buttercream and licks it clean.

'Why aren't you furious that you won't be able to turn the house into flats? I'm surprised you're being so calm about it.'

'I'm surprised too. But I think I was kind of going off the idea of taking on the house, anyway.'

'Because it's a millstone?'

'Not really, though it is a total money pit. You're a good fit here, Annie – much better than me. That's obvious from seeing you with everyone today. And I've been thinking about what you said on the beach about me disappointing Alice and it hit home. I do actually miss her, you know.'

Lines furrow his cheeks when he screws up his face and Toby – this time Toby Two, the version who cares about people – doesn't shy away when I give him a hug. He is family, after all.

An hour later, as the sun is casting golden beams across the ocean, I screw up my courage and tap the cake knife against my glass. The gentle tinkle hardly carries and no one takes any notice of me until Kayla yells 'Oy! Listen up!' at the top of her voice.

'Can I say something?' I squeak, all wobbly at the very thought.

'The bride giving a speech isn't terribly traditional,' shouts Jennifer, who's knocking back Baileys like there's no tomorrow. She's been dancing with Arthur, who, it turns out, can do all the actions to 'Y.M.C.A.' when he's had a few.

'I'm not a terribly traditional sort of person.'

'True enough,' she hiccups. 'You go, girl.'

'I just wanted—' My voice fails and I clear my throat. 'I just wanted to say how much Salt Bay and all of you mean to me.'

Storm starts miming sticking her fingers down her throat, but I'm not deterred. If your own wedding isn't a good time to come over all schmaltzy, when is?

'When I first came to Salt Bay last year, I had no family and no future really. I thought Salt Bay was awful – the back of beyond with nothing but rain and seagulls and not a patch on exciting London.'

'Don't mince your words, love,' shouts Gerald.

'But I quickly realised how wrong I was. There's a brilliant sense of community here and I'm so proud of our wonderful choir, who sang so beautifully during the wedding ceremony and laid on this fantastic reception. You'll never know what you all mean to me and how much I love belonging here in Cornwall with Josh and Storm and Emily and Barry and my great new in-laws. With all of you in fact. So thank you.'

Lovely Mary is crying and even Arthur is looking suspiciously tearful.

'I'll shut up now but finish by saying it's sad that Alice isn't here today. But thanks to her and to my dad's generosity, Tregavara House and Salt Bay are my home and they always will be.'

Everyone cheers and raises their glasses. And I raise mine as well – to my beloved great-aunt and the wonderful old house in front of me that's been the scene of so many Trebarwith weddings in the past. I'm a part of Tregavara House's past and present and now a part of its future too.

The house is sleeping when I slip out of bed at dawn the next morning and sit at the window with my chin in my hands.

Josh is snoring gently behind me and I'm dead tired but my mind is full of images from yesterday: the church filled with flowers, Storm and Amanda hugging, Kayla doing the hokey-cokey, my dad giving us thirty thousand pounds. I crane my neck to make sure Barry's cheque is still safely tucked under the lamp on the chest of drawers. First thing on Monday morning, that'll be deposited in the bank and Tregavara House will have her new roof.

We'll have to be careful with our day-to-day finances, but the B&B option is still a possibility and I just know we can make this place work. We'll stay in Salt Bay and life will go on as normal except for Kayla not being around. I'll miss everything about her – except the way she uses paperclips as dental floss. But it's right that she's leaving with Ollie, and Keswick isn't as far away as Sydney.

Plus, don't forget, chips in my inner voice, *everything changes eventually and even difficult change is often ultimately for the best.* Blimey, that's the most profound thing my inner voice has ever said. All it does normally is hurl personal insults my way. But I've never felt this peaceful before or so much at home.

Ooh, this is all a bit heavy for seven o'clock. I lean out of the window and take a deep breath of fresh Cornish air to clear my head. The sun is a pale lemon ball just above the horizon and only a few wispy clouds are scattered across the translucent sky. There's a September nip in the air, but it's going to be another gorgeous day in Salt Bay and ideal for our post-wedding picnic on the beach. Anyone who wants to come is invited and Peter and his friends are primed to ferry us there and back in their rowing boats.

The sun hits my window as it creeps up the stone of Tregavara House and I shield my eyes from the sudden glare. There are people on the cliffs even though it was dark just a short while ago.

I squint through the bright light at the fuzzy outline of three people – a woman with long fair hair and an older woman with white hair holding the hand of a small child. Suddenly I can hardly breathe. The younger woman raises her hand as though she's waving. But when I blink to clear my vision, they've gone. It must have been a trick of the light.

Epilogue

Two years later

'You're so lucky to live in such a beautiful place. Have you owned this house for long?'

'Only a couple of years but it's been my family's home for over two centuries.'

Stephanie, a tax inspector from Milton Keynes, stretches out on the steamer chair under the apple tree and gives a deep sigh of contentment. She was so stressed out when she arrived two days ago she could hardly speak but Salt Bay is working its magic on her already. By the end of the week she won't want to leave. None of our guests do.

Emily wanders into the garden in Alice's old apron and places a frosted glass of lemonade on the side table next to Stephanie. Her attentiveness is one of the reasons why our B&B visitors are so keen to return and we couldn't run the business without her.

She pushes hair from her eyes and waves at Josh, who's sitting on a rug at the back of the garden, where the shadow from the cliff provides shade from the sun.

'It's such beautiful weather today, a real Indian summer. Shall I get Millie a drink?'

'That would be lovely. Thanks, Emily.'

Josh beckons to me as Emily heads for the kitchen and I walk over in bare feet, enjoying the feeling of grass between my toes. It's been hot recently though temperatures haven't topped the heatwave summer we had two years ago when we took wedding photos on the cliffs and the garden was filled with family and friends. So much has changed since then but the important things have stayed the same.

I bend down and brush my lips against Josh's before sweeping a giggling Millie Alice Joanna Trebarwith Pasco into my arms. She'll curse us when she starts school and kids find out how long her name is, but I'll explain how proud she should be of her names and her heritage and she might forgive me.

'This dreadful child thinks I'm a climbing frame,' says Josh, lying back with his hands under his head. 'I thought she'd settle down and sleep back here where it's cooler but she's stubborn like her mother.' He grins when I play-kick him in the shin and closes his eyes. 'I think I might have a little snooze if you're on monster duty.'

Millie throws her chubby arms around my neck and snuggles into my shoulder. Her last bottle was a while ago, but she has a sweet milky smell and I take an extra deep breath to drink it in.

Enjoy every moment because they don't stay babies for long, says Maura, and I'm trying though it's not always easy when she's yelling the house down while guests are sleeping. And as for cracked nipples, don't even get me started. Florence is disgusted that I've given up breastfeeding, but she'll get over it.

I wander with Millie towards the front garden so she can see the bright blue of the ocean and, if we're lucky, the stray black cat she adores that stretches out on the harbour wall. 'Cat' is likely to be my daughter's first word and Josh and I are well aware of where we come in the pecking order.

'Hey there, can I come in?'

The gate squeaks when it swings open and Millie starts bouncing up and down in my arms. She's always the same when she spots her Auntie Kayla.

'I was out for a walk and thought I'd check how my gorgeous god-daughter's doing. Still causing you grief in the early hours?'

'Oh, yeah. She had us up twice in the night and the last nappy just before dawn was a right belter.'

Kayla wrinkles her freckled nose and squeezes Millie's bare feet. 'I did warn you about the joys of parenthood. Having spoken to the Smug Marrieds about kids the other day, just be grateful you have any pelvic floor left. Have you heard anything from Freya?'

'So far so good. She rang her mum yesterday and said she was having a wonderful time and Toby was about to take her to an ice rink.'

'No way! I can't imagine Toby on skates.'

'Me neither but at least he's trying and having Freya to stay with him in London is a big step. I'm sure he's mellowing a bit.'

'You always do think the best of him, though he doesn't deserve it.'

Kayla starts waving frantically at Jennifer and Roger, who are about to go for a walk across the cliffs. They've reached the foot of the winding path and appear to be arguing if Jennifer's body language is anything to go by.

'Those two are seriously weird,' says Kayla, pushing her sunglasses into her hair. 'There's definitely no hanky-panky going on, but they spend loads of time together and seem devoted to each other.'

'In their own grumpy, complaining way.'

'Yeah, maybe it's the mutual moaning that turns them on.'

'Talking of which…'

Storm is coming out of the front door lugging an art case the size of a small country. She drops it with a clatter onto the path and it falls against a shrub that's already been partly flattened by summer winds and squalls.

'There's no way I can carry this about in London without taking out a few tourists,' she announces. 'They're all going to hate me on the Tube – the passive-aggressive staring will be legend. Do you know Millie's trying to shove her entire fist into her mouth? That kid is messed up.' A soppy smile spreads across her face. 'But I'm gonna miss her apart from the appalling smells.'

Millie's going to miss her aunt too. We all are when Storm leaves for London in a few days' time to stay with Barry in his swanky new flat and study art at college.

I thought Amanda had lost it when she sent Storm an easel and painting kit a couple of Christmases ago. But it turned out to be the best present ever – Storm started sitting on the harbour wall with her paints when she got bored and produced some breathtaking pictures. One of the best – a riot of broad grey and green brushstrokes that captures the changing sea and brooding sky – is hanging in the sitting room and often admired by guests.

'Do you need a hand with your packing later? I can help this evening when Millie's asleep.'

My daughter starts wriggling in my arms at the sound of her name and I sit her down carefully on the grass. She mostly stays upright these days but has the occasional topple when we're not looking. And so far, she's not fussed about crawling.

'Nah, you're all right. I can't take too much 'cos Barry's car is so ridiculously small. It would make much more sense for Mum to pick me up and I don't know why Barry's insisting on driving down.'

No doubt because he's keen to snatch time with the granddaughter who's stolen his heart. He doesn't get to Cornwall much these days now his song-writing talents are in demand – Weirdo Wayne has shedloads of contacts in the music business and Barry has taken full advantage of them. But when he does pay us a visit, he turns into a besotted granddad the minute he kicks off his trainers.

'Anyway, I'm off to say goodbye to Serena and will be back later. I was going to show her my latest pictures, but I can't be bothered to take the case on the bus so put it back in my room, will you?' Storm hurries past us and calls out as she's scooting up the road: 'Bye, Kayla. Are babies allowed to eat flowers, by the way?'

Probably not. I stick my finger in Millie's dribbly mouth and pull out a masticated daisy. This baby lark took me and Josh by surprise – we weren't expecting me to get pregnant so quickly after we started trying – and we're still feeling our way through it.

But Marion is a brilliant babysitter and everyone in the village seems more than happy to give us advice when we're out and about with Millie in her pushchair.

'Hey, Kayla. I didn't know you were here.' Josh is wandering across the grass, waving a feeding cup. 'Tom brought this out for the bubs. Here you go, sweetheart.' He stoops down, places the lidded cup in Millie's tiny hands and strokes her wispy fair hair before getting to his feet. 'Mum just called and offered to babysit on Monday night if you fancy seeing the new Bond film. Our last chance of freedom before school starts again and you go back to work.'

'Sounds great,' I say, pushing down a flutter of anxiety at the thought of leaving Millie. I'm only going back to the charity part-time and she'll be well looked after by Marion and Emily but it's going to be strange.

'Why don't you and Ollie come too?' asks Josh. 'We can double-date and snog in the back row.'

Kayla grins. 'You know what a Bond freak Ollie is. He'll love it so count us in. Ooh, it's so brilliant to see you all and be back in

Cornwall.' She links her arm through mine and takes a deep breath of fresh, sea air.

She and Ollie moved back to the area a few weeks ago after Ollie made such a success of boosting sales for his company up north, he was asked to do the same in the south-west. I doubt they'll stay around for long because Ollie's got the travel bug and is talking about working abroad, but I'll enjoy their company while I can.

'Right, I can't stand here chatting all day. I have things to do, people to see and Roger to annoy,' says Kayla, bending down and kissing Millie's soft cheek. 'So I'll see you on Monday if not before and you must come and have a meal with us soon in our tiny hovel.'

The cottage they're renting in Trecaldwith is small, admittedly, but it has a sea view and a back garden that slopes up towards the moors so calling it a hovel is pushing it.

Kayla waves before walking off towards the village and I turn my back to the blinding sun to watch her go. She put on weight after moving to the Lake District – apparently extra calories were essential to cushion her against the bitter climate – and it suits her. The green sundress she's wearing complements her auburn colouring and looks fabulous.

'Do you think the monster will drop off if we take her out in the pushchair?' asks Josh, stifling a yawn. 'If she doesn't sleep soon, we'll have to try and keep her awake until bedtime which'll be a nightmare for all concerned.'

Millie grizzles when she's strapped into her pushchair but her eyelids droop and have closed before we reach the village green. The sun is starting to sink towards the horizon and cottages are bathed in gorgeous golden light that reflects off the windows and sparkles in the rushing river.

'Cyril's still out and about,' says Josh, steering the pushchair towards the wooden seat near the telephone box where he often sits on a sunny afternoon.

Cyril spots us and gives a wave when we get closer but doesn't try to get up. He's become increasingly frail since a bad bout of bronchitis last winter and moving hurts. Pain has etched its mark on his lovely old face, but he uses a walking stick and still manages to get to choir rehearsals. Roger and Gerald have promised to link arms and give him a chair-lift if he ever can't make it.

'How's the bonny babe?'

He smiles and strokes Millie under the chin while Josh and I pray she won't wake up. She shuffles slightly in her pushchair and sighs but carries on dreaming of milk and cuddles and cats on harbour walls.

'She's doing fine,' I tell him. 'How are you?'

'I'm not so bad and looking forward to choir starting up again on Wednesday. Have you sorted out what we'll be practising for the Christmas concert?'

'We're coming up with some options at the moment though it seems ridiculous thinking about Christmas when the weather's so gorgeous. We've got some potential new members coming along which is exciting – the young couple who've moved in to Enid's old house and a bloke from Trecaldwith who's impressed by our prize-winning reputation.'

Cyril chuckles. 'It's good to have new blood to take the place of us oldies who are dying off.'

I bend and kiss his wrinkled cheek because the thought of Cyril not sitting here on sunny afternoons watching the river rush to the sea is so sad. But the cycle of life and death goes on in Salt Bay. Villagers die and new ones take their place – like Millie and two-year-old Henry, who'll soon have a new brother or sister. Pippa told us she was pregnant again in the pub last week.

After spending a few minutes with Cyril, we push Millie past the church where she was christened and Maureen's Tea Shop where we take her for tiny cubes of Madeira cake that she mashes into her mouth. Then we head past Jennifer's shop and the pub for the rising fields that mark the end of the village.

Pushing Millie over rough ground is risky. But she's so deeply asleep the rhythmic bumping doesn't disturb her and we park her pushchair in the shade of a windblown tree when we arrive at the bench.

Technology is gradually creeping into Salt Bay and even Jennifer has computerised her stock system, but you still need to stand on this bench and wave your mobile in the air to get a decent signal if your landline goes down. It's mad – and yet strangely, peacefully wonderful.

'What are you thinking about?' Josh shuffles his backside close to mine and puts his arm around my shoulders.

'I'm thinking that we'll need to go and visit Storm sometimes when she goes up to London.'

Josh groans. 'If I must but I'm worried you'll realise what you're missing and insist we all up sticks and move up there with her.'

'I think I might miss this place rather more. Aren't we lucky!'

'We are,' says Josh and there's no need to spell out why because our good fortune is laid out here in front of us.

I glance at Millie, who's snoring softly as a warm breeze tickles her toes and push my hand into Josh's. Then we sit in silence for ages, looking across the valley while his thumb caresses the back of my wedding ring.

Salt Bay is the same as it's been for generations. Cottages are clustered together around the green and the squat tower of the church and there, where the village ends, is Tregavara House with its shiny new roof. Beyond it, the sun is glowing red as it sinks towards the silver sea and streaks of orange and pale gold are painted across the sky.

'Come on,' says the man I love with all my heart. 'Let's go home.'

A Letter from Liz

Hello – thank you so much for reading *Annie's Summer by the Sea* and I really hope you enjoyed it. Writing about Annie in Salt Bay has been wonderful and I felt rather tearful when it came to typing 'The End'. This book is the last of Annie's adventures but I like to imagine that village life goes on, the choir carries on singing, and Annie and Josh will spend many happy decades together in their gorgeous Cornish house by the ocean.

If you want to be the first to know when my next book is published, please sign up to my mailing list using the link below. Your email address will never be shared and you can unsubscribe at any time.

www.bookouture.com/liz-eeles/?title=annies-summer-by-the-sea

If you enjoyed *Annie's Summer by the Sea*, can I ask a favour? I'd love it if you'd write a review, not just because a positive review makes this author's day (though it does) but because reviews encourage new readers to give my books a try. And do get in touch if you'd like to say hello – my new website and blog are now up and running, and I'm slowly getting my head round social media and can be found on Facebook, Twitter and Instagram.

If this is your first Salt Bay book, you might like to know there are two more – *Annie's Holiday by the Sea* and *Annie's Christmas by the Sea*. These tell how Annie and Josh first met (Josh's Mini got dented in the process), how new life was breathed into Salt Bay Choral Society, and how Annie reacted when Barry and Storm turned up on her doorstep out of the blue (clue: it was a bit of a shock).

Right now, I'm working on my next book, set in the beautiful Cotswolds, which is an area I know well because my family have lived there for generations.

Until we're next in touch, I wish you many happy hours of reading fabulous books!

Liz x

        : www.lizeeles.com

        : lizeelesauthor/

        : @lizeelesauthor

        : lizeelesauthor

Acknowledgements

Huge thanks, as always, to Bookouture without whom I would still be an aspiring author with only dreams of being published. I feel incredibly fortunate to have the backing of such a talented team. Particular thanks to Abigail Fenton for being so endlessly encouraging, patient and wise – in short, everything I could wish for in an editor. Abi, along with Emily Ruston, provided loads of astute advice while this book was being written and I'm so glad to have them in my corner. Thanks also to publicity maestros Kim Nash and Noelle Holten, who look after their authors with such a passion.

My family and friends are awesome. After putting up with me banging on for years about wanting to write a book, they've been delighted for me and fabulously supportive since my dream came true. Thank you to all of them and also to the wonderful readers and book bloggers who have helped make the last year a very special one.

Finally, a special mention to my lovely husband, Tim, who talks me down when I get to the 'this book will never get written' stage, and to Cornwall for being an endless source of inspiration and such a wild and beautiful place.

Lightning Source UK Ltd.
Milton Keynes UK
UKHW011807091218
333730UK00015B/559/P

9 781786 813268